KILLER
COMMUTE

KILLER COMMUTE

❖

Marlys Millhiser

ST. MARTIN'S MINOTAUR

NEW YORK

www.minotaurbooks.com

Library of Congress Cataloging-in-Publication Data

Millhiser, Marlys.
    Killer commute / Marlys Millhiser.—1st ed.
        p. c.m.
    ISBN 0-312-26610-3
        1. Greene, Charlie (Fictitious character)—Fiction.   2. Women detec-
tives—California—Long Beach—Fiction.   3. Long Beach (Calif.)—Fiction.
4. Literary agents—Fiction.   I. Title.

PS3563.I4225 K55 2000
813'.54—dc21

                                                                    00-040255

First Edition: October 2000

10 9 8 7 6 5 4 3 2 1

For Joy and Mike,
Long may you love

ACKNOWLEDGMENTS

Thanks to Wendy Hornsby and Jan Burke for the Long Beach update and to Kate Gonzales and Mary Maggie Mason for their sense of humor.

KILLER
COMMUTE

CHAPTER 1

❖

CHARLIE GREENE TURNED her Toyota into the drive and stopped at the obelisk. White and pink obscenities already marred its new coat of dark olive paint. She stuck her card into its slot, knowing the black metal grate of a gate wouldn't open for her without further persuasion, and stared between bars into the courtyard with a sigh so deep it had a trace of voice in it. Bags of groceries redolent with celery, ground coffee, and spicy cold cuts filled the seat beside her, and the backseat, too.

She could see the gate to the alley clear across the courtyard in the dimming dusk. Mrs. Beesom's light was on over the door to her kitchen, lighting up a raft of bird feeders and the rear of her ancient Olds 88. Libby's Jeep Wrangler was gone.

Charlie stepped out of the Toyota. Her feet hurt, her head hurt, her stomach hurt—even her hair felt like it had an ache. Time for a break.

One whole week without the killer commute, the telephone glued to her ear, worried writers, prima-donna writers, office politics, studio execs, and harried producers. No teleplays, book proposals, manuscripts, pitches, or story treatments. No office meetings, business lunches, screenings.

The point of the obelisk opening the gate to the courtyard was so you didn't have to get out of the car and expose yourself

1

to roving gangs of criminal kids, increasingly Asian and ruthless, who were supposedly responsible for the graffiti that graced convenient surfaces.

Charlie slugged the obelisk in the appropriate places and caught her foot before giving the damn thing a kick, having almost broken a toe last night. She noted some new obscenities on the compound's wall—all in English and spelled correctly, like their predecessors. And some squiggles that suggested petroglyphs.

When the gate swung open, she grabbed her card, jumped back in the Toyota, and gunned it into the compound before the portal closed on the big bad world.

Charlie swung in beside the looming Oldsmobile and stepped out into her own little fortress—well, she and Libby shared it with three other households. But tonight it seemed exceptionally secure because she was home, yet she wasn't home.

A bag of groceries in each arm, she managed to open the kitchen door, switch on the lights, and kick off her shoes. Back out in the free air—rich with the ocean smell of the bay tonight, though her home was some blocks inland—she felt the cool of the concrete through the feet of her pantyhose.

That was another thing—no pantyhose for a week. Just sloppy sweats and comfortable shoes, shorts on a warm afternoon. On her last trip to the car, Charlie nearly tripped over Libby's cat who, instead of hissing with surprise and mauling Charlie's hose with her in them, rubbed his jowls and neck against her leg and mewed—like a real cat.

"Libby must not have fed you again." But Tuxedo's food bowl beside the refrigerator was about a third full of dry food mixed with foul-smelling meaty food. He always saved a portion of his dinner for a postmidnight snack so he could regurgitate it on the stairs to the second floor on his way to bed.

2

Tuxedo was the one part of her vacation she could have done without.

But once she'd changed into sweatpants and shirt and fuzzy slippers she figured she could even put up with the cat. Charlie could hear him still outside meoyowling as she filled the refrigerator and cupboards with provisions for her getaway. This was not only her home and her fortress. This was Charlie's hideout.

She nearly forgot and answered the phone while making herself a fried-egg sandwich with ketchup. Betty Beesom's voice on the answering machine in the living room reminded Charlie not to answer the phone because she wasn't home.

When she took the sandwich and a tall glass of milk out to the patio, Tuxedo Greene grew more insistent, pacing back and forth, pinning her with those big, luminescent eyes.

"If you want to go in the house, you've got your own door. Shut up and let me enjoy my retreat."

The sea breeze washed the car exhaust from the air. Night birds called in the trees. Airliners circled overhead. The roar of rush hour sounded far away. The egg and bread soothed her stomach, the milk seemed to wash away her aches.

Maggie Stutzman's house was dark, her parking spot next to Jeremy's Trailblazer empty. Her house and Charlie's faced the street and formed the front corners of the compound. Jeremy Fiedler's house and Mrs. Beesom's fronted the alley and formed the back corners. High masonry walls coated with stucco and topped with rolled razor wire and broken glass attached the small homes, forming what the city termed a "condominium complex."

Betty Beesom and her husband had at one time owned a small house in the middle of a large lot. In the boom days, before cuts in military spending hit Long Beach hard, a builder had talked the widow into the scheme by practically giving her one of the houses.

There were few secrets inside these walls with muted lighting spaced along them. Charlie didn't know anyone outside them in the surrounding neighborhood.

Each of the houses had a sunken patio, with identical flower boxes arranged for privacy and the parking spaces in between them. Visitors had to park in the street. Jeremy also had a Ferrari but kept it in a private locked garage some miles away. He was an odd duck who kept odd hours. His Trailblazer was there, but his house stood dark. He worked out in a health club not far from here, might even now be walking home.

Charlie sprawled on a lounge, letting go of tensions incrementally, sucking in sea salt and dead-fish smells.

Tuxedo Greene exploded onto the glass tabletop beside her, knocking over her empty milk glass. If cats can bristle, he did. A tiny, malnourished kitten when Libby found him abandoned in a McDonald's parking lot, he'd grown into a sleek, slender teen who was now a formidable, muscular tom. His coat was black, his toes and a V-shaped blaze on his chest, white. At the moment his coat and tail puffed to make him twice his size, and the white of his chest and the yellow of his eyes stood out as if animated.

"I take it you are trying to tell me something, cat."

Cat meorowelled. They don't really meow; they do all kinds of irritating language things, if you listen to them—which Charlie preferred not to. She didn't like cats, particularly this one. But she loved her daughter beyond all reason. And Libby loved this animal.

This animal puffed some more and then exhaled. He jumped onto her lounge, close enough for her to smell the horrid cat food on his breath when he said something else, then leapt to a planter full of blooming plants. Tuxedo stared at her over his shoulder, his eyes expressionless yet weird and some-

4

how momentous. Then he disappeared, dispersing petals.

Charlie relaxed into the lounge again, feeling chilly and drowsy, trying to persuade herself to take her dishes in and sprawl on the couch instead, watch some TV. Options, so many options—that's what this disappearing act was all about.

We aren't trying to talk ourselves into anything here, are we? I mean, we aren't afraid of a real vacation for once, right?

Charlie's inner voice was in the habit of voicing her fears and uncertainties, just so she wouldn't overlook them. She ignored it, but there was now an edge to her mood that even the commute and the cat hadn't managed to generate.

Charlie was almost to the kitchen door with her dishes when she dropped them to break on the quarry-tile paving of the patio because the cat screamed.

"If you was home, I'd tell you how sick I'm getting of these cat fights, that's for sure," Betty Beesom said, careful not to look at Charlie.

Charlie, with whisk broom and dustpan, had cleaned up the shards of glass and pottery as well as she could under the light above the kitchen door. She set them carefully on the edge of a planter before putting her arm around the older woman.

"Mrs. Beesom, just because I'm taking my vacation at home doesn't mean you can't talk to me." The home vacation had actually been Betty's idea, after Charlie's disastrous, if profitable, one in Las Vegas last fall.

"Oh, I know I'm just a nosy old lady who gets on people's nerves. But we all worry about you. We want you to get a decent rest this time."

The woman *was* a nosy old lady who got on people's nerves, but Charlie worried about her, too. Her eyes were always red and teary. She blinked a lot. "You're a neighbor and a good friend. Let's go look for those cats so you can get some sleep tonight."

Tuxedo sat on top of Jeremy's Trailblazer. He and Hairy Granger ruled the night—in the compound and the alley, anyway. Hairy was middle-aged, so Tuxedo, in his prime, reigned as king of the hill at the moment. Hairy lived with the Grangers across the alley from Betty, and until about a year ago cleaned Tuxedo's clock regularly. Now it was the younger cat's turn.

The turf wars were noisy. If you kept the cats in, they kept you awake. If you let them out, the neighbors suffered. They were both neutered, but when Tuxedo started spraying the baseboards, Charlie had a cat door installed.

"Libby's at the Esterhazies' tonight, and Mr. Esterhazie called to say he'd see she stayed out of trouble and got home all right," Betty said.

"You know Ed Esterhazie?"

"Well, I know he's Esterhazie Cement."

"Concrete."

"Concrete. And he called Maggie, who told me. Maggie's out with that man again. Jeremy's home and said not to bother you. Here I am talking to you."

"You're not bothering me." I kind of love you. I *must* need a vacation.

They were circling the Trailblazer, their eyes on the cat on its roof. He hissed and spat, arched his back and quivered his tail.

"Think he'll bite us?"

"I guarantee it, if we can catch him. Let me do it. You just keep him nervous on that side. If Jeremy's home, why aren't there any lights on in his house?"

"Maybe he went out again. Maybe—Charlie, something moved in there—" Betty backed away and Libby's cat flew off the Trailblazer, his forelegs out like a falling squirrel. Charlie

6

looked into the vehicle and the manic stare of Hairy Granger.

"This is the whole problem, Mrs. Beesom. Hairy'd—" But Charlie registered that Hairy wasn't alone in there just as she opened the door. An arm and a hand and a head hung out over the seat. Some part of the man's body dripped blood onto the concrete courtyard as Hairy flew into Charlie's arms.

The cat trembled. His breath smelled a lot like Fancy Feast fishy supreme. He was a lush longhair, and when he puffed up he looked like a porcupine on helium. He was black and white, too, but all over in patches, like a cow. Feminine instinct told Charlie she should comfort him. Common sense told her she should see if the man hanging out of Jeremy's Trailblazer was dead and then call the proper emergency folks.

But plain old selfishness uttered, "Shit, my vacation doesn't even start until tomorrow."

Before she registered that Betty Beesom's face had disappeared from the car window opposite (but after Hairy Granger detonated a thick layer of cat hair in her face, racked a set of razor-wire claws down her cheek, and erupted out of her arms), Charlie realized that the man in Jeremy Fiedler's Trailblazer was Jeremy Fiedler. And he was quite dead.

CHAPTER 2

❖

VEHICLES WITH LIGHT bars flashing packed the compound, fortress, retreat. But they were oddly quiet.

Maybe Charlie was in shock. Maybe she was in denial. The
official personnel spoke low if at all, gestured, nodded. Cameras
took pictures with flashes but no sound. Video cameras made
barely perceptible whirrs. An occasional beeper prompted
someone to bleep a cell-phone number, speak in secretive
monosyllables and *hmmm*s. In the old days, like maybe a year
or two ago, Charlie's fortress would have filled with the static
of two-way radios.

The only real racket now was two cats squaring off out in
the back alley.

"They" wouldn't even let Charlie comfort Mrs. Beesom,
who had come to and then passed out again when she saw
Jeremy and the blood on Charlie's sweatshirt.

"Hairy flew out of the car and I caught him but he panicked
and scratched my cheek," Charlie told the guy next to her in
one of the cars. He was clicking computer keys while another
official person got some more footage of her in her fuzzy slippers and bloody sweats, picking up sound on a small mike on
the camera's front. Next they'd be taking DNA with a tech-
nomagic spoon.

"Harry. There were two men in the Trailblazer?"

"*Hairy,* the cat, he—"

"Cats don't fly."

"Neither do men."

"All that blood on your shirt came from a scratch on your cheek left by a cat? I want that shirt."

Charlie started to pull it up over her head and thought again, but not in time. "I forgot. I'm not wearing a bra."

"I noticed."

"Well, I just started my vacation and vowed to be seriously comfortable for a whole week." She didn't have much in the way of boobs, anyway, which was cool when she was growing up and totally slender was in. Now you had to be slender and buxom at the same time.

"Some vacation." He glanced over at the backs surrounding poor Jeremy, kneeling, standing, measuring, all bent forward to study him in this last indignity.

"Mason," Charlie's detective yelled, and a woman cop helping a wobbly Betty Beesom to stand looked over at his car.

"Mary," Detective Amuller yelled from downstairs as Charlie stripped off her sweatshirt and slipped into another.

"Maggie," the woman in the black uniform yelled back and made a face.

"Mary Maggie," came the reply from Charlie's living room.

Officer Mary Maggie Mason shrugged, shook her head. "That kid needs help."

Charlie didn't think they were related but they both had a chipped front tooth and silly, sort of loose, uncoplike smiles. She followed Mary Maggie downstairs, where the detective swore under his breath at the little computer on the coffee table. Officer Mason moved behind the couch to look over his shoulder, still holding Charlie's bloody sweatshirt.

9

"Don't be so ham-fisted," she advised.

"Charlie Greene, first twelve out of five thousand," he groused. His name sounded German but he looked to Charlie like a blond Irish Presbyterian from New England.

"Press the CA button on the tool bar."

"What's that, California?"

"Criminal activity," the lady cop said and giggled.

"Charlie's no criminal." Betty sat uneasy in an easy chair, red-eyed and weepy, washing her hands over and over in her lap with nothing but air.

Charlie knelt beside the chair and clasped those hands to still them. They were icy. "You all right, Mrs. Beesom?"

"Poor Jeremy—why? I'm scared, Charlie. A murderer walked right in here. Those cats didn't even warn us."

"I don't think cats warn you. I think it's dogs that—"

"*All right.*"

"*Bingggg-go.*" Officer Mason's voice had a falsetto tone to it, and she kept trying to tuck recalcitrant hair behind her ears.

"You work in Beverly Hills and live here?" Detective Amuller slopped an astonished grin. "That's a killer commute."

"Tell me about it."

"They've even got your DNA record on file." Mary Maggie's grin faded. She came around the couch to sit beside her cohort. "They usually only do that for people who've been arrested. Jesus, J. S., keep scrolling."

Finally, both cops looked up at her and blinked—his expression quizzical, her mouth hanging open.

"Mr. Fiedler isn't your first murder victim, I see. You've been busy the last few years, huh?" Officer Mason pushed her glasses back up her nose. They slid down again the minute her finger moved away.

"I have never murdered anyone. That's not *my* criminal ac-

10

tivity." Charlie was simply an absolute genius when it came to being at the wrong place at the wrong time.

"Charlemagne Catherine?"

"My father was a history professor."

"How did *he* die?"

"Heart attack." Of course, his heart had been fine before Charlie announced she was pregnant at sixteen.

"Oregon, Beverly Hills, Utah, Boulder, Vegas."

They'd been bobbling between the little screen and Charlie, but when the phone bleeped and then bleeped again, the Long Beach Police Department watched Charlie not move.

"Aren't you going to answer?" Mary Maggie said finally, her jaw returning to the ajar position the second she stopped saying it.

"She can't," Mrs. Beesom said. "She's not home."

"She's on vacation," Detective J. S. explained.

"Oh."

"Charlie," Richard Morse of Congdon & Morse answered Charlie's message on the answering machine, "I know you aren't home and I'm glad you didn't answer, but I just wanted you to know Ferris signed at dinner tonight. I'm calling from the Celebrity Pit. Congratulations, babe, you got a sweet bonus coming on this one. Have a great vacation, toots."

"Toots?" Officer Mason held Charlie's bloodied sweatshirt up to the light of the table lamp next to Betty's chair.

"That wouldn't be Rudy Ferris?" Detective J. S. asked.

But Officer Mary Maggie interrupted, "Mrs. Greene—"

"Miss Greene."

"Whatever. Did you handle Mr. Fiedler's body?"

"No."

"Then how do you explain the bloody smudges on the inside of the sleeves?" She cradled her arms.

And Charlie and Mrs. Beesom chimed in unison, "Hairy."

"I want that cat," Detective Amuller demanded. Just like he had for Charlie's sweatshirt.

❖

"Uh, this isn't going to be as easy as the sweatshirt," Charlie informed the Long Beach Police Department.

"Those animals are darn near feral," Betty Beesom agreed and reached for the key under the fern-plant pot to unlock the gate.

"This gate always kept locked?" Detective Amuller took the key and opened it himself, careful not to touch the gate, or let them touch it, either.

"We only use the alley for garbage pickup," Charlie said. It was normally left to homeless drunks and cats, homeless or not. She had never seen it so full of people before. Neighbors she'd never met filled the alley on the other side of the gate, had to shuffle aside to let them out of the courtyard. They were quiet, too. Too quiet. The world had seemed so unrealistically silent since Jeremy Fieldler all but fell out of his Trailblazer. Maybe Charlie's ears were plugged.

But she heard Detective Amuller speak softly behind her. "Which of you ladies called in about finding Mr. Fiedler's body?"

Both Charlie and Mrs. Beesom whirled to stare at the detective. He and Officer Mary Maggie stood in a sea of faces with emergency-vehicle lights strobing off eyeglasses and foreheads.

Charlie decided she must be in shock—seeing and not hearing things the way they really were. Jeremy had lived in the same fortress with her for over five years.

"I don't think we did, did we, Charlie?" Mrs. Beesom didn't look too good either.

12

"Somebody must have," Charlie said. "You suddenly showed up. I remember thinking how fast you were. I'd just gone around the Trailblazer to find Betty passed out and she came to but passed out again when she saw Jeremy and you all showed up."

"Do you have any idea how long it was after you discovered Mr. Fiedler that we appeared?"

"I really don't. This is the strangest evening. Maybe one of these people called."

"J. S., we could be looking at shock here. Take it easy." Officer Mary Maggie took a close look into Charlie's eyes.

J. S. seemed to have lost interest in the cat. He asked Charlie to introduce him to her neighbors.

"I don't know them."

"Not any of them?"

"I spend my whole life working, commuting, raising a daughter, and sleeping." And not nearly enough of the latter.

"This is Wilma and Art Granger." Betty offered up the couple standing beside her. "They live with the cat that scratched Charlie you was looking for."

Wilma and Art blinked behind their eyeglasses in the blinking light. They stood between Betty and Officer Mason. It was probably just a reflection of Charlie's present state of mind, but they looked like four owls in a cage with the gate-bar shadows crossing their faces.

"We came out to see what all the lights were about," Wilma said. "Seemed like the alley was safe enough—all the commotion being over the wall there." She was short and pudgy, her husband tall, stick thin, and stooped.

"What do you know about Jeremy Fiedler?" Detective Amuller asked and Mary Maggie stared at the heavens, shaking her head.

"Don't know any Jeremy Fiedler." Art Granger straightened

13

to look the young officer eye-to-eye. "Know Betty here because she belongs to our church."

Betty didn't know any of the others in the alley, but the Grangers knew another man who knew another couple who knew two women who identified one of their neighbors. Everyone seemed to live in houses or apartments that backed on the alley in some way. Nobody claimed to know Jeremy or to have called the police, either.

But all kept their voices low—not, Charlie thought, out of respect for someone dead, nor out of fear or curiosity.

More out of remoteness.

The bystanders, the paramedics, the police, the crime-scene specialists, the homicide detectives—one and all remote from the crisis of Jeremy. Even Charlie and Betty. And that quiet. Something was wrong with that quiet.

J. S. garnered as many nods, head-shaking nos, and shrugged don't-knows as he did whispered answers. And others in the alley crowded around, leaned into the conversations to hear, and kept silent themselves so they could.

Charlie could even hear the sea-laden breeze stir the fronds of Mrs. Beesom's sentry palm into slithery whispers and rustling *clacks*.

"The press," Charlie said much too loud and everyone in the alley turned to stare. "There's no press."

"Well, thank a kind Lord," was Art Granger's fervent reply to that and several amens supported him.

"So many crimes reported in L.A. they can't get to them all," Mary Maggie said, and opened her face in a huge grin. "Kinda nice, huh?"

That garnered more amens.

But since there were no pesky journalists, a shrieking cat fight soon shattered the peaceful crime scene.

CHAPTER 3

J EREMY'S HOUSE, LIKE Betty's, had its front door and two windows on the alley boarded up—stuccoed over on the outside and plastered over on the inside. The windows on the inside of both had been transformed into recessed, arched art niches. Betty's were adorned with Jesus Christ on black velvet in one and a painting of the Last Supper in the other, both bought in a Tijuana street market for bargain prices.

Jeremy's niches sported expensive metal-sculptured nudes of women in various stages of sexual congress with each other.

The upstairs windows fronting on the alley were heavily barred on the outside, as were all outside windows, up or down, in all four houses of the complex. These windows pulled inward so they could be washed. Jeremy's always gleamed because he had a cleaning lady who actually did windows. Her name was Kate, but her heritage was definitely Latino. An older, no-nonsense woman, she refused to work for beans. Both Charlie and Maggie were on her waiting list for clients. She was the best, and Charlie figured Kate would be retired before Charlie made it to the top of the list. Interestingly enough, Kate Gonzales refused to clean for the very wealthy because they preferred cheap, illegal labor and would not pay her price.

Maybe vast mansions didn't show the grit and kitty litter like Charlie's little nest.

Detective Amuller studied the metal sculptures in the niches in Jeremy's living room. "What kind of a guy was he?"

"He wasn't poor, I think—"

"I mean sexually?"

"Never bedded him."

"I mean did he like women or men or both or animals or—"

"Since I've lived here, Jeremy has had a succession of younger women living with him for short periods—teens, mostly."

"How old a man was he?"

"Mid forties, early fifties, I'd guess. He worked out constantly, so his bod was hard to gauge. Hell, you got my DNA report on your little computer. You should be able to call up his life history."

"Not on record. In cyberspace he never existed. No Social Security number, no credit records, no tax records. Nothing," Officer Mary Maggie said, stepping into the room from the kitchen. "He's what's known as one suspicious character."

Officer Mason had stayed to see Betty Beesom settled for the night. She had been doing a great counseling job with the frightened witness when Detective Amuller insisted Charlie come to Jeremy's with him.

Two uniforms and a lab type had gone over every inch of Jeremy's condo for clues to his murder as well as his life. They were gone now, but Charlie was still to touch nothing.

Officer Mary Maggie had insisted that you can't catch a cat by chasing him. You had to ignore him until he came to you, curious about why you stopped chasing him and what you were going to do next. Charlie was skeptical—she'd never heard of anyone understanding cats. But sure enough, another uniformed officer followed Mary Maggie with a struggling cloth bag in each hand.

Just to be sure, Detective J. S. had both cats combed and

clipped and pricked for blood samples. They moaned that eerie warning as the technicians tortured them on an old *Wall Street Journal* across Jeremy's kitchen table and at each other. When the torture was finished, Officer Mason handed Tuxedo to Charlie and sent Hairy home with a gofer cop.

Tuxedo didn't hiss or yrowal or moan or scratch at Charlie. He trembled and clung to her. Charlie was afraid to move. Tuxedo hated Charlie.

"Well, you could comfort him with a little snuggle or something," the female cop said with disgust. "*He's* not as used to murder as you are."

By the time Libby and Maggie Stutzman and "that man" drove into the compound within minutes of each other, Charlie was shaking worse than the cat. Officer Mary Maggie and the gofer cop were all that remained of the Long Beach PD. Jeremy was gone, the Trailblazer was gone. The blood was still on the pavement where Jeremy had dripped it.

"Glad to see you're human," Mary Maggie said. "Some people go into shock and delay the normal reactions." Besides a regular cop, she was a community outreach and liaison officer. Part of her job was to temper the impact of necessary police-work on victims, their families, and communities, and to train volunteers to do the same. Her ridiculous falsetto voice was comforting, and when her smile tightened up from sloppy, it was unexpectedly shy. "Want me to call your doctor?"

"God, no." Charlie's only doctor at present was a gastro-intestinal type who treated her incipient ulcer. "He only wants to talk to me when I throw up blood. How do you know so much about cats?"

"I don't really. Got two dogs myself. But I've seen chickens traumatized by murder."

"You're kidding. Chickens?"

"Honest. Tuxedo and Hairy, now—they witnessed something they can't tell us about. Wonder what they'd say if they could."

Charlie took another look at Libby's cat.

Both Libby and Tuxedo Greene slept with Charlie in her bed that night. Except when they went back to visit grandma in Boulder, Libby hadn't done this since the monster-under-the-bed or in-the-closet phase. Then she was tiny and blond and cute and forceful. Now she was about three inches taller than Charlie, drop-dead gorgeous blond and forceful.

"Mom, we've got to stay together for protection," she'd said as she and her cat crawled into bed and fell protectively asleep while Charlie lay awake.

Maggie Stutzman and her stockbroker boyfriend, Mel, as in Clayton Melbourne, had no more than entered the fortress than the press had arrived in the form of a news helicopter. It dropped low enough to froth the fronds of Betty Beesom's sentry palm into a frenzy, suck dirt into the air from nowhere, and shatter the the peacefulness of the murder scene.

"Nobody's luck holds forever," Officer Mason said with an exaggerated shrug. She shepherded them all into Maggie's house, the closest door. Tuxedo hung over Libby's shoulder, relaxed as a rag doll. All was well now that his pal was home.

"Is Maggie short for Margaret?" Charlie's best friend asked the cop when Charlie introduced the two Maggies.

"For Mary," Officer Mason said and took Maggie Stutzman aside to grill her on where she'd been all evening and what she knew about Jeremy Fiedler and who might want him dead.

"I don't know that much about him, I guess," Charlie'd heard her friend answer, with a regret and sadness that belied her words. "But if it wasn't for robbery or something, my guess is there ought to be some angry fathers out there. He dated only the nubile."

Charlie's hearing was so acute, she often overheard conversations meant to be secret. It was both a blessing and a curse.

"Any names you can give us?"

"They just had first names, stock names like Stephanie and Michelle and Lisa." Maggie's name was more German but she looked Irish. Lush black hair, pale, perfect, almost translucent skin, and snapping blue eyes. Maggie was a lawyer whose bottom was growing out of proportion to the rest of her. She was one of the dearest, most trusted people Charlie had ever allowed into her life.

Maggie was a total idiot to trust Mel-the-swell-stockbroker with her heart, body, or finances. And everybody could see it but Maggie. Even Jeremy, who lusted only after the nubile, could see that. Mrs. Beesom had dubbed Mel *that man* in protest, and that was his nickname around the compound.

Even now, Mel, who was married to Mrs. Mel but on the brink of a divorce any second for at least the last six months, was watching lovely Libby instead of Maggie. Maggie glanced over at him and didn't notice.

Unlike Charlie, Maggie needed a man. Nobody needed this guy.

When questioned, *that man* admitted to knowing Jeremy Fiedler only from a party Maggie had given on her patio one night to introduce Mel to the neighbors and a few friends from her legal life. He hadn't stopped smoking the whole time and had impressed only Maggie. Nobody wanted to say anything to hurt her. So they hadn't then. Still hadn't.

Charlie had finally just fallen asleep when screaming outside roused her yet again.

CHAPTER 4

❖

CHARLIE AND MAGGIE sat on either end of Maggie's couch in their sweats, bare feet tucked under the center cushion, and raised some serious coffee in a toast to poor Jeremy.

It was a sort of a morning drunken spree without alcohol. Maggie had a cappuccino machine and had made them lethal lattes. Nobody but Libby and Tuxedo, still tucked up in Charlie's bed, got any sleep last night. Well, maybe Jeremy's spirit, somewhere.

They sat bleary-eyed, baggy-eyed, preshowered, preshampooed, even pretoothpasted. It took a community to face murder in the morning, a community minus the press and the *how-do-you-feels*. The silly doves were cooing their haunting mourning-mornings in the chilly air out there. In here it was cozy, and blessed with the vigorous smell of the coffee bean, freshly ground.

That man had left before Maggie, too, had heard the scream. Even Mrs. Beesom, asleep at the back of the compound, had heard it. No cat this time, but a man very literally frozen in shock on the front of the front gate. A reporter for the Los Angeles *Times,* he'd decided to skip the glass and razor wire on top of the wall and climb over the front gate.

"I'll sue you," he yelled as the ambulance types came to take him away.

"Two questions." Charlie started the salvo. "One: Why, with all the murders in this combined city, would the *Times* be interested in the murder of Jeremy Fiedler?" Females between the ages of fifteen and twenty-two seemed to get murdered every five minutes. Of course, that was true everywhere. Maybe it wasn't news any longer. "And two, who wired the gate?"

"One, I don't know. Two, Jeremy. I thought you knew. He wired the back gate, too. And all on his own nickel. It was a good deal, Charlie, for all of us. Comes on only at night."

"But why, and when? And what if Libby came home some night and didn't know, or one of her stupid boyfriends stopped by?"

"Jeremy pointed out that the high wall was not sufficient—anybody could climb the gates. He wired everything, Charlie, even the wall and razor wire. And Libby knew. You were probably on one of your trips—I think it was when you were in Las Vegas, and your stories were so horrendous we all probably forget to mention it. Or maybe we did tell you and you forget it. You're so overwhelmed at work and everything."

"So where's the switch that turns it on and off? And can that reporter sue us?"

"I don't know."

"But you're the lawyer."

"I'm not that kind of lawyer." Until recently Maggie had specialized in workmen's compensation suits—a sort of legal housekeeping that went nowhere and thus ended up in the hands of women. She'd burned out and was now with a firm that specialized in estate planning. "Maybe we could counter-sue for attempted trespass."

As if on cue there was another scream outside, really more

of a shriek this time. Neither woman jumped to her feet and ran to see what it could be.

"You know, Charlie, I'm beginning to regret your decision to vacation at home."

"We haven't even had time to discuss poor Jeremy's murder."

They carried their soup-bowl coffee cups and wandered out into the courtyard, disheveled and barefoot and beyond caring who saw them that way, too.

This time it was a reporter for the *Press-Telegram*. He'd managed to escape the electricity and razor wire and broken glass embedded in the top surface of the fortress's eight-foot wall by pole-vaulting into Mrs. Beesom's sentry palm. And the shriek had been Betty Beesom's.

The sentry palm had a history in the compound predating Charlie and Libby Greene. It was the tallest tree inside the walls, although there was a far-taller palm in front of Charlie's condo-house in the area between the curb and sidewalk. The sentry palm had been a gift to Betty from her church upon the death of her husband, and had special meaning. It was also a noted example of its type, and had been written up with its picture and hers in a garden section of the L.A. *Times*. A disintegrating copy of this newsworthy event still clung to the door of Betty's refrigerator with the help of a magnetized hummingbird.

That tree, by its very name, stood vigil over the compound, and the old lady was sure it looked after her safety just as her dear husband always had. Eventually, with some misgiving, she'd extended its protective qualities to include her neighbors within the stucco-covered walls.

Four rough trunks grew out of a base somewhere underground, the highest being maybe thirty-five feet and the shortest maybe twenty-five. Its spread among the drooping fronds was something like nine feet, and it had hung blessing over Betty's roof and the wall, too.

It now had three trunks standing and one fallen across Mrs. Beesom's patio—and across a very surprised journalist. He managed to wiggle out from under the palm trunk, narrowly avoiding poking out an eyeball on the pointed end of a sword leaf.

"Hi, I'm Mark Gifford from the *Press-Telegram*. And I'd like to ask you a few questions about . . ." Mark Gifford from the *Press-Telegram* was backing away from the three advancing woman even as he spoke.

"I hate strangers before breakfast," Charlie said, meaning every syllable of it. She had a low, throaty voice that some people found sexy and others found threatening, and others still, depraved.

"And I am an attorney," Maggie added, looking every inch a disgruntled housewife-before-makeup. "And I'll see you and your newspaper sued for breaking and entering, invasion of privacy, and unwarranted trespass. And my firm will see it through the Supreme Court."

But it was Mrs. Beesom who slipped the key from under the potted fern and opened the gate behind him so he'd backed into the alley before he realized it. Mark Gifford was showing that *oh-you-panicky-women-always-overreact* look and was about to launch into a routine to intimidate them into apologizing when the old lady slammed the gate in his face and locked it.

❖

The fortress's surviving occupants gathered in Charlie's kitchen for a breakfast of scrambled eggs and Betty's sinful cinnamon rolls with powdered-sugar frosting, hot from the oven, which nobody could figure out how she could produce at a moment's notice. And more coffee, this time from Charlie's percolator.

Maggie, the health conscious, brought segments of sweet California oranges that probably came from Mexico and squirted juice across the table at every bite.

Charlie had a dining room table in the next room covered with paper—mail, catalogs, and such, which she periodically dumped when the piles began slipping onto the floor. The amount of money she had lost by not sending in her sweepstakes card from Publishers Clearing House must amount to billions, and could certainly buy out Ed McMahon twenty times over.

But her breakfast nook in the kitchen, a high-backed booth with a table that caught the afternoon sun through its barred window, was a favored neighborhood chat place, any time of the day. And since only four of the human inhabitants were left, it had plenty of room.

And the topic of the day was finally Jeremy Fiedler's death, his life, and his secrets.

"How did Hairy Granger get inside the Trailblazer with Jeremy?" Charlie asked. "Was that where Jeremy died? I mean, I was in and out carrying groceries and then sat out there to eat a sandwich. I'd have seen anybody around the Trailblazer, except when I was putting the food in the cupboards and changing clothes. He was still dripping blood, so it doesn't seem likely he was already dead when I got home."

"Maybe he killed himself." Libby had showered, her hair still wrapped in a white towel that contrasted with the even, light tan of her presently flawless skin. Dark eyes mocked the older women, and she flashed the perfect smile for which Charlie had payed the orthodontist dearly. "And, Mom, do you actually know how long people drip blood after they die?"

"Not really."

"Listen to us, talking blood dripping, and the poor man's murdered." Mrs. Beesom looked toward the end of the table

24

where Jeremy had usually pulled up a chair from the dining room if they'd all gathered at once.

They looked in that direction as if expecting him to appear, to right the imbalance his sudden death had created in the concept of home.

"I feel as bad as you do, Mrs. Beesom. I was probably closer to him than anyone, but I didn't realize until that Maggie cop asked me directly how little I knew about him." Maggie the attorney, like Charlie, was still in her sweats and dishabille. Mrs. Beesom still wore her housecoat and sleeping cap that kept her thin, white curls safe between bimonthly visits to the hairdresser. Three different generations of women here around this table. Only the youngest seemed to be coping with things. "That never bothered me when he was alive. Now it does. But we need to talk this out, no matter how crass it seems. We can't let it fester."

"All I know about him really is he liked to work out and he had a weakness for girls young enough to be his daughter," Charlie said. "Neither is an unusual personality trait in the business I'm in."

Now they were all looking at Libby.

"Hey, don't worry there. Jeremy wasn't that dumb." The willowy girl/woman cut her sweet roll in half. "He knew there was one person in our complex capable of murder if he fooled around with me. And who'd hear any naughty suggestions if he even whispered them."

Now they were all looking at Charlie. "What, you think I would kill somebody if he—"

"Threatened your kid in any way? Yes," Maggie Stutzman, Charlie's best friend, said with no hesitation whatever.

Charlie's kid, all five-foot-nine of her, slithered out of the booth with her half of a frosted cinnamon roll and sashayed off to the hair dryer before her hair set-dried into permanent snarls. The cat on the refrigerator jumped to the counter and then to the floor to follow his buddy, sounding like a falling elephant with each landing.

Now they all stared at the remaining half of Libby's cinnamon roll.

Maggie and her butt won (maybe lost) as she reached for it first.

"Okay, what's the back story here?" Charlie finished up the scrambled eggs. "Why did Jeremy electrify the compound? Did he have enemies? Something worth stealing?" And why hadn't it occurred to Charlie to worry about him noticing Libby before now?

Betty Beesom scraped up the crumbs and melted frosting from the cinnamon-roll pan and licked them off her butter knife. "What I want to know is who called the police last night, Charlie? It wasn't us, and it wasn't either of the cats. I say it was the murderer of Jeremy himself."

"Maybe he had his cell phone in the Trailblazer with him and made the call as he was dying," Maggie offered. "Maybe he knew he was in danger so that's why he wanted the compound wired. So how did the murderer get in, then?"

"Maybe one of Jeremy's young lovers had a card to the obelisk," Charlie said. "Maybe her father found it and got in to murder the pervert who had ruined his innocent daughter. But even stranger—they can't seem to find Jeremy in any records, in cyberspace, nowhere. He has no existence."

"That's impossible," Maggie said. "Unless he wasn't really Jeremy Fiedler, but somebody else. His cars had to be registered to somebody. Maybe he just got deleted."

"Yeah, I've always worried about the lack of a paper trail now that everything's going electronic. Or maybe the Long Beach PD isn't that computer savvy."

How *did* Hairy Granger get inside the Trailblazer with Jeremy? What was Tuxedo Greene ~~tying~~ *trying* to tell Charlie and Betty when he sat on top of the vehicle? "Could you really disappear electronically and turn up dead anyway? And why didn't we get a shock off the back gate when we went out in the alley last night?"

"Maybe that part of it doesn't work," Betty Beesom answered.

So many questions. Only maybes for answers.

CHAPTER 5

❖

*C*HARLIE HAD JUST stepped out of the shower when Detective Amuller rattled and banged at the security grate covering her front door.

The obelisk originally had a buzzer and a speaker for each house to communicate with the gate as well as a button to open it for those permitted within, like the door release in an apartment building. Only the release buttons remained because vandals kept breaking the obelisk speaker or yelling obscenities into it when the fortress dwellers preferred to sleep. Visitors now had to park in the street. They could use the front doors of the two condos in front and call ahead for the two houses on the alley, where no one was expected to venture but the garbage man, cats, and homeless. One never put out the garbage or collected the empty cans at night.

There was only one bathroom in Charlie's house, and it was downstairs. And of course she hadn't bothered to bring a robe. Yelling for Libby to let in the police, she raced upstairs and threw on clean sweats.

"See you're still not home," J. S. Amuller commented when she came down trying to sort out her messy mass of wet curls with a wire brush. He was watching Libby ignore him. "How is it she survived in this institution with a practicing nubiphile?"

"Jeremy never bothered Libby."

"He wouldn't dare. My mom'd kill him."

"Libby—"

But the kid had trounced out the door, pulling her car keys from her pocket.

"Kind of chilly for shorts today," the cop said, starting to follow her, but he'd hesitated at her wonderful pronouncement long enough to give her a head start.

"She's slinging at the diner today. Green shorts, pink shirt." The Long Beach Diner was better known for its meatloaf and mashers than its color scheme.

There was room only for one car for each house in the designated parking between patios, and Libby usually parked next to their patio heading out. She had the Wrangler started and through the gate before the detective could reach her.

They stood on the steps of Charlie's sunken patio watching the gate close. "I'd like to explore that last statement of hers. Have to catch her at the diner, I guess. What's this about Art Corry from the *Times* getting a real shocker off that gate last night?"

"Hey, that's nothing. We had a guy from the *P-T* pole-vault over the wall and break Mrs. Beesom's sentry palm this morning." A seagull sat statue-still on the pink-tiled peak of Jeremy's roof, like he thought he was a pigeon. The gulls were everywhere out here. They fought the cats and drunks for edible garbage in the alley.

"Against the law to electrify security systems without displaying warning signs."

"Don't look at me, I didn't know anything about it. Jeremy apparently had it done and paid for it himself while I was out of town last fall. Nobody thought to tell me about it until this morning."

"Convenient. Everything about this murder is so convenient. For some people."

29

"Then it was murder for sure, not suicide?" The gull activated effortlessly and glided over the compound, feet flattened up under his tail feathers, gray wingtips on his underside.

"Mr. Fiedler was suicidal?" Detective Amuller's blond hair was clipped short, but still it curled. It gave him a babyish appearance at odds with his considerable height—six-two or -three.

"Not that I ever noticed. But we survivors were talking about it this morning—like it would have been a way for Jeremy to die while I was watching the courtyard and the Trailblazer."

"I'm afraid things aren't *that* convenient, Charlie Greene."

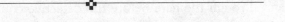

Charlie and J. S. Amuller stood with Maggie Stutzman in Jeremy Fiedler's living room.

"What does J. S. stand for?" Charlie asked him, distracted. There was something wrong with the script here. Or was it the set? She loathed it when people talked cinema—life was too surreal anyway. Now she was doing it. Even in her thoughts. Jesus.

"Stands for 'Just Standard' for cops, okay? I don't want to hear that question again. Understood?"

"No problem. I'll ask Officer Mary Maggie."

"I am looking for clues into the life of a man you two have been living close to for years and tell me you know nothing about but didn't realize that until he was murdered."

"What I want to know is why he thought he had to hotwire the compound." Charlie reached a hand to the art-deco angular light fixture hanging way off center from the ceiling. "And why you didn't get a shock when you opened the back gate last night."

"*Don't* touch anything. Either of you," the homicide man yelled for the umpteenth time.

Maggie straightened and pounded her chest. "He's making me afraid to breathe. I'm not getting enough oxygen."

"Okay, you both make great comediennes, but we have a murder and those who live here are at the top of the list as suspects. If you get my drift."

"No." Charlie reached for her friend. "She's on allergy medication and it makes her heart beat funny. This has nothing to do with you, J. S., honest." But even as she said it, she saw the disbelief in the detective's eyes. Some people are just never convinced that there is anything that has nothing to do with them.

For some reason it was at this point that Charlie Greene had a glimmer as to how deep this shit could get here.

Detective J. S. stomped across Jeremy's living room and up the two steps to the dining-room ledge. (All the living rooms and patios in the complex were sunken, for some reason that escaped Charlie altogether). He wore a longish raincoat like he was auditioning for a TV movie. Under the raincoat he wore the same sport coat and pants as last night. The result was rumpled, again suggesting a TV cop circa the 1980s.

Maggie mentioned the *M* word and it turned him off so, he was speechless. His grimace, as loose as his grin, made the chipped tooth add to his boyishness.

Maggie lay on the floor with her bottom up against Jeremy's couch and bent her knees, putting her lower legs and feet on its seat, her hand over her heart. Charlie laid her hand over Maggie's and after a few minutes she could feel the tempo of the heartbeat's sudden return to normal.

"You're too young for menopause, Maggie—what forty, forty-one? Has to be those allergy pills. You've got to get off them. So your nose runs all the time—"

"I haven't taken them for three months. Charlie, my clock's running down." Those snapping blue eyes dripped tears into her ears.

J. S. groaned. "I hate to bother you two at such a dramatic moment but—"

"Kate said it was estrogen deprivation and not to let the doctors talk me into heart disease. They're so set on getting women for heart trouble—don't distinguish between the sexes."

"Kate? Kate Gonzales? Is she—?"

"Started last week. I was at the top of her list, Charlie. You're next. Now with Jeremy gone, you should—"

"Who is Kate Gonzales, and what did she have to do with the murder victim?" Drops of sweat beaded the detective's forehead.

"She cleaned this house, every other week." Charlie helped Maggie to her feet. And great, now we have another reason for me to want Jeremy dead.

"You take the word of a cleaning lady over a medical doctor?" the cop said, as if he'd stumbled into an Alzheimer's unit.

Lots of glass and triangles in Jeremy's house, like triangular tables where the narrow end wouldn't hold anything, where if you put anything heavy on the wide end it would tip it up and dump it. Jeremy'd always come to parties at Charlie's house and Maggie's, too, but she'd only known him to throw one at his house in the time she'd lived here. Granted, everyone worked a lot and entertained little. Still.

Even that once, when filled with people, it didn't take so many people to fill these little houses, this one had never looked that lived in. Even when his young lovers were in residence, if they smoked or chewed gum, they had to do it out on the patio.

Why did all this seem strange only now that he was dead?

32

CHAPTER 6

"DID YOU LIKE Jeremy Fiedler, Charlie Greene?" Detective Amuller asked as they walked upstairs. He'd dropped his silly raincoat on the floor below and looked a lot cooler. You so rarely saw raincoats in Southern California.

"You know, I kind of did. I'm not sure why, considering his taste in females."

"I know what you mean," Maggie said behind them. "He was always so dependably *here*. But he never demanded anything of you."

"Yeah, anything happened, you call Jeremy and then the police. Even Betty Beesom did."

"So, you like having guys around if you don't have to do anything for them?"

The stairs in these houses crawled up one wall of the living room. He turned at the top to bar their way. Charlie looked back at her friend. They both nodded—but thoughtfully.

"And you don't find that a selfish reaction?"

Charlie and her friend shook their heads—but thoughtfully.

"I don't get this. Here you are in the guy's house, you sort of like him, he's been murdered, and nobody sheds a tear except for wound-down clocks. Fiedler's clock will never strike again."

"We didn't really know him that well," Maggie said. "It's

33

not like he's Mel. Not like we won't *miss* Jeremy."

"Jeez, he could have been a dog." The representative of the Long Beach PD lifted his arms in the air like the ceiling was about to fall on them. "I gotta be dreaming. You're professional, educated women."

"Jeremy wouldn't have shed tears for us," Charlie said, trying to help. *It's not as if a homicide detective wouldn't have served in far worse neighborhoods than this one.*

"Yeah, but guys don't cry."

Jeremy Fiedler's bedroom didn't look slept in anymore than the rest of the house looked lived in. Then again, Charlie and Maggie weren't allowed to look in closets and drawers, and obviously their dead neighbor hadn't slept here last night. A short stack of *Business Investor's Daily* on the nightstand was the only reading material evident.

Charlie dropped to her knees for a quick look under the bed.

"What, you think the experts haven't already looked there?" the detective condescended. "Maybe we should have this Kate-the-cleaning-lady up here for some expert advice?"

"That's not a bad idea." Maggie looked at him, surprised.

"If anybody knew Jeremy Fiedler, it would be the person who cleaned up after him," Charlie agreed. *Even if she's a woman, you jerk.*

The second and last bedroom was given over to Jeremy's office. Curiously, it was the largest of the two. Angled drawing board under the window, a computer/fax/phone/answering machine thing. Printer/copier/scanner.

"Now I know what's wrong here. What's wrong here is this place has been searched in a homicide investigation and it's not a mess. Either everything's been put back together or it hasn't been searched."

"Been searched, videotaped before and after, and carefully

arranged as was," J. S. announced triumphantly, back on familiar ground, "so that his neighbors, friends, acquaintances might comment on what they see. Ladies, what is it you see that is different?"

"First time I've been up here," Maggie Stutzman said.

"I see a home office of a landscape architect that looks as if it's never been used," Charlie offered.

"Did you ever meet any of his clients?"

"He always went to their houses or offices—I thought, anyway," Charlie said.

"Which of you, would you say, knew him best?"

"I did," Maggie assured him. "If the mornings were nice, we'd often have our coffee together on his patio or mine before work. I'm going to miss that."

"I didn't know you two ever met for morning coffee." Charlie felt cheated, and she could hear that fact in her voice.

"You always left for work long before we did. Jeremy worked at home and my commute's only about twenty minutes."

"Did he talk about his clients? His designs? His little girls? What?"

"Mostly about his workouts, his vacations to Mexico and Costa Rica, Mrs. Beesom's nosiness, whatever."

"Did either of you ever see him carrying around armloads of rolled drawings? Did he ever discuss plant and tree types, ground covers?"

Charlie and Maggie looked blankly at each other, embarrassed, then shook their heads.

"That doesn't mean he didn't and we just didn't notice because it was so expected of him." Charlie tried to save the day but knew that was a weak answer. How could she not have questioned these things before now?

Because you're a selfish shit all wrapped up in your own life

35

and problems. And now Jeremy is dead and you never got to know him. You put the guy in the "no problem" folder and never took the time.

"I guess mostly we talked about me and my job and problems." Maggie Stutzman admitted what Charlie didn't want to. "He always asked about you, listened to you, if he wasn't in a grouchy mood or something. Seemed interested but not judgmental—"

"Never offered advice unless asked," Charlie chimed in. Wow, I'm going to miss him too. "Kind of strange for a guy, I guess."

"This health club he was so proud of—"

"Judy & Gym's Age Buster," Charlie finished. "I know it exists because I've driven by it."

"Judy and Gym Malakevich and every one of their ten employees swear they have never heard of a Jeremy Fiedler and could not identify him from a photo of him dead. He carried no photo I.D., no driver's license, and there's no record of his registering his cars."

"But you can't drive without a license or having your car registered," Maggie said.

"You can until you're pulled over once," Charlie pointed out. "Have you ever been pulled over? I haven't—but I know it's going to happen eventually, so—"

"Exactly," Amuller told them. "Illegal vehicles and drivers on the streets are everywhere."

"Maybe Jeremy knew a hacker who got everything erased from the computers," Charlie said.

"You can't erase anything—there are even better hackers—most of them five years old—who can reconstitute crashed files, or whatever," Maggie insisted.

"The Pentagon didn't believe those kids could access their secrets just for the fun of it, either. But they did. Police departments have so much information to enter, compare, and access, and limited budgets to do the entries and the accessing and keep their computer systems up to date. My vote is they lost Jeremy somehow. I mean, they can't afford these new computer geniuses." Charlie noted raindrops on Jeremy's windowpanes and Amuller threatening to implode.

"Excuse me, I had no idea I was in the presence of such intellectual geniuses. Have I just been given all the answers to the meaning of life here or what?" He led them back downstairs and put on his raincoat, catching their exchange of smirks. "It *is* going to rain, you know."

"Already raining. I just never see raincoats much around here. I see those in Manhattan," Charlie said.

"You two have opinions on everything—medicine, menopause, computer systems, police investigations, the Pentagon, and the weather. I suppose I should ask such knowledgeable ladies for stock-market tips."

"I like financial institutions and pork bellies," Maggie said. "But Merck and Oracle would be—"

"Huh-uh. Automatic Data and Stryker are better bets, and stay away from pork—"

"Now stop that." The red patches crawling up Amuller's face from his neck and spreading to his ears and into his hairline, deepening. "I hate sitcoms."

Maggie ignored him and started crying again. "I really am going to miss Jeremy. I feel terrible about not getting to know him better."

"Me too," Charlie chimed in, but without the tears. "I just thought there was plenty of time. I didn't know he was going to die. But Detective Amuller, could Jeremy have gotten lost in the Y2K computer thing?"

"Maybe he could, if he wanted to." He turned up his collar and motioned them out into the rain, past the yellow police tape and into the courtyard where Jeremy Fiedler's blood was washing away. "Question is, why would he want to? Question is, what makes you imagine that I could believe you two have no answers to that question?"

CHAPTER 7

◆

"*H*E KNOWS WHAT happened to Jeremy." Charlie tipped her wineglass toward Libby's cat. "He and Hairy Granger."

She and Maggie had the grill lit on Charlie's patio, hamburger patties ready to go, and Libby was bringing barbecued beans home from the diner. Maggie had tossed a salad, and of course Mrs. Beesom was baking a pie.

Well, they were all suspects in a murder. They had to keep busy.

Besides, the air smelled so fresh after the rain and they were each so glad *they* hadn't been the one murdered. She and Maggie kept looking at Tuxedo, who did not appear responsive, and over at the vacant parking space where Jeremy's blood was no more than an outline in the shape of a huge amoeba and a rivulet stain running toward the drain in the middle of the courtyard. It was just a year ago February that Jeremy had somebody in to flush out that drain. He always took care of things like that. Who would do that now? Charlie wouldn't even know who to call.

"How do we know the murderer isn't still around?" Maggie uncorked another bottle of red. She was getting tiddly, and Charlie was trying to. "I mean, why should he be done yet?"

Charlie had been asking herself that question since the police left the compound last night. In her experience, which was growing considerable, one body tended to lead to another. "I suppose you are going to want to crawl in bed with me and Libby and the damned cat tonight."

"No, but I do think we should break the rules and sneak into Jeremy's house and find out more about him. I mean, the police have such a caseload they'd do anything to pin this on someone in the compound and get on with their jobs and lives—hell, I would too. Charlie, as an attorney, I have learned that you cannot depend solely on an attorney to vet a contract for you. As an investor I have learned you can't depend on a broker to ignore the latest 'tip' and really study the fundamentals of a company. As a shopper, I have learned you can't depend on a retailer's advertising to give you the real story about a product. Why should we expect the police to be any more concerned about our welfare when trying to do their job? Everybody has an agenda, you know? Especially cardiologists, gynecologists, and pharmaceutical companies."

"Whoa, back up there—stockbrokers? Mel?"

"He's a wonderful man, Charlie, but no great shakes as a financial planner."

And here Charlie thought she'd known her best friend so well. "But he's your broker and has been for years."

"I just use him to do the transactions, not to tell me what to invest in."

"So you're not advising all those geezers planning their estates to take his advice about turning over their 401Ks at retirement?"

"No, we have several bankers and financial planners we recommend. How do you choose your investments?"

"Mostly through my boss. He read *The Beardstown Ladies*. He's into compounding and dripping and stuff." Charlie had made some money in Las Vegas last fall and garnered pretty good commissions. Richard Morse had talked her into investing some of it. "You're not really into pork bellies, are you?"

Maggie's eyes danced. "I couldn't help baiting Detective Amuller."

"Baiting him is one thing, breaking into Jeremy's is another."

"Oh, come on, Greene. Where's your sense of adventure?"

"The answer is absolutely not. That's the wine talking."

"Okay, we'll wait until after coffee."

Charlie was feeling the wine, too. She poured herself another glass and sat down in front of the cat. He perched on a flower-box ledge so he could look down at her with disdain. "So what happened to Jeremy last night? And how did Hairy get in the Trailblazer with him? I know you were trying to tell me something."

He didn't even blink. Nothing can look as evil as a cat when it decides to. But he lost interest in tormenting her when Libby's Wrangler roared into the drive and stopped in front of the obelisk.

"Jeremy was one of the original occupants of the compound, wasn't he?" Charlie asked Betty Beesom over probably the best hamburger she'd ever eaten—complete with lettuce, tomato, pickle, sweet red onion, ketchup, and mustard. She could hardly get her mouth around it. This was not the first time she'd noticed how good life tasted after the trauma of someone else's death.

Betty's watery eyes teared even more but she took a mouthful of the diner's barbecued beans, a sinful delight and favorite carry-out for miles around. "I moved in first, and him second. Our doors fronted on the alley then. Wasn't long before we both saw the mistake in that, I'm here to tell you." She reached into the elastic waistband of her polyester slacks for a tissue. "But Jeremy, he isn't."

Doug Esterhazie put an arm around her shoulders and gave her a hug. He'd come home with Libby, probably when he heard about the beans and the murder—and in that order. He would eat here and very likely again at home later. The kid was pushing 6' 3" and not done yet if he was to grow into his feet. He was all bones and braces.

Gawky, in love with Libby since he first laid eyes on her, he'd settled into the best friend role rather than nothing. Charlie hoped he'd hang in there until Libby's good sense caught up to her hormones, because when his body caught up to him he'd be a worthy foil for her shallowness. His father was also Esterhazie Concrete, which meant Libby might at least have a chance to survive her stupid career choices and settle into a life that had possibilities past the age of twenty-two.

What? You're talking husband material for your daughter, right? Hypocrite, her inner self reminded her. "Just like your mother did for you, and see what happened."

"What happened?" Libby leaned around Betty Beesom. "Who's mother did what for who?"

Betty and Maggie and Tuxedo stared at her, too.

"Get that damned cat off the table." Charlie tried to rescue her credibility.

"I thought we were talking about Mr. Fiedler, the murder victim," Doug Concrete said, ketchup dripping down his chin as he bit into his third burger. Charlie hoped Betty's pie was filling because they were out of beef and beans. And what was left of Maggie's salad wouldn't hold him till his second dinner tonight.

❖

If it hadn't been for the wine, Charlie would never have let them break into Jeremy's house. She and Maggie had pretty much decimated three bottles, and even the heavy meal hadn't doused the effects.

She had bought enough to have a glass before dinner each night while on vacation—not planning to finish it off the second night.

It wasn't like they had to break in. Mrs. Beesom had the spare key to his house and he'd had hers, just as Maggie and Charlie had exchanged house keys. If you lost yours you could go to your neighbor, or if you left town someone had a key to check out your house for burglars.

Sounded good, neighborly—the sense-of-community thing. And after living with her growing daughter in a bed/sitter in Manhattan behind a six-inch-thick metal door it had seemed sort of free and pioneerish or something. But the fact was, if Charlie thought there was a burglar in Maggie's house, no way would she go in there, key or not. She'd call the cops. No— she would have called Jeremy, and *then* the cops.

The cops, of course, had not used Jeremy's key and lock. But when the two back houses in the complex had their front doors on the alley boarded up and stuccoed and plastered over, the city had pointed out that the fire code demanded two doors of egress for each home, so Jeremy and Betty had been forced to add a door inside the compound—but it had to be a certain distance from the other door. Since two sides of their houses were essentially fortress walls and the once-back-doors opened off the kitchens, they were forced to add a door abutting the side wall. Mrs. Beesom's was operable, but all but hidden behind a trellis of some cloying flowers gracing a vine and the sentry palm, and it was never used. Jeremy's was completely hidden by a torrey pine he'd planted after the inspectors left, and on the inside it was disguised by a media center on rollers that you could move if threatened by murderous burglars or a house fire.

Charlie had heard about this arrangement but forgotten it, as she did most things not of continuous threat or worry. Hers was a busy world, after all. And she was surprised when Betty brushed between the branches of the torrey pine and the stucco with her key. The tree allowed her to open the door far enough to permit Doug to slide in and push the media center inward over a new layer of carpeting.

All five of them gained entrance without disturbing the crime scene protection on the outside. They had two flashlights among them. Three of them wore pairs of Mrs. Beesom's gardening gloves. Libby wore a pair of gloves she'd used as a prissy librarian in a school play—convincing she was not. Doug wore rags wrapped around his hands, again compliments of Betty Beesom. Charlie had explained that fingerprints were not the only source of identity you could leave behind. You left skin flakes or follicles or something wherever you walked.

Maggie quickly brushed that aside. "They've already tested for all that. Besides we've already been inside and they have no reason to do those tests again. They are very busy people. And as long as it takes to test all the evidence anyway, Jeremy's murderer will probably be known by then."

Half of Charlie was afraid Maggie was right. The other half hoped the lights would suddenly come on and Detective Amuller, in the company of a gofer or two, would swish his raincoat and announce, "Aha, we knew you would try this— and now explain yourselves."

Well, that's how she'd write the script.

Charlie, babe, this is not a script.

"I know, but—"

"You know what?" Libby squeaked, stopping in front of

Charlie so abruptly they both stumbled into one of the triangular coffee tables which upended and dumped its arty but empty vase, luckily on carpet so it didn't break. "Whoa, you can't even breathe in this place."

"I feel like Nancy Drew," Doug Esterhazie said without enthusiasm.

"You look like her, too," Libby came back.

They all started when the refrigerator shut off. Even that slight white noise had been loud compared to the emptiness that replaced it. The house smelled empty, too. No lingering scent of soap or cooking or aftershave on the still air. It felt more than just forsaken, it felt void of Jeremy.

Mrs. Beesom opened the refrigerator and they all gathered around like ghouls, the light flattening and whitening their faces. Yogurt, bread, oranges, raisins, milk, vodka, vermouth, and gin—and a vegetable bin stuffed with plastic bags they didn't open.

The freezer side had ice cream, frozen pasta dinners. At least he ate here.

Charlie rolled back the top of a modern version of a rolltop desk (it was white, for one thing) in the dining room which, like in all the houses, was on a ledge level with the kitchen, two steps up from the living room.

A blank notepad, some pens, stamps, blank envelopes. No business cards, check blanks, credit-card receipts, bank statements. "How did he pay his bills? How did he pay Kate Gonzales?"

"He could have paid Kate in cash and other service and repair people," Maggie said. "You can pay a lot of bills by direct debit of a checking account. I don't know about all of them. I wonder if he paid taxes."

"He paid in full for this house, I know. So he wouldn't have a mortgage payment," Mrs Beesom said, lowering herself to a stair with a grunt. "But he'd still have taxes. I just figured he sold another bigger house and put the money into this one."

"Must have had a lot to hide," Doug said, "to go to all that trouble."

"By now Detective Amuller and crew have to have contacted, say, the phone company or Edison to find out how he was billed and how he paid. If it was a debit to a checking account, that account had to have been in somebody's name who had ID—Social Security at the least."

"I don't know, Charlie. If you had your money in a trust fund, you could have all your bills sent there and the fund managers would pay them," Maggie said. "Of course, your trust fund would know who you were."

Charlie came as close to wetting herself as she had since the latter stages of pregnancy when a voice came from upstairs: "This is Jeremy . . ."

CHAPTER 8

———❖———

CHARLIE AND MAGGIE were nursing hangovers with skinny lattes sprinkled with nutmeg the next morning, their toes tucked under Maggie's center cushion, when Officer Mason called ahead to be sure someone would let her into the fortress. She'd called Charlie's house, but Libby never answered the phone before noon on weekends.

When she arrived, Maggie Stutzman made the officer a latte and crawled back on the couch.

Mary Maggie looked at each of them several times and grinned, "Saturday nights suck on Sunday morning, right?"

They were again in their uncouth, uncombed, unbrushed, just-out-of-bed modes, and their senses of humor wouldn't show up for a couple of hours.

The scare last night had nearly forced them to go to Betty Beesom's church this morning. We're talking a serious fright here, that no loose cop grin could budge.

"How are the cats?" she tried again.

"Recovered." Charlie slugged down the last of her latte and waved the empty soup-bowl cup at her hostess, not yet up to *please.*

"You won't stop peeing for a week."

"I'm on vacation for a week."

The officer took too deep a draft of her latte, blinked back

47

tears, pushed her glasses up her nose, and gave Charlie a conspiratorial look. "Any more . . . *interesting* ideas on Jeremy Fiedler's death?"

"Nobody disappears their identity that completely in this computer age."

"Computers make mistakes. People make even more. Not nearly enough of the people responsible for things can keep up with the technology. All you have to do is hire a hacker and disappear." Maggie Stutzman sang the same refrain.

"Shut up and make coffee."

"You two sound married. So, what'd you do besides drink last night?"

The unmistakable voice of a dead man coming out of the upper reaches of a more-than empty house had sent the conspirators scattering and then back, clutching. Charlie thought Doug Esterhazie would crush her head into his breastbone. God, they make kids hard these days.

"Officer Mason, do you think Maggie's hypotheses about technology overpowering the official brainpower in this country has any validity whatsoever?"

"Well, let me put it this way." Officer Mason took another gulp of her latte and fished in a uniform pocket for a tissue. "And I will never admit to saying this in a court of law—"

"We got the room bugged—but go ahead." Their hostess poured steamed milk into Charlie's latte cup.

"We are reportedly looking into hiring, at minimum wage, a few underaged geeks for a summer recreational workshop to look into the possibility of recovering lost, stolen, deleted, or screwed-up files of interest, because we can't afford Bill Gates's programmers or their fresh-out-of-high-school replacements-in-training."

"This sounds like really classified information." Maggie handed Charlie her second serious jolt.

"Well, let's say that if we need a middle or junior-high group of experts to handle this admittedly serious problem, we won't be able to afford community-outreach types like me."

"But aren't you worried those kids will go home and hack into stuff you don't want them to, once you give them the information to retrieve what you want them to? How are you going to keep them from babbling or selling the information they retrieve?"

"That's exactly the problem," Mary Maggie said, looking impressed.

Why did people assume literary agents were stupid? Charlie was expecting Mary Maggie to say, "So, you broke into the murdered man's house last night without disturbing the crime-scene foils, huh? Congratulations. What did you find? Hand it over before I take you to jail."

Actually the most impressive thing they found last night was the difficulty of getting back out the way they got in. If that media-center cabinet didn't want to push in for them over the new carpet, it turned really rebellious when Doug tried to pull it back in place. There was nothing to grip it with, and it was wider than the door and would be noticeable if left standing out a ways in the room because the indentation in the carpet would show between it and the wall concealing the door. And tugging too hard could knock some stuff off the shelves to be left on the floor and attract the attention of the next cop to enter and put the chief suspects, the neighbors, in an even more difficult spot.

Finally, Libby and Doug, probably because Libby's mom and her best friend were several sheets to the wind and Betty Beesom was crying again, took charge. They shooshed the three incompetent adults out the secret side door and closed it. Then they pushed the recalcitrant piece of furniture back in place and scratched the new indentation out of the new carpet and crawled out of the window. Since it was inside the compound, that window was not barred, and whatever crime-scene secret gizmos they might have set off somewhere did not send a team of LBPD types out to investigate. Of course, the problem now was there was no one inside to latch the window shut.

"Mo-om," Libby had assured Charlie, "everybody but Doug's DNA could be in the house before the murder. And we don't have to mention him. And the first person who goes in surreptitiously locks the window and—"

"Surreptitiously?"

"Now stop that." Libby left in a huff to take Doug home and left Charlie calculating all the ways Douglas Grant Esterhazie could be linked to the Greenes and the compound.

"This is Jeremy Fiedler," the message on the answering machine upstairs in the murdered man's house had said last night to scare the sense out of the neighbors who'd sneaked in illegally. "Please leave a message."

"But I didn't hear the phone ring," Doug said.

"Fiedler," said the man leaving the message. "I'm on to you and I'm going to blow your sick little world to pieces."

"Sounds like a father all right," Maggie had said. "He's just a little late is all."

Jeremy never answered his wired phone and had turned off the ringer. The neighbors reached him by cell phone. He'd always been unlisted. Charlie was, too. So what?

"I've got it," Maggie Stutzman said now. "Jeremy was in a witness protection program."

"Their identities are falsified but they still have credentials," Charlie told her, and turned to the policewoman. "Did Jeremy have his cellular with him in the Trailblazer when he died?"

"I'm the one who's here to ask the questions, Ms. Greene. And with your recent history, you might think you know all there is to know about murder investigations, but we can see in a weekend more murder victims than you've seen in the last three years." Officer Mason set down her half-filled cup and stood. "Now, if you'd be so kind as to wake your daughter for me, I'd like to ask her some questions."

"You'd be wise to let her shower first. She's not good in the mornings and doesn't have to go to work till noon."

"You sound like you're afraid of your own kid. It's not like she grew up downtown, even if her mother did lay one on last night."

They were halfway across the courtyard, Charlie and the lady cop, Charlie still cupping her coffee bowl in her hands, the coffee buzz beginning to cut through the wine hangover and sleep deficit.

"Just because you've seen countless disadvantaged and self-destructive teens in your work, officer, and are raising two dogs, does not mean you are up to Libby Greene this early on Sunday morning and before her shower." But Charlie escorted the cop to the second floor, knocked on Libby's door, threw it open, and hurried downstairs and out into the courtyard to finish her coffee.

The air smelled clean and cool. The morning fog had burned off early and the sky was a California blue. Her little lemon tree was in bloom and smelled sweet. You need to notice these things when you're on vacation, especially the kind of vacation Charlie was having.

Her flower boxes were a riot of color—lots of pansies and she didn't know what else. Charlie had finally given in to her neighbor's pleas and hired a "gardener," who was a totally different animal from a landscape architect, Jeremy had informed her, to plant the boxes and come around now and then to pick off the dead flowers and clean up plant debris on her patio and front yard.

He was one of Kate Gonzales's sons, and his name was

Leroy. That was a strange family. He'd rigged up a little timed-drip system that kept things watered. Charlie'd thought it a total waste of money but had grudgingly come to admit that if she was going to be a full-time literary agent and a mommy, too, she had to hire help with the small stuff.

She looked around her now and made a point to enjoy it. Most days she left for work before daylight and got home at dusk or after dark, and was too tired to notice Leroy's work.

The seagull who thought he was a pigeon posed on top of Jeremy's roof again. Okay, it probably wasn't the same one, but he did appear to be doing his statue thing in the same place.

Mrs. Beesom's sentry palm clattered merrily even though it was only three-fourths of its former self. Charlie must ask Leroy if he could help dispose of the dead fourth. Jeremy would have taken care of that once.

How could Jeremy have been so indispensable and still such an unknown quantity, and why hadn't she or Betty or Maggie raised this question while he still lived? Such mysteries can be fun—but not when they happen to you and your neighborhood.

Officer Mason slid out the back door and slumped into the deck chair across from Charlie. "She's taking a shower."

"Good plan."

"We're going to talk afterwards. I'm sticking with dogs."

"Another good plan."

"How can some young snit with three huge zits make a cop feel like a leper? Even if she is a blond?"

"Zits? Oh, there is a God." Charlie's buzz hove to and she stood. "Want some breakfast?"

"Already had my bagel." But Mary Maggie followed her into the kitchen and watched her poach an egg and heat milk, pour it all over a piece of toast. "I've heard of hang-over medicine, but—you're not going to eat that?"

Charlie grabbed some leftover orange slices and took her breakfast to her sunken patio to enjoy the birds flitting around Mrs. Beesom's feeders, the wonderful scents and colors of her own private patio garden, and what promised to be a beautiful day. She was on vacation, and would not obsess over the poor cop who'd stayed in the house to interrogate Libby, or even a murdered friend and neighbor. Not right now. Every minute counts in this crazy world. If you can enjoy one, grab it.

Even her commute—often two hours each way, if not held up by an accident or construction or whim of the freeway god—offered chances to grab some time to do something or enjoy something, like eat a bagel or dry her hair while sitting in gridlock and talking on the cellular to New York which was three hours ago on the wrong time and maybe already out to lunch.

The options were endless with her notebook computer and e-mail, her electronic scheduler. Gridlock used to be an ulcerating, unscheduled hassle in an already frantic day. But Charlie had adjusted, and now she was woefully behind in her day and makeup et cetera if there was no grid to use to get ready for the office. She'd been known to arrive without her pantyhose on. No way could you drive a freeway and put on pantyhose.

It was the return journey at night that was the problem. As she'd increasingly lost any pretense of control over her only child, she'd sort of given in to the exhaustion besieging her on the return trip and risked drowsiness and death from inattention.

But in Charlie's crazy world, this day had become special suddenly, and she spooned up the rest of the warmed eggy milk with a satisfied sigh. Three whole zits that weren't there yesterday. What more could the mother of a teenaged girl ask? Libby Abigail Greene was about to have her period.

CHAPTER 9

◆

CHARLIE UNLOCKED HER mailbox, one of four silver doors in a black metal casing on a pole carefully lettered with a number of crude suggestions. It stood outside the compound, and she had to step aside when the gate swung open and Officer Mason strode out to the street and her car.

Before the gate could close, Libby and her Wrangler roared out, too. Thankfully, the cars headed in opposite directions. Neither female saw Charlie, or pretended they didn't. Both looked royally pissed. Charlie figured Doug Esterhazie had lost his anonymity with the Long Beach PD.

Maggie slipped out her front door as if she'd been watching for them to leave. She opened her box and Mrs. Beesom's. Whoever got to the mailboxes first usually brought in everybody else's mail and left it on their doormats. It had been Jeremy's idea, so anyone coming home after dark wouldn't be exposed to mugging. The same key worked for all four boxes. Charlie and her best friend stood looking at Jeremy's box.

"I don't remember ever bringing in his mail," Charlie said.

"You're usually the last one home. I took his in when he went on trips." Which wasn't very often.

"He must not have picked his up Friday, either, if he didn't pick up ours. Maggie, when you took in his mail, was it addressed to Jeremy Fiedler?"

"I'd think I'd have noticed if it wasn't, don't you?"

"You don't remember." They stood talking to each other but looking at Jeremy's mailbox, like they were talking to it. Neither wanted to admit what both knew they were about to do. "If he got mail, he had to have an identity recorded with the post office. I mean, they won't just deliver to an address. Will they?"

"We better hurry before someone sees us."

Charlie emptied the last mailbox and both of them rushed to her front door. She'd blocked open the security grate that guarded it from a surprise visit from the big bad wolf.

"What happened to your key? You're going to lock yourself out again."

"It's just easier to block it open. You know, there'd be one way for sure to prove Jeremy had no identity—if he didn't get any offers from credit-card companies to lend him buckets of cash at twenty-two percent after six months." Charlie rummaged through her mail, all junk, not even a doxy magazine for her teen, and threw it at the pile already overloading her dining room table. They settled at the breakfast nook with the rest.

"We should be wearing gloves," Maggie said.

"Too late now." Charlie helped her best friend sort through their dead neighbor's mail and then looked up, astonished. "God, they actually send credit-card stuff to Occupant?"

"Do you suppose they have those phony checks made out that way? There's no bank statement or bills."

"Mine and Libby's was all junk the last two days, too. Even Edwina e-mails now or calls. What did you get?"

"Hardly anything of importance comes through the U.S. Post Office anymore, when you think about it." But Maggie fanned out her mail on the table, too. Two mail-order catalogs and her ten-million-dollar winnings from Publishers Clearing

House came to Maggie—the rest came to Occupant or to Resident.

"You didn't get a bank statement, either."

"My bank's gone electronic."

"So has mine. Do you think if you are totally electronic you can escape your identity?"

"Charlie, there's always the IRS, and the city and county and state governments have to keep track of you for tax purposes."

"The IRS has gone electronic for filing and billing simple tax statements. If you could get access to their computers, which are rumored to be medieval anyway, you might disappear yourself."

"But what about your Social Security number? Have you noticed how we keep changing sides in this argument? You scare me."

They looked at Betty's mail. Three mail-order catalogs for sensible shoes, *Stylish, but with big toe boxes and slender heels, for the mature, stylish woman.* One birdwatcher's newsletter. A glossy quarterly report from Sara Lee. Three glossy brochures spouting the advantages of Celerium, the antiaging pill. *How to live longer and enjoy it. The miracle cure for cataracts and senility. Orgasm for those over eighty!*

"Maggie, these are all addressed to her, at least. We all worry about our personal business, buying habits, finances, and health problems becoming public knowledge to whoever buys the right mailing list."

"Vibrators? Porno videos?"

"Look—here's a come-on from two brokerage firms. They know she's got Sara Lee, and she probably has other investments. They know her age, probably that she's widowed, may even know what she has in her checking account. Here's something from her bank, looks like. It's all addressed here, and to her. She's targeted. Ah, here's AARP. See what I'm saying?"

"I don't want to."

"What are you talking about?"

"They make dress shoes with big toe boxes and narrow heels? How come I can never find any? And if I order a catalog like this, they'll give the AARP my name and address and the people who want me to have orgasms after I'm eighty."

"Maggie, the important thing is, almost everything is known about Betty Beesom. Almost nothing about Jeremy Fiedler. He didn't seem like the hacker type, but if the Long Beach PD can hire some hackers, he sure could."

"To get himself erased from all electronic records. But there are still paper records on him somewhere—backup copies of computer disks and CDs."

"Could be hard to find. Software changes, and companies don't back up the dated versions long anymore."

"Yeah. Look, they've even got pumps like mine—but with a wide toe box and a narrow heel."

Outside, the gate grated open and Betty's Olds 88 roared in. They looked across the table at each other, sharing a familiar thought. The old lady drove only to church, the supermarket, doctor, dentist, and beauty shop. To the homes of a few close friends, and even fewer restaurants. She did much of her shopping by mail. But it was only a matter of time before she and that juggernaut hit something. Charlie and Maggie dreaded the day Mrs. Beesom could no longer drive. Particularly now that Jeremy was gone.

Maggie took Betty's mail over to her and Charlie forgot and answered her phone. It was Ed Esterhazie. Officer Mason of the LBPD had been for a visit. Ed was on his way over.

The Esterhazie mansion wasn't that far away, but Charlie was still surprised at how soon the doorbell rang. She opened the front door and then the security grate to the president of

Esterhazie Concrete just in time to surprise two young things laying wrapped flowers up against the front gate of the compound. When she called to them, they turned and ran.

"Wait." Charlie ran after them, leaving poor Ed to hold the grate open. When she returned moments later, one of the floral offerings exploded, and just the percussion knocked Charlie to the sidewalk. Seconds later another explosion sent pieces of the iron driveway gate flying. One twisted bar embedded itself in the front of Maggie's house. And if Charlie had thought the world a strangely quiet place when the compound filled with emergency and official officials to investigate the murder of Jeremy Fiedler, it was totally without sound now. She couldn't hear herself swallow, or the sound of her shoes as she staggered to her feet and wove her way toward Ed, who lay sprawled across her front step.

He'd let go of the security grate and it had slammed shut, but it didn't matter because the front gate was open to all now. Permanently. Charlie giggled and couldn't hear it either, her ears should be ringing. Panic at the thought of a permanent disability seeped into her consciousness with an odd and horrid tingling.

"Ed," she felt her mouth and tongue and vocal cords say.

His eyes were open and blinking. Blood on his forehead trickled off into the inverted V of his hairline to one side of his widow's peak. Charlie collapsed to a sitting position next to him and blinked back.

Just around the corner, the girls had jumped into a waiting car which had no discernable license plate and whose driver laid rubber for a block getting them out of the neighborhood. Now she knew why.

Ed was talking to her, struggling to pull a cell phone the size of a thin billfold out of his shirt pocket. Pretty soon you'd be able to make a phone call on a pinky ring.

"I can't hear you," she told him, and couldn't hear herself. Was she making sound?

Maggie and Mrs. Beesom appeared as one out of the void and Ed handed Maggie the cellular billfold. Ed was a good-looking fiftyish, in a prosperous way—

That doesn't make sense, Charlie.

I know. At least I can hear myself think.

Ed sat up with Betty's help and gave Charlie a pitying look. What, her nose had been blown off, too? She was almost blind without her contact lenses, couldn't hear, no nose—what else? Well, she could smell. She could smell blood.

And Charlie could feel. She could feel herself tipping over where she sat.

Jeremy Fiedler sprawled on the lounge on Charlie's patio stroking Tuxedo and Jennifer. One of them purred. Jennifer sat alongside him and Tuxedo on his lap. He stroked the nubile on the head just like the cat. Jennifer hadn't grown into her nose, her hair was untidy, and her eyes red, but her legs were well shaped.

"What do you see in girls young enough to be your granddaughter?" Charlie asked him.

"Their acute intelligence," Jeremy said and Tuxedo grinned and Jennifer smiled with her reddened eyes and her whole face. She looked triumphant and transformed. And suddenly lovely.

Charlie sat in a morning grid on the 405 talking to Joe Putnam at Pitman's in New York about Keegan Monroe's novel. "So, what do you think?"

"Keegan Monroe can't write novels, Charlie, you know that. But I love the films he pens."

"You *have* read the manuscript—"

"I don't have to. The buzz is screenwriters can't write novels. You know that. He could always do a novelization, but he's too famous. Call me back when—"

Charlie was halfway into her pantyhose when traffic started up again. She almost spilled her coffee. And people used to obsess over being taken to the hospital in dirty underpants. Her shoes on the seat beside her, the foot on the gas wearing one side of the pantyhose to the knee, the one on the brake side bare, coffee cup in one hand and steering wheel in the other, and the cell phone in her pinky ring rang and she spilled coffee down her front to answer it but it was the wrong hand and how the hell was she supposed to show up at the Universal meeting in a ruined suit and she switched to the hand that held the wheel to answer her other pinky and Jeremy said, "Jesus, Charlie, watch out—" and there was this semi headed for her windshield and the driver lopping a wrapped floral arrangement at her and Jeremy saying out of the car radio which she was pretty sure she hadn't turned on, "Charlie, don't keep all your money in the stock market. Keep some in cash."

"Cash doesn't earn dividends and it doesn't drip," she told the radio just as the world exploded when she and the Toyota rolled right up over the bumper, the mile-high grill, along the hood, and through the windshield into the cab with Jeremy and Tuxedo and Hairy Granger, too. They were all grinning.

CHAPTER 10

❖

*C*HARLIE GREENE COULDN'T even hear in heaven. And the bright light touted by people who die but live to tell about it? It wasn't at the end of any tunnel. Figures, information being so screwed up these days.

No, the light came from above.

Charlie waited for the Anglo-Saxon, blue-eyed guy with the white beard to stare down from the light and point an accusing forefinger at her.

Maybe heaven didn't have any sound. Maybe that's what made it peaceful.

But it wasn't just one head that came between her and the heavenly light. There were lots of guys, and she knew them all. Lovely Larry looked ready to cry.

Don't cry, Larry.

Richard Morse just kept shaking his head. Maybe Charlie was still in her coffin and the light was a ceiling light in the mortuary.

Damn sight more likely than your going to heaven.

Oh shut up. Shit, her inner voice wouldn't let her be—even when she was dead. Oh, please don't let Libby's head appear in that circle above. I couldn't stand it, especially if she looked sad and especially if she didn't. Oh God, and not Mitch Hilsten either, please, please. He'd try to resuscitate me even after my

61

blood was drained and I'd been formaldehyded.

Ed Esterhazie was up there too, leaning over her. She had an insane desire to sit up very slowly and moan or something, but of course she couldn't. Could she?

The three men were so very different in their looks and reactions—she'd never noticed that before. Charlie knew she tended to lump all guys into sort of a separate grouping that held few individual qualities, kind of a guy profile. It made it easier to avoid personal relationships.

Her boss at Congdon & Morse, Richard Morse, his nose looking more bulbous from this angle, his short, clipped, curly hair kept carefully dark except at the temples, dressed pretty spiffy for a Hollywood agent. They were known for wearing pink or yellow shirts with brown suits and like that.

Richard was known around the office and behind his back as Richard the Lionhearted. He'd had his eyes done several times but the bags were forming underneath again. He had protruding eyeballs and could make a blink stick halfway down and still not look like a wink. But the eye jobs were gradually reinventing the term *wide-eyed*, even for him. He was short but dapper, savvy in so many ways, seriously clueless in just as many others. An enigma, as were they all, really.

Larry Mann, her assistant (secretary) at Congdon & Morse turned heads wherever he went, and made a fun escort because of that. Trouble was, he turned heads of both women and men, and his own preference was for the latter. Which made him a safe as well as fun escort. He was also, next to Maggie Stutzman, probably her best friend. Which made him a comforting and dependable date. He worked at Congdon & Morse solely as a way to make contacts in his chosen profession as an actor. Which was true of a fourth of the residents of Southern California. Another fourth were writing screenplays and novels. Which left the other half of the population of the area to work at real jobs to support them and the general economy.

Larry Mann was known at the office as Larry the Kid because he'd landed a part in a beer commercial as a cowboy and made the mistake of returning to the office in costume after a shoot. He had caramel-colored hair that swept across his forehead, and an incredibly expressive face. He had a carefully maintained and muscular body but a relaxed, lazylike posture and flowing movement that, along with the sardonic expression, mocked your expectations.

Charlie would miss them both, bless them.

She didn't know the president of Esterhazie Concrete well, but his expression was a combination of concern and anger. Which made sense. Because of Charlie's family, his had become involved in a murder. His son was infatuated with her daughter. Libby had once schemed to get them married because Ed belonged to the yacht club and she wanted entrance to the teenage social set and activities available there.

But Ed had been about to marry for the second time—Doug's mother having moved to Florida with his sister and a new husband. Dorothy and the second marriage lasted about a year. And Edward Esterhazie was once again an available millionaire or billionaire or whatever the rich did now. Wealth was so relative these days.

Ed's handsome was a more responsible one than Larry Mann's. A white bandage around his head, the craggy face of a sea-going yachtsman, the latent good humor of a man who'd made it.

The mortician must have left her contacts in because she could see them so well.

Hey, hold on here. How come you see when you're dead but not hear?

And then a sharp pain in one ear as if God had grown impatient and hit her up the side of the head. And then far

63

away and barely discernable, Maggie Stutzman said, "Hey, Greene, you going to loll around all day?"

And her stupid pale face with the snapping blue eyes joined the guy faces above Charlie. Next was Libby, who said nothing but did look like she cared, and who still sported three healthy zits.

"I'm not dead," Charlie heard herself say but as though through several feet of cotton.

Charlie sat upright in a hospital bed trying to convince Maggie and Larry that the compound had to be watched tonight because somebody blew the gate apart to get entrance to Jeremy's house to steal tons of cash he must have stored there in order not to have to write checks for things. He could take cash in to a bank and get a money order for big stuff, pay the rest in cash. Probably what he was murdered for. That's why he wired the compound. Her hearing may be almost destroyed but her mind was working pretty damn good, and she was dizzy with relief to not have been formaldehyded. Charlie knew she was babbling while slurping down clear broth, Jell-O, tasteless tea, and buttered toast.

Charlie was being held for observation and without bail at Community Hospital. She'd been scanned and X rayed and probed and prodded, all bodily fluids microscoped, her eyes and ears and nose tested by instruments of torture too numerous to remember. Nobody would give her an opinion on anything. But the layer of cotton lurking between Charlie and the world of sound seemed to grow thicker. She could hear herself now, but when Maggie and Larry talked it was distant, muffled, impenetrable.

"Wait, can somebody lend me some money?" Her purse

had accompanied her, probably because it contained her identity and insurance card, which here was the same thing. But her cash, which was minimal, had been removed to a safe somewhere to be returned to her upon her release to protect the hospital from responsibility. Her credit cards were still there, though. Maggie handed her ten and Larry a twenty.

Charlie knew the denominations only because she held the bills an inch away from her eyeballs. Maggie had thought to bring her lens case and solution and her eyes were soaking. Her contacts had been in too long with her eyes closed and needed it.

She knew her two best friends watched her, slid glances at each other, and were talking, but she couldn't determine if they were talking to her or to each other about her on the other side of the yards-thick cotton. She couldn't understand a word. Had they understood a thing she'd babbled? The panic tingles were so much worse now that she couldn't really see, either. She feared they'd stop her breathing next. She tried to keep the panic out of her voice so she could convince them of the urgency here.

"No, you see, you, Maggie, Mrs. Beesom, and Libby are in grave danger if these twits come looking for the cash tonight. And why wouldn't they? The LBPD is going to come to the same conclusion I have and the perps will have to act fast."

The aid who came to take her tray seemed delighted to find a resident who could eat that sludge and put her beaming face into Charlie's and nodded when her patient ordered scrambled eggs, coffee, and more toast for dessert. This hearing-impaired Hollywood literary agent and mother would need all the strength she could muster.

"I mean if these people are capable of using explosives, they're capable of blowing up the whole compound to find what they want—or do it out of spite because they can't. They could hold the neighbors hostage, even torture them if they suspect they know anything about the cash."

Her friends mumbled meaningless sounds, patted her hands to make any kind of contact, while she gobbled down another dinner.

"They could be Asian gangs who steal from, torture, and murder their own because they know these fellow Cambodians, Humongs or whoever keep so much cash in their houses because they don't trust governments or banks. If they've heard about Jeremy's cash supply."

But her friends rose and Larry patted her on the head like Jeremy did Jessica and Tuxedo. Maggie wrote in large letters on a hospital note pad, *We'll come back tomorrow. I'll bring your glasses. Stop worrying. Everything's going to be fine. Get some sleep.*

Yeah, right.

Charlie slid the bills under her pillow and stuffed the pills a nurse gave her into her cheek.

The minute she was alone in the dark, she spit out the pills, grabbed the cash and her sweatpants, T-shirt, and Keds out of the metal locker and her lens case off the nightstand, and closed herself in the bathroom.

Her best friends hadn't believed her. There was only one thing to do.

CHAPTER 11

◆

N ow THAT SHE was one, Charlemagne Catherine Greene
would never make fun of a handicapped person again.
The whole trip sneaking out of the hospital was terrifying without enough sound to gauge boundaries, to hear if someone
followed.

At least she could hear a little, she kept telling herself the
whole way, tears of self-pity trying to wash out her contact
lenses, making her stupid nose run—at least it was still on her
face. She'd had time during her escape to check out her face
and everything seemed to be pretty much there. She still had
Hairy Granger's scratch on her cheek and a bruise on her forehead where she'd hit the sidewalk. Nothing permanent there,
at least.

Her body worked fine now that she knew she was alive,
even after two dinners of hospital sludge. How could anybody
wreck scrambled eggs? Nothing bled there that she could find.
It was just the almost absence of sound—more tantalizing
maybe than no sound at all because you did hear a trifle bit
that suggested the part you didn't hear was what made sense
of life.

First things first, Charlie babe. Get yourself home in one
piece.

She walked boldly into the reception area and asked the guy

at the desk to call her a cab, expecting some orderly thug to overtake her at any moment while she waited. But when the cab arrived she could give the cabby her address, had cash to pay him, could see him talking and gesturing to the windshield, but she didn't have a clue what he was saying.

Charlie worked up the courage to tell him, "I'm deaf and I haven't learned to lip-read yet." It was so final, so awful to admit out loud. Made her want to throw up. That was another thing—she had an incipient ulcer to contend with, too, and no, antibiotics didn't touch it. It wasn't viral, it was caused by living. She just knew it would love being hearing-impaired and she started crying again.

The cab driver might find her so helpless he wouldn't take her home—just rob her and rape her and leave her at the side of some road. She actually could not believe she was still in the same body with the tough, worldwise, old Charlie Greene she'd been last night at this time.

I won't be able to hear the stupid cat fights, the mourning doves in the morning, hear when Libby sneaks in after curfew at night. Do they let deaf people drive? Jeeze.

No way she could travel the 405 to Beverly Hills, go to screenings and important party events with Luscious Larry on her arm, even talk to New York on the cellular before its three-hour premature lunch hour. What would she do to support herself and her kid?

Charlie was actually surprised when the cab pulled up in front of her fortress compound where Larry Mann, Detective J. S. Amuller, and Officer Mary Maggie Mason stood guard at the blown-away gate.

All these people were talking at her and she didn't know what to do. She'd returned home in a panic because she knew no one would be guarding her fortress and her child, and here they all were. Maggie Stutzman, Mrs. Beesom, and Libby Abigail Greene with a disgusted-looking Tuxedo over her shoulder appeared out of nowhere, too. That's what it's like when you can't hear people coming. They're just there.

But it was when Officer Mary Maggie said out of the blue, "Boy, do you look better than the last time I saw you. All tipped over on the sidewalk with your nose bleeding your guts out," that Charlie lost all semblance of control. She grabbed the startled officer in a hug of relief.

"I heard you. My nose was bleeding my guts out, you said." Charlie knew she was wigging, as Libby used to say before the language changed again. But for someone whose hearing had been so acute it was at times painful, this was an emotional experience.

"Mom can hear again, Tux. Say meow." Libby stuck her cat in Charlie's face and Tuxedo Greene hissed and spat. But Charlie did hear it.

"Hey, boss, did they release you from the hospital?"

"I released me. And see, I got home and I could hear. So it was the right thing to do. Did you tell Detective Amuller of my suspicions?"

"You won't believe this, Charlie Greene," J. S. answered for himself, "but the Long Beach Police Department was actually capable of coming up with some suspicions of their own."

"I knew you would." Charlie backtracked fast. "I just didn't know it would be this soon. Maggie, what are we going to do about the gate? Jeremy would have taken care of it. I'm hungry again."

"She may be hearing," Larry said, "but she's not tracking. My vote is we get her back to the hospital."

People talk *about* you and not *to* you when they think you have no control and they must make your decisions. The panic began to bubble again, and Charlie's heartbeat wasn't racing like Maggie's but it was sure getting forceful.

"Now, don't scare her, you." Betty Beesom pulled Charlie toward Maggie's house. "First we feed the poor woman. She must be recovered if she's hungry."

Charlie truly hated being perceived as helpless, but sat meekly at the table while Maggie warmed the mushroom pizza that had been the communal feast in her absence and Libby shoveled some leafy salad onto a plate for her. Betty poured a glass of milk. She could only consume half the meal, but it tasted wonderful.

"Before I send you back to the hospital, Ms. Greene," J. S. Amuller said when he stepped through the door, "I'd like to know where you think all this cash could be hidden."

"I'm sleeping in my own bed tonight. I'm not leaving my child here alone—"

"I'm going to the Esterhazie's," Libby said.

"—and I have no idea where he'd hide the money. But, since all the houses are the same, it must be someplace I'd know. And have you checked his computer? There has to be some way to trace him on it or get information about him from it."

"Tanya told me everything on Jeremy's computer was encrypted," Libby said and tugged a string of cheese off the cardboard box. She dangled it for Tuxedo, who was partial to cheese.

"Tanya," Betty said, wiping her teary eyes with a tissue stuck under her trifocals.

I can hear, Charlie thought. I can work, commute, talk to New York, support my child. . . . "Was she one of Jeremy's girls?"

"You didn't tell me that," Detective J. S. said.

"You didn't ask." Libby's tone had grown dangerous.

"I didn't know you knew any of Jeremy's girls," Charlie said.

"I knew most of them. Some of them went to Wilson."

"You didn't tell me that." Charlie might be hearing again, but it wasn't as good as before.

"Mom, you don't talk about things like that with your mother." Libby's disgust made Tuxedo look around for someone to bite.

"I can't leave Betty and Maggie here. . . ."

"I'm going to the Grangers," Betty said.

"And I'm going to Mel's."

"And I'm taking Tuxedo with me, so you have no excuse not to go back to the hospital."

"Before you go anywhere, Miss Libby, I want you to tell me all about these girls."

"We don't talk to cops about our friends, either."

"Libby, they weren't your friends. Jeremy was murdered, you can't—"

"They could have been my friends. We don't rat on our own."

"Own what?"

"Our own generation."

All Charlie could do was shrug helplessness at Amuller.

"What, you don't know the people in your neighborhood?" He turned on Charlie. "Even Fiedler, who lived within these electrified walls, and you don't even know your own kid? You do not make a very reliable witness. Murderers don't, either."

He continued to speak. Charlie could see it. But unfortunately, those were the last words she heard before the terrible silence enshrouded her with batts of cotton again. It was devastating. Very much like dying.

Outside, Officer Mary Maggie Mason gave her a hug but drove her and her silent world back to the hospital prison. And loner Charlie had been so surprised and grateful to have all these friends and people on her side.

CHAPTER *12*

———◆———

W HEN CHARLIE AWOKE in the morning, the world was still lost in deafening silence. But her mood was not as murky and hopeless because the sun was outside her window. Because she had once again cheeked the pills and spit them out. Because she'd slept like a tank from exhaustion and the knowledge that her fortress and loved ones were guarded.

And an inkling of an as-yet unplanned revenge.

This attitude of yours is the normal grief and denial of your condition, the therapist reassured her right after the gag-awful breakfast. *You have issues to deal with now that you've never faced before.* This assurance came by written word and than by a series of hand signals suggesting orangutan foreplay. *I'll come back when you've resigned yourself to your horrible fate.* Okay, that last sentence wasn't her exact words but it certainly was the meaning she conveyed. It fed Charlie's angst.

Hospitals were wonderful places to visit other people.

You couldn't tell nurses from aides from housekeepers from the boy next door anymore, but the doctors you can, and the one who arrived next brought a person whose handwriting was legible to translate his garbled message into script for the newly hearing-impaired who'd not yet had the chance or the right attitude to learn to sign.

The wonderful irony of this was that her hearing returned

again and she actually heard what he said to the person chosen to be the interpreter. God didn't slap her up the side of the head this time, but it did hurt for a second and she used every muscle in her face to hide that fact from her well-meaning but busy tormentors. Hell, Charlie knew busy.

What he said in effect, although she wasn't to read it this way when he left—interpreters are probably worth gold—was that, since she'd had no recurrence of reinstatement of her auditory faculties since being bludgeoned by the explosion, she should hold out little hope of recovering her hearing. And should cooperate with those who could teach her how to cope with this loss and lead a productive and satisfying life, as most do when they learn this coping thing.

She read the pad, which put it a little less bluntly, and motioned for the translator's pen to pen a question. *Life as what? What occupation can I pursue to support my child now?*

"Oh shit," he said clearly, "tell her there's government help for the handicapped and any number of vocations she can pursue but I'm just the doctor and that information will be available from other specialists and social workers. What time is it?"

No one had bothered to tell the doctor that Charlie's hearing had returned for a short period when she arrived home. Maggie was right. Specialized information didn't travel well, particularly when everyone was so preoccupied with their own business.

Charlie had no idea if her problem would return or for how long or when, but she did know that the only expert she could count on was herself. She'd been involved in crimes and murder before, but this was the first time it had hit home, and she was angrier than she'd ever been in her life. All she could think of was revenge.

You sound like a guy movie.

"Shut up," she told her good sense.

She didn't trust the hearing return to be permanent, so she made a quick call to the compound, where her daughter actually picked up. "Hey, Mom, can you hear again? That's great."

"I don't know how long it'll last, so be quick and tell me what happened last night."

"Nothing. Except the police are taking Jeremy's house apart looking for that cash. Mr. Amuller's here, want to talk to him?"

"Wait a minute, why aren't you in school?"

"Because Detective Amuller wanted to talk to me. Gotta go, bye. Here, it's my mom."

There was some background shouting and then Amuller came on the line. "You know Charlie Greene, next to you, your daughter's the most exasperating, uncooperative female I've ever met."

"I've been totally cooperative. Where'd she go?"

"Off to school, I guess. She refuses to identify any of Fiedler's girls. Called me a snot wad. Couple nights in a jail cell ought to do her a world of good."

"You'll only make it worse. Trust me. I'll work on her. She said nothing happened last night?"

"Nothing, and we can't find any cash stashes either. Maybe your theory was wrong. Imagine that." And he hung up on her.

Sounded like she'd have to make another escape. Maybe she could get home before her ears gave out again. And before they served lunch here. Charlie picked up the *Press Telegram* that had come with her breakfast tray, noticing a familiar name toward the bottom right side of the front page because the paper was folded that way.

Long Beach Police are looking for information on this man, the murder victim at the Belmont Shore condo complex, found in his car last Friday night. He went by the name of Jeremy Fiedler but might have other names.

A hotline number was listed along with one of those drawings you often see rather than a photo because there isn't one, and witnesses are trying to remember features, etc. This time it was probably not a composite but a sketch of a dead man with the artist imagining how he'd look alive. Charlie didn't think it looked much like Jeremy, but the name ought to bring a few angry daddies out of the woodwork—and did Jeremy always part with the young nubiles on good terms? Maybe a few of them would surface, too, so J. S. wouldn't feel the need to put Libby in a jail cell.

But it would also attract more attention to the defenseless compound, which Charlie doubted Amuller and company would want to continue to guard against intruders.

Charlie was dressed and on her way down the hall with the newspaper tucked under her arm when a nurse met her with a wheelchair and an already written note: *You are being discharged. Here is the card of the specialist, Dr. Rodney, who will take over your treatment.*

Well, Charlie's insurance company came through after all—wouldn't pay for another night of observation. Charlie took Dr. Rodney's card and sat in the chair. Down at the front desk, another note read, *Who should we call to come and get you?*

Charlie looked the nurse right in the eye and said, "A cab."

Like Charlie had a raft of caregivers who sat home all day instead of working, waiting to pick her up. Made her feel like an old woman. It was insulting.

❖

Betty Beesom sat at her ancient redwood picnic table with Art and Wilma Granger when Charlie entered the compound, her hearing still unimpaired. They waved her over and made her eat a tuna-salad sandwich with real mayonnaise and real potato chips, as in fried and salty. Charlie figured that making people feel guilty about buying real food is what made them eat out so much.

"Think your hearing will last this time, Charlie?"

"I don't know. It comes and goes without warning. I'm afraid to get my hopes up."

The breeze was a little cool for a picnic today, but the absence of the fourth trunk of the sentry palm left the patio open to the sun and the high fortress wall radiated back the heat, making it quite pleasant. "Eventually, something good comes of everything," Charlie's mother, Edwina, always used to say. At least until her daughter got pregnant at sixteen and her husband died six months later.

"Art's brother had something like that happen to him back in Iowa," Wilma said cheerfully.

"Wasn't either like that. No explosion. Ned fell off a tractor. Landed on his ear." Art hit himself up the side of the head. "Hearing came and went for about a week, then was gone. Deaf as a post the rest of his life."

"What'd the doctor say?" Betty passed the bag of chips around again.

"Said to go to a specialist." Charlie pulled out the card. "Dr. R. Rodney. Wonder if that's Rodney Rodney. Richard Rodney. Rupert. Rufus."

"Probably isn't pretty, or he wouldn't just use his initial," Art said.

"Don't forget to ask Charlie about the eye specialist." Wilma never quit smiling, even when she chewed.

"I thought your eyes had been bothering you lately, Mrs.

77

Beesom." The way the light hit Betty's face out here Charlie thought she detected a smoky film on one of them.

"She's been scared to death it's macular degeneration." A fragment of the leaf lettuce protecting the bread from the juicy filling stuck to Wilma Granger's smile. "Then she read about cataracts and how easy they are to fix."

"He was a laser doctor you went to, wasn't he?" Betty asked. "They do cataracts too now, I hear."

Charlie had to admit she hadn't gone to see that doctor yet. Friends and family had been after her for months to see about laser surgery for her myopia. Mitch Hilsten and Edwina had even sent clippings and pamphlets on this wonderful new procedure that cost two to three thousand dollars an eye. The office manager at Congdon & Morse, Ruby Dillon, assured Charlie that insurance wouldn't cover it.

"I haven't had the time or money to look into it. And people who do it seem to be putting drops in their eyes all the time." Charlie didn't like to go to doctors. But she still had this ophthalmologist's card in her purse, too. She handed it to Betty and Wilma grabbed it.

"But you bought all that stock," Betty protested.

"Well, Libby might want to go college after all. And that commute is wearing out the Toyota and I don't have medicare." Charlie was sitting next to Art across from the two women. Wilma was still smiling, but her eyes and Betty's were beseeching.

Jeremy would have done it.

Charlie looked over at his house—the crime-scene tape much in evidence—but the search damage must be all inside. There was a seagull posing on the pitch of his roof again.

You owe it to Jeremy and to Betty.

What if I go deaf and can't drive us to the doctor?

78

"Tell you what, I'll make an appointment for both of us to go in and see if he can help us. How's that?"

Wilma closed her smile on the lettuce, nodded, and bit her lip.

Betty Beesom broke into tears. "I just can't face it alone, somehow. Guess I'm getting old."

The seagull on Jeremy's roof took flight and Charlie savored the *whumping* sound of his wings.

Charlie choked on a potato chip when Jeremy Fiedler's red Ferrari came slowly down the alley, paused at the back gate, and drove on.

CHAPTER 13

◆

WHEN CHARLIE WALKED the few steps back to her house, Leroy Gonzales was pinching dead blooms off the plants in one of her flower boxes.

"Leroy, did you take care of the broken trunk on Mrs. Beesom's sentry palm?"

"*Sí*. Hall in thees place needs much help."

Boy, you can say that again. Something weird about a guy named Leroy talking pidgin, though. But an even bigger surprise waited inside.

Kate Gonzales was having a personal chat with Tuxedo. And an even bigger surprise than that—Tuxedo was paying attention. Charlie did not understand the conversation because it was in Spanish. Kate spoke softly, waving a finger in front of Charlie's nemesis. Both knew she was there but ignored her, and Charlie would not have dared interrupt.

Tuxedo Greene might be a royal pain in the ass, but Kate Gonzales was a legend in her own time. Tuxedo perched perilously atop a pile of stacked junk mail on Charlie's dining room table, looking down at the legend who spoke with her voice and with her index finger. That cat followed the movement of that finger back and forth for entire pages of foreign script, and when it and the voice stopped, the cat reached out and brought the finger to his face and bit it.

The feline and the house cleaner stood that way forever. The magazines and pleas from hard-up banks—companies who could go under without Charlie's fee for usurers and all the other crap she tossed these days—trembled. Hell, most of those poor companies needing her so badly could afford glossy. It was a wonder how that slippery pile stayed upright with an impressive-sized tom on top.

The bite had not been a hard one like he would have delivered to Charlie and then run off, but Tuxedo continued to hold on to Kate's finger with one paw. Finally, Kate laughed low in her throat and looked away. The devil cat moaned warning and leapt into her arms as the plastic wrap slipped from under him and the whole pile tumbled to the floor.

Kate Gonzales, the legend, turned to look at Charlie over Tuxedo's head, the smile still on her lips. "Cone-grat-u-lations, Sharlie Greene. You haff made thee top of my list."

Officer Mary Maggie Mason arrived as Charlie was enduring the telephone run-around trying to get a hold of J. S. Amuller to tell him about Jeremy's Ferrari. So she hung up and told the woman cop instead.

"You can hear again. What did the doctor say?" was the out-of-context response.

"Said I was to see a specialist and come to terms with the probability of permanent hearing loss. Test results aren't back yet. What about Jeremy's computer? Was it really encrypted?"

"Results aren't back yet. So where did Mr. Fiedler keep this Ferrari, and how do you know it was his?"

"I don't. It's just that it was red. Have you to talked to Kate yet?"

"Kate who? And did this doctor know that your hearing

had returned for a while before I took you back to the hospital last night?"

"I didn't tell him, did you? And Kate was Jeremy's cleaning lady."

"Jeremy had a cleaning lady? Why didn't you tell me that?"

"I told J. S. Wouldn't he have written it in a report somewhere? What does J. S. stand for?"

By now they were out at the back gate. There was no red Ferrari in the alley, but Charlie had seen Jeremy's there any number of times. He had a special key to the lock and would drop off things or little girls at the back gate. He never left the car there for long, though.

Officer Mary Maggie drooped, tucked her hair behind her ears. "I haven't had time to read the reports. We got a backlog of homicides and victims' families demanding the justice they got coming. You know, you help me out of a little bit, I just might tell you what J. S. stands for. I could use a little fun. It'll be months, maybe years before Fiedler's computer comes back from the FBI. And the lab tests, too. Everybody's swamped these days. So where did Jeremy keep this Ferrari?"

"In a garage somewhere, not too far away. He'd drop off a sweet young thing at this gate and take off to park the Ferrari and maybe ten minutes later he'd arrive on foot and let himself in the front gate."

"This is the screwiest setup. I just can't believe he lived here with three women and a teenaged girl and nobody got curious about his comings and goings."

"I can't either, Officer Mason. Mrs. Beesom was always nosing around. We could ask her, but I think she's taking her nap now. I wonder if my lab reports will take months, too."

❖

"Oh, a meestery. I luff a meestery," Kate Gonzales exclaimed from the stepping stool she'd hauled up to Charlie's room where she swiped tons of crud off the top of the door moldings. "Thees house will take a few visits to bring hup to snuff, you know?"

"That's fine," Charlie said quickly, already impressed with the way the windows and mirrors sparkled. "So Jeremy didn't pay you in cash?"

Officer Mary Maggie, stonewalled because Kate refused to go over to Jeremy's until she'd cleaned Charlie's house, paced and glowered, her expressive face convoluting in uncoplike expressions of impatience.

"He pay hevery six months. He pay ahead. I am going to miss poor Meester Fiedler very much. His company pay my company. It go right into my account in thee bank."

"What was the name of his company?" Officer Mason came to a halt.

"Fiedler Henterprises."

"Well, finally we've got something. What's your bank?"

"HHTP of thee Pacific."

The cop pulled out her cellular and stepped into the hall.

"Did you ever see any checks with that company name on them?" Charlie asked. "Or cash lying around?"

"Mr. Fiedler very tidy. Nothing left around and Hi don look in desks and drawers. The young ladies leave things out, but not heem."

Kate had streaks of gray in dark hair wadded into a knot on the back of her head, dark eyes full of mischief, and a sure and easy posture that wasted no energy on unnecessary or clumsy movement. She sort of flowed around the room, plastic bags tied to the belt loops of her jeans offering up cleaning rags and spray bottles that left the odor of oils and vinegar like a salad on the air instead of chemical cleaners. It was hard to gauge her age—Leroy had to be well into his thirties, and there were lines in her face, but her skin glowed, and before she left she hauled a heavy-duty vacuum upstairs and down with little effort.

Charlie wrote her a check on the glossy empty tabletop in the dining room and wished she'd gotten someone in sooner. Kate Gonzales accompanied Officer Mason over to Jeremy's. When they returned, appearing the best of friends, Leroy had his mother's vacuum and mops and bags of rags and cleaners stashed in the back of his pickup.

Charlie and the cop watched them drive off from the ruin of a security gate. "It was nice of you to be patient with her. You could have pulled your official rank."

"Sometimes it's easier to get what you want with honey. That's why I'm here right now instead of J. S. He's about to blow his toupee."

"Detective Amuller wears a rug?"

"No, but he will by tomorrow if he keeps pulling his hair out over this case."

"Officer, I think you need to talk to Libby. If you can win over the legendary Kate Gonzales, you might stand a chance of keeping J. S. from doing something stupid that will make my daughter clam up for good."

"That's also why I'm here."

"Are you up to meatloaf with mashed potatoes and gravy?"

"You cook?"

"Libby works at the diner tonight. Gets off at nine. How about it?"

"The L. B. Diner? I haven't had Jell-O in months. You're on."

"Detective Amuller thinks I'm the murderer, doesn't he?"

"Look, you and Betty Beesom were the only two people in

this little group of domiciles when Fiedler was killed. You are both prime suspects but you look a lot better than Betty. Help me find some other people in Fiedler's life we can add to the suspect list. He's a known nubiphile and your own daughter lives here and it never occurred to you to worry about it. He's dead and you now have a cleaning lady many people would kill for. I've seen her stuff. She even likes pets. And thirdly, if we're counting, you're the one coming up with all the false leads here. If you're guilty, we're going to nail you. If you're not, we got to know that, Charlie."

"Ohmygod, there it is."

"What? There what is?"

"The Ferrari—get the license number, quick. My eyes aren't that good."

A red Ferrari had cruised by the compound as they parried and sped up when the driver saw them.

"What, mine are?" But the woman cop was out in the middle of the street staring after the disappearing vehicle, pulling out her cellular.

Charlie said, "There was a license plate but it was—"

"Smeared with mud. Old ploy. See you at the diner at seven for meatloaf." And she was in her black-and-white with the sirens blaring and off down the street, leaving Charlie to turn back to the scary fact that her fortress was unprotected, and her hearing could leave the country forever at any moment.

And Jeremy wasn't here to know who to call to fix the gate.

CHAPTER 14

◆

*L*IBBY SERVED THEM Southern-fried chicken with mashed potatoes and gravy instead of meatloaf. This place was so bad it was sinful and thus crowded, but Charlie and the woman cop had Jell-O anyway. "You want meatloaf, you got to get here by six. We're famous for it. Hey, Mom, you still hearing? Means I better get home tonight on time, right?"

"How can anybody with three zits that size sashay her little butt around like she owns the joint?" the cop asked, turning in the booth to watch the sashay hustle down the aisle to the kitchen door.

"Well, she's young and blond and this is Hollywood," Charlie offered ruefully, and sat back at the sudden change in Officer Mason's expression.

"That's it. It's been driving me nuts. I knew I knew your face from somewhere. I guess I expected you lived in some mansion in Malibu or some place. It's not your name so much as—your face has been around."

"What are you talking about?" But Charlie knew. She always felt the one place she was safe was in Long Beach. You can't be anybody if you live here.

"You're Mitch Hilsten's girlfriend. I feel so dumb." Mary Maggie Mason slapped her forehead and then had to readjust her glasses. "Jesus."

86

"You had my DNA info on your computer and not that?"

"As we both know, modern technology is not perfect."

"I'm beginning to think it's a nightmare. But I'm just his friend, not his girlfriend."

Mitch Hilsten, superstar, was still successfully overcoming the female preteen craze for pasty-faced adolescent-looking twentysomethings. Mitch Hilsten was a fair actor, classically handsome, midforties. Charlie'd had untold fantasies about him in her own teens. Through a series of impossible events, which were becoming standard in her life, she ended up spending some time with him at the most vulnerable time of her month. In fact, a couple of them. Libby hated him and the publicity. Charlie just wished he'd get over it.

"Is he really as aloof and moody as he seems?" Officer Mary Maggie gazed off into some remembered fantasies of her own.

"Actually, he's quite sensitive and friendly."

"That smile and those eyes. He doesn't take his teeth out at night or anything?"

"No, but they're capped. Officer Mason, don't mention him around Libby, okay? We want her cooperative."

As it turned out Libby was quite cooperative on her own.

The diner was long and narrow, with booths and tables spread out to either side of a sizable semicircular counter complete with bar stools and foot rest and revolving-glass pie displays. The carpet was threadbare, the decor in pastel shades of green and pink. The waitpersons wore shorts all year round and T-shirts with L.B.D. lettered on front and back.

Charlie's daughter slid her green shorts and pink L.B.D. shirt into the booth beside Charlie and good-naturedly admitted to the policewoman that she didn't really know more than two of Jeremy's girls, and one of those only by sight. They were the only two who went to Wilson. She'd just been torqued at Detective Amuller. She didn't know Tanya's last name but had walked home from school with her one day, and Tanya had confided that Jeremy let her use his computer. "And she said it was encrypted."

"He never made any sort of advances toward you?" Officer Mason asked. "Like squeezing your bottom, wanting to hug a lot, or sit close and put his hand on your thigh?"

"Never touched me. He was usually helpful and he could fix things, knew what repairman to call if he couldn't. He was good at geometry and stuff, would most times help me out. I never felt like I knew him very well, but I'm going to miss having him around."

Officer Mason leaned forward, leveling a squint through her eyeglasses that reminded Charlie of Tuxedo's intense bird or bug focus. "What's this 'usually' and 'most times' all of a sudden? It's always been good old dependable, reliably unchanging Jeremy with you guys."

"Well, sometimes he'd be grouchy. Hey, sometimes I get grouchy, right, Mom?"

"I don't remember him being grouchy very often. Distracted maybe. Self-involved at times."

"How would you know, you're never home. And when you are, your mind's still at work."

"All you have to do," Charlie told the officer, "is check for Tanyas on the class lists at Wilson."

"Maybe it was Tony," Libby said and left to find Charlie a styrofoam doggie box for the half of her dinner she didn't eat.

Back at the compound Mary Maggie drove her squad car into Jeremy's space and got out.

"You going to spend the night?"

"Charlie, I want you to come see something." The officer took Charlie's arm and walked her down the driveway and turned her around. "I want you to tell me what you see."

"I see unchecked access to my home and to Maggie's and

Mrs. Beesom's, and to our cars—we're wide open."

"Now I want you to look down the street both ways and then I want you to turn around and check out the houses across the street."

It was dark, but streetlights lit up some things. Most things Charlie knew from memory anyway by coming and going twice a day. "I see houses and trees and lighted windows and parked cars—what you'd normally see in a neighborhood. What I've been seeing for five years."

"No, what you haven't been seeing for five years. Describe what's right across the street."

"A car parked at the curb, a palm tree like mine, a sidewalk. A house with flower boxes on the porch. A car in the driveway, flat roof—what?"

"You still don't see it. People nowadays really astonish me. Tell me what's not there that's here."

"No signs of explosion. The sidewalk leads right to the front door like here. Look, I'm tired. Get to the point."

"The point, Ms. Charlie Greene, is that there's no gate to blow up. Never was. No walls with razor wire on top. Do you see anything on this street as fortified as your house and fellow condos were? No. Christ, this is Belmont Shore, the safest part of town."

"But they're all single-family. Apartment and condominium units have security gates. Whole subdivisions in the newer parts of Long Beach are gated. There is nothing unusual about security gates in Southern California. We even have an alarm system." Charlie pointed out the little sign on the front yard that boasted, DOG ALARM SYSTEM. "Hey, they haven't shown up yet."

"They'll get around to it if they're still in business. They know we'll have been and left by the time they do. And, Charlie, two or three blocks north of here there's an apartment complex that's not gated. What I'm saying is this place stands out like a sore thumb in this neighborhood. Mrs. Beesom told me that the walls between the houses were part of the original development. But the razor wire, the gates that needed locking, the alarm system were all Jeremy Fiedler's idea, and the new widow felt very vulnerable. And he paid for it all and she was grateful."

Charlie looked at Mary Maggie Mason long and hard. "I think you should be heading up this investigation. And maybe, like Betty, we all didn't want to doubt or question Jeremy Fiedler because we appreciated the convenience and safety we felt he provided living among us."

"Looks to me like you were all wrong about the safety part." Officer Mason ran a hand over the obelisk. It was bent over like the neck of a grazing giraffe.

Charlie walked back to the center of the compound and did a full circle here, too. She decided she preferred Jeremy's excessive security system, especially now that she might lose her ability to hear.

Swallowing back the terror that thought brought up, she told the cop, "I can't believe Jeremy could have owned a home in this city without having an identity. I can maybe see driving an unregistered car hoping no one would stop you, but you'd have to renew license plates somehow. He must have owned things under a different name. If we could find that name, we could trace the Ferrari and find out more about him. Maybe Jeremy had a bunch of names."

"Don't know about the Ferrari or even the Trailblazer yet, but his house is officially owned by a trust administered for one Elizabeth Ruth Beesom. The trust pays all the bills."

"Electronically? Did Betty know about this?"

"Apparently not. Doesn't seem possible, but it's being investigated. We're trying to get the IRS interested in this but their computer systems are in a worse mess than ours. City started to upgrade a few years ago."

"Jeremy must have lived here what, ten years—long before electronic banking. What's the name of this trust?"

"Beach Enterprises. You know how many businesses in Long Beach use *beach* in their names? Can't trace it any farther. All computer data seems to have been lost in cyberspace."

"That information has to be backed up somewhere."

"That's the problem—*somewhere*. Too much *somewhere*. Not enough people and time to track it down. And you honestly never saw anything strange about this mysterious guy?"

"I thought he was something of an oddball, but he was so dependable. Hell, this is Southern California. My life's full of oddballs." Mitch Hilsten even believed in UFOs. "I really don't think Jeremy was ever on anything, but sometimes he'd forget he'd asked you the same question a day or two before. But stress plays havoc with short-term memory for all of us."

A car engine started somewhere up the alley and headlights suddenly revealed Tuxedo hunkered down, sniffing a wrapped bouquet of flowers leaning against the back gate this time.

"Cover your ears," Officer Mason yelled and yanked Charlie down behind her squad car, just as Libby's Wrangler pulled in from the street.

CHAPTER 15

◆

I DON'T BELIEVE I ever met Mr. Fiedler," Ed Esterhazie told Charlie. "Doug mentioned him once or twice. They had any response from the ad in the *P-T?*"

They sat on Charlie's picnic table, watching the bomb squad disperse. The wrapped floral arrangement had been just flowers this time.

"If they have, they haven't told me. But then Betty and I were the only suspects in the compound when he died."

"With your history, Mrs. Beesom doesn't seem the likely candidate."

"Her stock must have gone up some when they discovered Jeremy's house had been her's all along. Since they can't find anybody else who knows him, they don't have anyplace else to look."

"I think your idea of an enraged father makes sense. Anybody working that hard to hide his identity must have had enemies he needed to hide from. And I don't think it's possible to own a house and not know it. Not unless it was an all-cash deal and no bank was involved."

"Jeremy did pay cash for it. Betty figured he'd sold a bigger house and put it all in this one. And all this new computerization and constant upgrading doesn't leave people time to learn one software before they have to learn the next because the first will 'no longer be supported.' An awful lot of stuff can fall through the cracks. And if it's being purposely manipulated by someone who knows how to do it . . ."

"Yeah, we just changed over to a whole new system at Esterhazie Concrete and lost hundreds of thousands of dollars in the process. I'm told it's going to be worth it, but you have to trust the people doing the installing and the training. Kind of a helpless feeling. Speaking of which, do the doctors think your hearing has returned for good?"

"The doctors don't know it's returned at all. No more vacations for me, that's one sure thing. Too stressful."

Ed had come in shortly after Libby and before the bomb squad arrived. He'd brought some flowers and a bottle of single-malt scotch, which tasted kind of good with water and a little lemon in it.

"Remember when Doug and Libby served us dinner out here?" Doug's father said.

"Yeah, Kraft Macaroni and Cheese from the box and Dom Perignon. And Doug served it in a sport coat and shorts with my dirty dishtowel over his arm."

"And they told me you would slit your throat if I didn't come to dinner. I expected you'd been cooking all day, wore aprons or something."

"And I came home from work, dead tired, to find a strange man in a dinner jacket on my patio."

"And me with no idea I was competing with the likes of Mitch Hilsten."

"Oh, Ed, I hadn't even met him then. And Mitch and I are really not an item. No matter what the tabloids say. Just friends. I know it's none of my business, but what happened to you and Dorothy?"

"She wanted to change everything, run everything. Me, Doug, Mrs. McDougal—even the house. I'm happy with the way I am. I'm not going to change myself for someone else."

"The saddest words in the English language: 'I thought I could change him.' "

"My fault. I'm old enough to know better than get involved with someone that close to my own age. Women over forty are set in their ways and know what they want, so if they can't find it they try to mold a man into the desired shape." Ed used to wear dark-rimmed glasses that Charlie thought made him look even more distinguished, but he'd had that laser surgery and didn't wear them now. He motioned to the concrete courtyard emptied of official cars and vans. "Looks like there'll be no protection tonight."

"I'm going to miss Jeremy and his electrified gates. It felt safe here. It doesn't now."

"I have a security system, but I don't have gates. I keep things well lit, but if somebody's out to get you . . . all that protection didn't keep someone from murdering Jeremy Fiedler." And Ed and Doug lived in a mansion worth breaking into with only their housekeeper, Mrs. McDougal.

In the light cast by the bulb over Mrs. Beesom's kitchen door, they watched Hairy Granger insinuate his fluffy self through the gate from the alley and disappear in night shadow, only to reappear around the end of a stone flower box on Charlie's patio. "It's okay, Hairy, our enemy's inside with his mistress."

She introduced them, and the cat joined them on the table while she told Ed about finding Hairy in the Trailblazer with a dead Jeremy.

"Dorothy had several cats who enjoyed riding in the car. He may have jumped in the open door hoping for a ride."

"Or maybe to get away from Tuxedo. They fight constantly."

"Maybe the door was open," Ed said, emptying his glass,

"while the murderer stuffed Jeremy into the car."

"Maybe the murderer opened the car door and stabbed Jeremy sitting behind the wheel and Tuxedo scared Hairy and he jumped in and the murderer slammed the door shut and I came home and the murderer hid someplace until I went in with the groceries and then got out one of the gates without getting shocked."

"Maybe there're ways of getting in and out without getting shocked Jeremy didn't want you to know about."

"Maybe you only get the shock trying to get in, but don't trying to go out."

Ed went in to refill their drinks and Libby came out in sweats and slippers. "I can't sleep. Can I come out and help you guys 'maybe'? Sounds like a lot more fun than lying awake."

"Okay, but watch for Tuxedo. Hairy's out here and we don't want them waking up Mrs. Beesom."

"I can't sleep, either." Betty walked around the parked cars from her patio to Charlie's. "Can I help 'maybe,' too?"

And being Betty, who could rarely drop in without bearing gifts, she carried a tray with a teakettle, cups, and packets of hot chocolate. So the four of them sat in chairs around the table drinking hot chocolate. Hairy perched on the table and kept a careful eye out for Tuxedo, who Charlie knew would explode from somewhere and ruin everything at any minute, and Hairy probably did, too.

"I couldn't believe it when that police lady told me I'd owned Jeremy's house all this time," Betty said. "He was such a nice man. Except once in a while."

"Except once in a while what?" Ed asked. He was having a sip of scotch and a sip of cocoa. So was Charlie, and it tasted good for no good reason.

"He could be mean. Didn't happen often, but—"

"Like how?" Charlie wanted to know.

"Like when he threw rocks at Tux and old hairball here," Libby said. "Rocks from that square patch under the pot with the fern plant where we keep the key to the back gate." She chucked Hairy under the chin and he lifted it to the night sky so she could reach it better.

"Well, they *was* fighting and screaming, Libby dear. But those are expensive decorator rocks. And I saw him throw them at a gull on top of his roof one day. And then next day he was putting out the fish scraps from his garbage on his picnic table. He come over to mine and we watched that gull swoop down and clean it up nice and quick as you please. 'Now that, Mrs. Beesom,' he says, 'is recycling at it's proper best.' "

"Did you ask him why he threw rocks at the gull one day and fed it the next?" Ed asked.

"Well, no. I wanted to, but he was always hinting around that I was a nosy neighbor, so I just didn't. But most of the time he was a perfectly reasonable man."

Charlie thought it odd that once one of them remembered something unusual about their murdered neighbor, the rest of them began to come up with a few examples, too. Sort of like ignoring the flaws in a parent because you want them to be stable and not a worry so that you could lead your own life without that complication. Until you're a teenager, of course, and then you pick at those imperfections, real and imagined, until something bleeds.

Things happened then, and so fast Charlie would never be able to sort out in what order. Tuxedo's predictable attack startled them all, anyway. When he hit the tabletop, Hairy leapt onto Ed. Ed dropped both his glass and his cup. The teakettle and two more cups hit the hard patio tile, which was suddenly awash in cocoa, hot water, scotch, broken glass, and pottery.

And the shadow of a woman, in a long coat that reminded

Charlie of Detective Amuller's raincoat, detached itself from the deep shadow of a post holding up Jeremy and Maggie's parking cover. It was, like Charlie and Betty's, meant more for sun protection than rain, a series of logs with latticework meant to hold flowering vines that had never seemed to take.

Windshields often spotted when it rained, and the ancient Olds 88 had faded patches in spots all over the roof and hood because it had to be parked in pretty much the same spot if Charlie was to park and be able to open her car doors, too.

The lights on the latticework made it clear that the shadow was that of a woman—and she didn't move like one of Jeremy's nubiles, either. An older woman with hair that swung like her coat as she ran—sensible, flat shoes. Charlie ran after her, pleading for her to stop. The woman kept on through light and shadow, throwing her heels outward because her pelvis was made more for childbirth than flight.

Charlie had followed her two blocks up and then crossed Ximeno for a couple more before the obvious brought her up short. What if the woman in the swinging hair and coat had left a bomb in the compound, and Charlie had run off and left Libby without warning her?

In a blink Charlie had lost sight of her quarry and found herself alone out in the big bad world.

Maggie Stutzman and that-man-Mel were there when she made it home, having run most of the way. Charlie was in no shape for running. And her ears were gurgling. Ed Esterhazie and Mrs. Beesom had most of the mess on Charlie's patio cleaned up. Libby had put her feet up on her lawn chair and watched, of course.

Mel and Ed took flashlights and looked all about the covered parking area across from Charlie, finding no signs of a bomb. Jeremy's patio seemed safe, too. But a window was broken in his house.

The dispatch person put them right through to none other than Detective J. S. Amuller, who informed them that since the L.A. county bomb squad had been there that evening, no one would attend to Jeremy's broken window until morning—have a good night. So, the bomb went off at about two-thirty in the morning.

But Charlie didn't hear it. Her ears had shut down again.

CHAPTER 16

❖

HALFWAY INTO HER unvacation, Charlemagne Catherine Greene traveled her killer commute again. But she wasn't behind the wheel.

It was an eerie, silent ride. Maggie drove. They couldn't talk because Charlie couldn't hear. Charlie knew every shopping center, curve, on-ramp, off-ramp, detour, ditch, shopping center, sign, palm-and-wispy-smog-finger-draped, red-tiled-roofed condo-apartment-housing development, shopping center . . .

There was only one grid, but this was late rush hour, surprisingly little difference now that she looked at it. Might as well, she couldn't hear it.

During this grid lull, Maggie wrote on the notepad, "I don't know how you stand this every day."

Charlie didn't bother to answer. She didn't trust her voice when she couldn't hear it—didn't need to feel any more embarrassed than she already did. And an answer would have taken more than a notepad could handle.

Charlie would give anything to be driving the Toyota now, drying her hair, eating her bagel, sucking in the smell of the French-pressed coffee she'd picked up at a drive-through on the way out of town. Talking with New York on the cellular, trying to put on her pantyhose and makeup.

And hearing it all. Car horns, tire screeches, diesels thundering, the air conditioner, NPR.

She could see and smell and taste, but it wasn't the same. She'd never assumed she was in control of the 405. But compared to now, she'd felt in control of her life, her work, her car. Her identity.

Charlie should be nicer to her best friend for taking off from her own work this morning to drive her to the specialist recommended by the bored doctor in the hospital. Wouldn't you know this specialist was just off Wilshire in Beverly Hills. Congdon & Morse's insurance wouldn't cover him—that's for sure. How they'd gotten her in this fast, she didn't know. Maybe nobody's insurance would pay for this guy. Maggie was to deliver her to the specialist, and Larry would pick her up and take her back to the office after her appointment to clean up a few things on her desk, and then he'd drive her home.

Charlie didn't want her colleagues to see her this way, and she didn't want to talk to the specialist because there might be bad news. And who knew what more could blow up in Charlie's fortress in the meantime?

Jeremy's house still stood, and at night, from the outside, it didn't look that damaged. The Long Beach fire department was first to arrive and quickly doused what little fire there was. Some of the upper story had relocated to the first floor, the windows were all shattered, and the door blown out, but the unofficial opinion of firefighters and police was that the structure could probably be saved. Charlie described the running shadow of a woman who'd fled the compound earlier. Specialists of a different kind—arson and bomb—were sifting through what little was left of poor Jeremy Fiedler's life.

Somehow the idea of an enraged father being responsible for all this seemed a little much by now. Maybe someone was looking for something—or trying to destroy something so it wouldn't be found. Maybe that somebody was the running shadow woman. She'd probably been trying to leave the courtyard unnoticed after placing the bomb in Jeremy's house.

Charlie had expected Maggie to drop her off at this clinic, but the lawyer parked and escorted her inside, apparently suspecting how tempted her friend was to bolt. While Charlie filled out one of those interminable forms demanding the scoop on her entire medical history—she didn't remember what childhood diseases she'd had—Maggie Stutzman had a long talk with the woman behind the desk, whose attention was constantly being demanded by the telephone and a toddler toddling into everything in sight while his mother never once looked up from her entertainment magazine. Finally, the woman no longer behind the desk nodded, smiled reassurance to Maggie, and grabbed the kid who was smearing snot on one of the cloth chairs. Maggie came over to give Charlie a hug and left.

Charlie had the nearly unbearable urge to cry.

By the time Larry Mann met her in the clinic's lobby after her appointment, she could no longer resist that urge. Larry is one of those people who rarely shake hands, rarely hug, never greet you with a kiss. Charlie knew a woman like that once, who refused to even nurse her baby because she didn't like being touched. So it took a minute for her to realize she was letting all her feelings run out her eyes and nose and mouth against his shirt and he was holding her, stroking her head like she was Tuxedo. And when she backed away to look up at him, her secretary had tears in his eyes. The woman behind the lobby desk brought them over a box of tissues, and they managed rueful grins for her and each other.

Her second-best friend and the handsomest man in the world drove her to the office on Wilshire, not that far away. Congdon & Morse shared the fifth floor of the First Federal

United Central Wilshire Bank of the Pacific building with a shrink and a coven of entertainment lawyers. The FFUCWB of P sat on a corner facing Wilshire with its drive-through banking across the side street, a paved alley running along the other side, and its first floor halved in size to provide covered parking in back and two levels of parking underneath.

Larry pulled into an agency space on the first level and they took the elevator up to the fifth floor, followed the carpeted hall to a discreet door with an intercom for those who didn't have a pass card. Richard Morse shared an even more discreet entrance at the back of the building with the shrink, but the help had to use the front door. Larry slid his pass card into the slot and unlocked the door that protected the agents from the wannabes. Before the receptionist was murdered several years ago, a semicircular desk had graced the middle of the lobby and all calls and all visitors and all clients were processed through that receptionist. Now everything was voicemail and the office manager, Ruby Dillon, had a regular desk to the side of the room, and couches and comfortable chairs took up the center. But you had to get by Ruby Dillon to see any of the agents, and those agents had to notify Ruby that you were coming. Somebody could announce on the intercom that he was Mitch Hilsten, Tom Hanks, or Clark Gable, but that door wouldn't unlock for him unless an agent or an agent's assistant had put that name on Ruby's list.

Charlie didn't even look at Ruby, but hung a right the minute she was inside and headed for the back hall and the ladies' room to put cold, wet paper towels under her eyes.

So you cried. So you're human. It's not like you have no reason to, and it's nothing to be ashamed of.

Charlie looked at the mirror and saw anger and defiance.

When she stepped back into the agency's lobby, they were

all standing there waiting for her. All standing in a row. It couldn't have been more horrible if this were a nightmare. Everybody was there but Larry. He probably couldn't stand the embarrassment, either. They all looked so sympathetic, so sorry for her. She was more than likely still looking angry and defiant. Nobody said anything. People don't talk to people who can't hear. Makes sense, right?

Charlie's was a competitive business—sharks would be right at home in it. Charlie was the only literary agent here. The others handled talent. Not that screenwriters and book authors weren't talented—but they weren't "talent." She was also the only one, except for Richard Morse, with her own assistant. Ruby Dillon was at his beck and call. The others had to share Tweety and resented it.

Luella Ridgeway was the first to come up and give Charlie a hug. The others lined up behind her like Charlie was the buffet table. Luella Ridgeway was what Charlie wanted to be when she grew up. Single, rich (one profitable divorce and an even more profitable widowhood), she had a fantastic house high on the Hollywood hills with a deck as big as Charlie's condo, and loved her work besides. She had the deepest blue eyes and arguably the most successful facelift in town, and knew how to dress stunning.

Next, Dorian Black, whom Charlie had detested from the get-go.

Why do I have to stand here and put up with this?

Because you never let sharks smell blood.

Then Howard Highsmith and Jonathan Gunn, both in brown slacks, one with a yellow shirt and the other pink. Then Tweety, her breath smelling of candy bar and peanuts. Then Ruby Dillon, probably the most unfashionable woman Charlie had ever come across. And last the boss, Richard Morse, who ruffled her hair with fatherly affection. Charlie's hair, a mass of unruly curls, was born ruffled and didn't need that. He whispered in her ear, "It's gonna be okay, kid."

Charlie, so awash in self-pity, was halfway down the hall to her office before she realized she'd heard him. And that she was hearing sounds in her head again, sounds bodies make routinely but you don't hear until you haven't heard them for a while, like whatever the air pressure does when you swallow and the *whish* as you inhale air up your nose and the puff when you exhale. The faraway, cricketlike sounds in your ears. The gurgle in her stomach sounded alarming after all that silence. There's even a soft click when you blink. Soon all were overcome by the air filtration and temperature control system and the chronic indigestion of the little refrigerator in the coffee-sink-water-microwave room.

Charlie walked very carefully, trying not to jar her head and make the world go away again. Larry Mann had a cubicle just inside the door to the hall that was so full of treatments, proposals, manuscripts, and the welter of doing business in the modern world that there was barely room for him. He was a good-sized guy. He put his head down in that endearing way he had so that he was looking up at her sardonically and grimaced, and if he knew she could hear he would have said, "See, you survived walking the plank again, boss."

Charlie grimaced back and passed him. Her office was twice the size it needed to be, and nice. She sat behind her desk and ignored what was on top of it. God, she loved her work. Sharks and all.

"So what did the doc say?" she heard her boss ask her secretary.

"Met her in the lobby, didn't see him. She didn't say anything. Wait, I'll write her a note and ask."

He came in with the note and an affectionate smile. He

cared. They all did, in a way. But if she had to be replaced, they'd forget her soon enough. Turnover in the agency was brisk. They all had to survive.

She wrote in answer that the doctor had not spoken to her because she couldn't hear, but the nurse had written they'd let her know when the results of the tests were in. Which is pretty much what had happened.

Charlie decided to continue her deafness so she could hear what was really going on at Congdon & Morse Representation, Inc.

CHAPTER 17

❖

*T*RACY DEWITT'S VOICE was the next to sound from the cubicle. Her office name was Tweety because whenever she exerted, little chirps came up her throat with her breathing. She was the niece of Daniel Congden, the Congdon in Congdon & Morse. He had an office next to Charlie's, and in the five years Charlie'd worked here, she'd never seen the man.

"Wonder if Richard will get a new literary agent in here. Most of us don't think we need one."

"We don't know that Charlie's condition is permanent. I wouldn't be too hasty to sing of her career demise."

" 'Sing of her career demise.' Gawd, neither one of you are from the real world. The written word is dead, you know—it's all going to be film and music—"

"Just because you can't read, Tweety . . ."

"Dirty fag." And Tracy waddled her bird breath off down the hall.

The only really new business on Charlie's desk was Rudy Ferris. There probably was more, but obviously Richard Morse was sending a message here. This had to be dealt with before anything else. She glanced over various transcribed phone messages, printed-out e-mails, deal memos, and contract changes, gathered it all together in a manila folder to take home with her, and sat back in her chair. Charlie was blessed in that the

106

palms had reached the fifth floor with their little sprout of fronds and she had a big window that looked out on them and the smog and the sky and the sun and the busy bird life among the fronds. She rarely took note of all this, of course, but they had become suddenly dear.

One end of her office sported a couch, two easy chairs, a lamp table, and a coffee table with a phony floral arrangement denoting the office of an important person. Her desk, a brushed gray wood, ran long and narrow along the back wall, her computer station at one end, and behind her chair, crowded shelves reached to the ceiling. A visitor's chair across the desk from hers. Several pictures of Libby in various stages of terrifying development in attached frames at one corner of her desk, book and film posters hanging on the blank wall behind which was the office of Daniel Congdon.

One poster for the film *Shadowscapes*, another for *Phantom of the Alpine Tunnel*, with Hilsten's mug all over it. The poster of A. E. Mous's mystery novel, *Dead Men Don't Need Jell-O*, had a history all its own. At one time the previous office manager had drilled a hole behind it to record Charlie's office conversations when the police were investigating the death of the office receptionist. It was just a cheap paper poster, unframed, meant for bookstore windows. A. E., like most published authors, had never advanced beyond the lower rungs of the midlist and didn't warrant cardboard. But he was one of her very first authors. In fact, as far as she knew, it was the only time a publisher had even bothered to produce a poster for him.

She imagined now that A. E.'s poster moved as if in an air current.

"Can't she at least write us a note about how she's feeling or something?" Luella Ridgeway's voice from the cubicle now. "This silence is freaking me out, Larry."

"Probably not as much as it is her," Larry said matter-offactly. "Look, right now she's a package of conflicting emotions—panic, sadness, anger, resentment, disbelief, denial. You know how much she loves her job and her kid. Libby will be off to college after next year. What will she do without either her career or her kid? Give her time, Lue. You know Charlie won't accept this until it's proven to be a lasting condition—not even then, probably."

Charlie's eyes teared over at that. And the *Dead Men Don't Need Jell-O* poster positively waved in the breeze that wasn't in the room. She blinked her contacts back into place. What if she had the laser surgery for myopia done and it made her blind? What if she lost her sight and hearing, too? Might as well jump off a bridge. But she wouldn't be able to find one.

"You know, for a guy, you are incredibly sensitive." Luella's voice softened.

"Goes with the territory. Us queens are like that."

"Why do all the sensitive guys have to be gay?" Luella's voice hardened.

"You're stereotyping again, Lue. Lots of gays are true jerks, trust me."

Charlie was halfway out of her chair when Howard Highsmith weighed in. He was the newest recruit. Charlie could only wonder where Richard found these guys. If Dorian Black was like used-car salesmen at their worst, Howard was like a clown who never washed off his happy face. She swore now she could hear the smile in his voice. He probably wore it in the bathroom, would carry it to a watery grave in an airliner crash.

"So, old Charlie's lost her edge, poor kid." This was followed by a deep, cheerful laugh. "She's a tough one, and in a funk now. But she'll come through, old Charlie will."

Old Charlie had a serious desire to kick his smile in.

"Seniority wise, I'm in line for this office," Dorian Black said. "The agency's too small for its own literary agent anyway.

TNT's only got two and they're five times bigger than we are."
His voice was either receding down the hall or the sound of
blood pounding in Charlie's ears was muffling it.

Chill, Charlie. Blood pressure might bring back the smoth-
ering quiet. Shut down the world for good.

There had once been a hole behind A. E.'s poster—was
there one there again, and was it air from Daniel Congdon's
office blowing the poster?

Was the silent partner in the business back in town? Finally
using his office? Surely her colleagues would be talking about
that instead of her, right?

"Oh, Larry, I feel so bad for Charlie. How's she really doing? She seems so stoney."

"She's doing fine, Jonathan, but nice of you to ask."

Like almost every known substance, gelatin, according to
the author, had once been touted as an aphrodisiac. Charlie
didn't doubt it. Newspapers are ever looking for medical
news—*Studies show that . . .* Charlie'd always wondered how
many of them reporters made up.

The poster of the book jacket was red on a black background—one of the cheapest ways to make a jacket. A bowl
tipped on its side, spilling out a blood-red glob with a hand
falling out of it on one side and a leg sticking out the other.

"Tell her I'll pray for her, Larry, like I always pray for you."

Jonathan Gunn had found Jesus and knew that Larry could
find help in God to become heterosexual. Larry had found
Stewart Claypool—probably the best thing that had ever happened to him. Jonathan had also informed Charlie that Jesus
forgave her for having Libby out of wedlock and that all she
need do is marry a good Christian man to give her life and
Libby's some balance.

How anyone with religion could work in the exciting but
squalid mire that is Hollywood Charlie couldn't fathom. When

she'd asked Jonathan about this, he'd reminded her of the Christian mission to work among the heathen in the world's least civilized places.

"Thank you, Jonathan. We both certainly need it." Everyone in the office was very careful with this dude. The Taliban and Kenneth Starr had made all zealots suspect, and unfortunately many innocent people who weren't zealots, too.

"Maybe this is God's way of giving Charlie a chance to stay at home and raise her child." Jonathan Gunn specialized in circus performers, stuntmen, soap opera actresses, and talent in religious programing.

Charlie slid the red and black poster for *Dead Men Don't Need Jell-O* aside. There was a hole again. A smaller one this time. An eyehole. With an eye in it.

CHAPTER 18

---❖---

CHARLIE KEPT UP her deceit until Larry drove them to a late lunch at Mamas' before taking her home. They both needed some serious chicken soup after the day they'd had. Charlie was in such a state of shock she just blurted out her order the minute Mama asked for it.

"So, when did you start hearing again?" They sat at the counter, which was understood protocol when the lunch rush was over and the place mostly empty and Mama's feet were tired.

"So, why didn't anyone tell me Daniel Congdon had come home? I mean I can't believe Tracy Dewitt wasn't chirping her head off about her big-deal uncle being in residence to promote his niece's importance. Even if I couldn't hear it."

Larry leaned over her, his caramel hair falling across his forehead, his prominent cheekbones shadowing the face below. "I asked you first. Didn't I, Mama?"

"God, kids drive me nuts. You are both getting big bowls of soup, and crusty fresh-baked bread. I don't wanna hear no sass. And you, doll"—she pointed her order pad at Charlie—"are getting a big glass of milk with it. You come late to the table, you get what we got. So, immature hunk, whaddaya want to drink? And we'll discuss dessert when we see how you behave. Got it?"

There were two mamas, lesbian, neither yet forty-five, both Jews from Manhattan with a flair for cooking and mothering. North Hollywood was a haven for gays, many dying, when these two opened a small cafe named Mom & Pop's to dish out what comfort they could for the misery AIDS had inflicted here. But a bakery with the same name and within thirty miles had brought suits, so eventually this place became Mamas'. This mama had even introduced Charlie's ulcer to the soothing effects of a soft poached egg over milk toast with salt and pepper. Charlie, a renowned rebel in her youth, always ate what this mama ordered. The other mama waved a soup ladle at them from the kitchen through the oblong opening above the back counter.

These two missionaries served food and comfort without preaching, their only agenda compassion. You didn't have to believe in any ideology. You just had to avoid starving. Nothing was wasted here. Volunteers carefully packaged anything left over in the kitchen and took it to those too sick to go out and to their caregivers. The homeless got their share as well as clothing from the café's semiannual clothing drive. These gals talked tough and melted your heart.

"I realized I was hearing when Richard whispered that everything would be okay when I first saw him at the office. It comes and goes without warning. Scares the hell out of me. Your turn."

"So you really didn't hear what the doctor had to say, but you did hear what your thoughtful colleagues are thinking now?"

"Right, but why didn't I hear anything about the return of the mysterious silent partner? You could have warned me, Larry."

"Congdon hasn't returned that I know of. Who told you he did? Oh, that's what you were up to when I came to get you for lunch. Peeking behind that poster—I thought you'd lost your mind as well as your hearing."

"Larry, there was somebody looking back. There's a little hole behind that poster, and it had an eye in it."

"Why? All you'd see is the back of the poster."

It was dumb, but Mamas' chicken soup with fat noodles, heavy on the salt and herbs with chicken hunks and real fat blobs floating on the broth really did make you feel better—not just Charlie, but everybody said so. Maybe it was just that you were afraid it would piss off the Mamas if it didn't.

Charlie was almost blissful when she crawled into Larry's Bronco with the doggy jar Mama insisted she take home and finish off for dinner. "You don't look good, girl," Mama said.

"I brought my jammies, boss. Can I sleep on your couch tonight?" Larry asked as they took the ramp off the 10 and onto the 405.

"Anytime, but are you sure you want to be around for the next pyrotechnics?"

Miles on down the freeway he spoke again. "I don't know how you stand this every day."

"I get a lot of work done, but you should see my car—my second office—without you there to organize it. There was somebody in Congdon's office, I tell you."

"I haven't heard anything, but they do get people in to dust it up a couple times a year. I tend to notice anyone coming down the hall that doesn't stop at our door, though."

The Congdon & Morse Agency was located on a corner of the building, with Charlie's office and Larry's cubical between Congdon's office at the end of the hall along the front of the building and Richard Morse's on the corner. Richard had windows on two sides. The rest of the agents had smaller offices along the side of the building and lousy views. Tweety had a central niche on the inside wall of Howard's office and no window. Ruby sat in the lobby itself, which was an inside room. So anyone walking past Larry's cubical could only be going to Daniel Congdon's locked door.

"Unless the cops hope to spy on you from there somehow."

"What cops? Beverly Hills?"

"They're cooperating with Long Beach."

"Amuller?"

"You hadn't noticed they'd been through your desk and files? Made copies of your computer files, too."

"They what?" Charlie took deep breaths hoping to slow the angry blood inside her head and forestall any hearing loss thinking of dropping in on her.

"Why?"

"They're looking for Fiedler's murderer, Charlie. I sure hope they haven't decided you're it and set out to prove it instead of investigating the murder, if you know what I mean."

Charlie did know. No witnesses, no leads. No traceable family, friends, or enemies of the deceased. Two people behind locked and electrified gates with the victim. One, an eighty-three-year-old frail woman. The other, Charlie Greene, whose unfortunate and widely recorded record showed an unlikely involvement with dead people. Unsolved murders made for unpopular cops—hell, they solve them weekly on television, don't they?

"But they can't think I'd set off explosions in my own little fortress."

"Not unless you had evidence to hide, evidence of committing a murder or a compelling motive to do so. Who had better access for planting bombs?"

"You don't honestly think I would endanger my daughter, my neighors like that? Or that I'd kill Jeremy?"

"No, I don't. But overworked, underpaid law-enforcement officers see you as a way to wrap a case—they'll look for the most likely suspect first, and maybe precious evidence that could convict an unknown person and free you of suspicion will disappear with time or be overlooked in their haste. The murder cases that are not solved right away stand a good chance of not being solved at all. If you fit a profile they think positive, they'll go after you at the expense of further time-consuming investigation."

"Where'd you come up with all this?"

"Keegan Monroe sent in a full screenplay—typed, not on disk. Charlie, it's devastating—which means wonderful. Amuller didn't find it because I hid it."

"Keegan? I thought he was trying to write another novel." Charlie's most successful client was in Folsom Prison and had decided to use his excess of spare time to write a novel. He'd been attempting that feat apparently since birth, but made him-self—and helped make Charlie and Congdon & Morse—a real living writing screenplays. In fact one of his most successful was written in Folsom during an attack of the dreaded writers' block. Most of Charlie's screenwriters wanted to write novels to have some control over their work and her novelists wanted to write screenplays to earn some money, neither side wanting to listen to the truth about the other's reality, all artful endeavors relying more heavily upon dreams. Charlie would be out of business if it were otherwise. Which didn't mean she was a murderer or deserved to be suspected as one.

"So, boss, I have decided to come to your house and help you investigate. I read a lot of mysteries, treatments and book proposals, scripts and stuff. Stew and I watch videos of movies in bed, which are mostly mysteries anyway. I can help you if you let me, and am going to try on this one even if you don't. That Amuller scares me. He's out to get you, Charlie."

115

CHAPTER 19

❖

RUDY FERRIS WAS on the TV when Larry and Charlie walked into her house. Libby, Doug Esterhazie, and Lori Schantz sprawled across the furniture in various catatonic poses. Tuxedo sprawled across Doug.

"Ohmygod, Mom, he's so gross, I can't understand how you can represent him."

"I don't represent him. The agency does. I just lined them up." Charlie grabbed a basket and began shoveling Taco Bell wrappers, boxes, napkins, and plastic forks into it. "Tell me the cat didn't eat any beans."

"Hey, you can hear again. Larry, I think Mom's faking this deaf bit so she can investigate Jeremy's murder, don't you?"

Larry's answer was to wad up a paper taco wrapper and lob it at her. She tossed it to Doug who threw it at Lori and it made the rounds twice before Tuxedo intercepted and dissected it. These three kids had been together on and off since Libby hit Long Beach. When one of the girls teamed with a boyfriend, the other two carried on until she came back to the fold.

Where Libby was tall, blond, and slinky, Lori was short, brunette, and bouncy. They'd both cut gorgeous, glistening long hair—Libby's straight, Lori's curly—last year and broke their mothers' hearts, as daughters have been doing for decades. Charlie had to admit now, they both looked pretty good.

"Sorry to hear about Mr. Fiedler," Lori said with an inappropriate but habitual giggle.

Charlie was mentally tabulating how long before one or all of them would be demanding dinner—the Taco Bell debris having originated from after-school snacking. Here was Charlie Greene, a possibly permanently handicapped, barely employable single mother and prime murder suspect living in a bombing zone, automatically calculating the relative merits of takeout, delivery, a quick run to Von's, or feigning deafness again. She could eat the rest of her lunch and let the rest of them deal with it.

Anybody with her problems should not have to be thinking about this. She looked at her assistant/secretary. He could organize the office, but Stew did the cooking at their house.

Rudy Ferris was one of the sleaziest talk-show hosts going—which says a lot. He talked, dressed, and acted like a carnival barker. Charlie'd happened to meet him on a recent trip to Manhattan, although he lived and worked in L.A. She was there to talk deals for several of her writers, and to suck up to the latest hot book editors, East Coast producers, and a few influential story editors in film.

Charlie had never quite convinced herself these trips paid off—she feared flying—but she didn't have to pay her way, and contacts are influence, after all. Still, most of her real successes had come from out of the blue, as unexpected as Jeremy Fiedler's murder—the sheer-dumb-luck quotient she'd learned to value over talent.

She and Rudy happened to be sitting side by side at a publisher's luncheon, she unhappy because she thought it was to have been just her, her client, his editor—Joe Putnam, and a representative of Pitman's marketing department. And Rudy Ferris happened to be fuming at his entertainment agent at

TNT. One thing led to another. He recognized her as having a connection with Mitch Hilsten, superstar. She gave him her card. He called her at the office the next week and she set up a meeting with Richard Morse. Sheer dumb luck beat out hard work any day.

"So what do you think everyone's going to—"

"Chinese, takeout/delivery," Libby said. "With crab-cheese wontons, and cold peanut rice noodles for appetizers and—"

"May I have dinner with you tonight if I promise to do the dishes?" Doug asked.

"Let's eat at your house and sleep at mine tonight so you don't get blown up," Lori offered. "You too, Doug, if you want to sleep with my little brother."

"And we can actually eat on the dining room table." Libby sat up to stare at that piece of furniture as if she'd never seen it before. "We've got a cleaning lady."

Charlie and Larry left them arguing over the menu and choice of delivery service to stand in front of Jeremy Fiedler's bombed-out house. It smelled of a fire that had been soaked down with water.

"There's no crime-scene tape, Larry."

"If they've found their murderer, they've found their bomber." He let her lean on his arm.

"Does Stew know you're spending the night here? I don't want anything happening to you."

"Stew's a big boy and so am I, Charlie. Neither one of us want anything more to happen to you."

"Do you think kung pao shrimp will blow out my eardrums for good?"

"Well, at least we'll know. Keegan Monroe's new script is filled with food. That's so unusual for him. He and most men write of breakfast, lunch, and dinner to mark time. Woman write of eggs or bagels, soup and salads or sandwiches, fettuccine or meatloaf or salmon, and always of desserts."

"Most women writers who can sell are selling novels. Most screenplays are guy stuff written by guys. But I'm not surprised that Keegan's getting into food, Larry. I expect the fare in prison makes him homesick for food."

Jeremy Fiedler's house had blackened patches on the stucco around the windows and a seagull on the peak of the roof.

Not-very-securely nailed boards blocked the doorway, almost like an invitation to danger. So they looked in the window next to it, into what had been the kitchen. A mangled light fixture hung on wires and cords almost to the floor.

"How could the police just walk in and copy my computer files, go through my mail and records, Larry? Don't you have to have a court order or something?"

"Apparently not. But I think you should look into getting a lawyer."

"Then they'll think I'm guilty for sure."

Larry walked around to peer in the window Doug and Libby had crawled out of the other night. "In my inexpert opinion I would say, Watson, that someone was attempting to destroy evidence here."

"Looks like they succeeded, Holmes." Charlie came to stand beside him.

The entertainment center/bookshelves piece had apparently protected the side door, and the torrey pine looked in better shape than the house. All Charlie could see inside here was dark, stinking, depressing. Tidy Jeremy would not have approved. Something inside creaked and snapped and a billow of ashy dust puffed out at them as if Jeremy had answered.

They both stepped back in time to see Mrs. Beesom crossing the courtyard carrying something in a newspaper. She saw them and winked, set the newspaper on Jeremy's picnic table, and walked over to them with a finger to her lips. A breeze ruffled the edges of the newspaper and Jeremy's seagull floated down from the roof to eat the fish scraps from Mrs. Beesom's dinner.

"Seems like there ought to be a memorial service for Jeremy." The old lady's lips trembled. "Maybe this is as close as we'll get to one."

"I hadn't even thought of that," Charlie said. "There should be some kind of service for him. But you're right, that bird is the only being we know outside the compound who knew Jeremy." Charlie wondered who would come if they held a memorial for him here. Or maybe at the seaside, how about on the bay? Would the woman in the long coat come? Would Charlie know her without the coat?

Charlie was really missing Jeremy. Larry was wonderful and beautiful, but if it weren't for the fact Jeremy was the victim in this travesty upon her fortress, he would have been the one she and everyone else who lived here would be counting on now. Weird. Major weird.

Betty looked into Jeremy's living room window and shook her head. "Don't seem possible, but the fire inspectors think the house can be gutted and rebuilt inside. If it can be, I'm going to have it built back the way it was, exactly. That will be kind of a memorial, too, for the poor man."

"Will you sell it, do you think?" Larry asked.

"No, I'll rent it to some nice young man we all can trust like we trusted Jeremy." Betty looked away quickly. She was always nice to Larry but never comfortable around him. Charlie wondered if that made Larry feel like being handicapped made her feel.

They put newspapers over the gleaming table in the dining room and shared mooshu pork and kung pao shrimp, sesame chicken, moo gu gai pan, beef and broccoli in garlic sauce, Tai peanut noodles, and wanton cheese crabmeat wontons, along with bucket boxes of steamed rice with soy sauce and endless cans of Coke—an oriental pig-out Charlie knew she would regret in the middle of the night when raging thirst and the need to pass all that Coke would strike at the same time. God only knew what her ulcer would be thinking when she staggered down the stairs to the bathroom. Whoever said you get what you pay for had it all turned around.

There would have been enough left over for another meal if Doug Esterhazie had not been with them. Larry confiscated a half-bucket box of rice he could microwave with cinnamon, sugar, and milk for breakfast to help alleviate his sodium hangover, and the rest was history.

When he and Charlie were left alone with the cat, they discussed a memorial service for Jeremy. "It would make Mrs. Beesom feel better—people her age are really into death and stuff and maybe somebody who could be a fellow suspect might show up. What do you think? I mean, I kind of feel lonely in the suspect role here—could use the company."

"You're the only one who actually saw the woman in the long coat running away from here before the blast inside Fiedler's house."

"And the only one who saw Jeremy's Ferrari come down the alley. Officer Mason saw it from behind later, going down the street, but the license plate was covered with mud and she didn't see the woman driving it. She has no proof I wasn't lying about it's being Jeremy's."

"I sure hate to tell you this, boss"—and he leaned across the crummied newspaper protecting the gleaming dining room table with one of his heart-stopping winsome looks—"but I can't see what more you could lose at this point. Unless the bouquet bomber's not done yet."

CHAPTER 20

—◆—

*C*HARLIE STOOD ON the crumbling cliff along the beach she'd never seen before. She wore a series of long scarves that blew in the sea breeze, something a sixties-type would have worn as an adult when Charlie was a kid. Major weird.

Larry Mann stood in Lawrence of Arabia garb at the edge of a cliff with arms raised, invoking the gods to give peace to the poor murdered Jeremy Fiedler, who stood beside Charlie's secretary, nodding his approval, and a seagull circled low overhead, looking for fish scraps. The breeze that blew Charlie's scarves blew Larry's robes and the long coat on the woman standing under a torrey pine that itself stood alone on this cliff. Betty Beesom, huddled on a rock nearby, her thin but careful hairdo gone ragged in the salty sea wind, smiled, nodded, and winked at Jeremy. And that was it—sea breeze, woman in the long coat, Charlie, Betty, torrey pine, Larry—all in motion with the wind. Except Jeremy, in his usual tan pants and striped shirt and seriously thinning hair, was undisturbed by nature. But that made sense, since he was dead.

Charlie's problem, besides keeping the scarves in some semblance of propriety in case Detective J. S. Amuller appeared, was her overriding thirst. She was halfway down the stairs in her condo on her way to the potty when the transition from sea cliff in sunlight to stairs at night seemed perfectly normal. Maybe because of the thirst.

Enough light from the streetlight penetrated between the bars on the window to reveal Larry Mann's makeshift bed was empty. She passed a few gallons of Coke in the bathroom and headed for the bottled water in the kitchen. No Larry here, either.

She found herself listening and holding her breath—good, she could hear the refrigerator and remembered now she'd heard the toilet flush. She hated these sudden and unreasonable panicky feelings when she remembered to worry about the loss of what had become such an unexpectedly vital part of her senses.

The floor tile felt cool and oddly lacking in grit under her bare feet. Why had she waited so long to hire a cleaning lady? They weren't that poor even before her recent successes professionally and her winnings in Vegas. It was just the memory of those struggling years trying to put food on the table while paying exorbitant rent for a bedsitter in Manhattan when she'd worked at a literary agency there. If her mother had not paid for Libby's day care and private school, Charlie wouldn't have made it. She'd felt so liberated having a home and a living wage out here, hated so having to depend on Edwina Greene, who had never forgiven her her teen pregnancy. Libby had to go to public school here, but they were a free family at last. Now that Charlie could afford private school, the kid didn't want to leave her friends at Wilson.

Charlie slipped into a windbreaker that hung on a hook inside the broom closet to one side of the kitchen door. It was scruffy but came down almost to her knees, covered the fact she slept in nothing but a T-shirt.

The patio tile was really chilly on her feet but she wouldn't be out here long, would just stand on the top step of her sunken patio and look around for her gorgeous secretary.

Maggie Stutzman's car was in its berth across from Charlie's Toyota. Her car, a loaded Subaru, sat lonely there without the Trailblazer. Charlie wondered what "they" had done with it. What "they" had done with the copies of her files. Charlie didn't think the Beverly Hill's PD could invade the office that way without some kind of court-ordered search warrant. But it was rumored the Feds did such things and worse in a secret investigation. Larry was right—she needed a lawyer.

Jeremy was something bigger than a neighborly murder. If he could disappear his identity . . . he could be a national threat. And if Charlie killed him she might be involved in this identity conspiracy, too.

Charlie was glad her best friend was home—even though there might be a bouquet bomber about. Even though their fortress was no longer protected. Mel the merry-married was a real threat, too.

A shadow moved away from the torrey pine at Jeremy's house, slid around the patio flower boxes, and disappeared behind Maggie's Subaru. It walked upright—so it was either man, ape, or big foot. It wasn't thick enough for a bear.

But Charlie regretted all that bottled water and moved ever so slowly backward down to the level of the patio—hoping she was in shadow, too—when something furry tickled itself between her ankles. She knew it was a cat, hoped it was Hairy Granger. He actually liked everybody. Everybody but Tuxedo.

Another shadow—this one had to be luscious Larry—moved away from Jeremy's house and toward Maggie's Subaru. Beautiful men have a way of moving their shadows—no explaining the laws of nature.

Charlie had just bent over to pick up Hairy Granger and keep him from tickling her into revealing her presence in the drama unfolding across the expanse of concrete courtyard only to find he was Tuxedo Greene instead, when the compound's all-but-forgotten security system kicked in. Cars with unofficial light bars (yellow in color, but flashing) roared into the newly ungated compound and disgorged middle-aged male figures with sizable beer bellies and sleek Dobermans upon Charlie's world.

There had to be a god of the inane and poor timing following Charlie through life. Suffice it to say that by the time the first Doberman reached her, Tuxedo had climbed to the top of her head and she had released some bottled spring water onto her patio for the Doberman to stop suddenly and sniff. His burly-gone-pudgy handler couldn't stop in time and took a nosedive over the attack dog in an attempt to land on top of Charlie Greene and her daughter's cat.

But Charlie and Tuxedo backed away in time to escape into the kitchen, only to find Hairy Granger right behind them, and the two felines, so happy to have escaped the Dobermans, were content to wage a sound fight that held to warning moans and occasional cat screams in Charlie's condo. While she could only guess what the flesh-eating canines and ghostly shadows and uniformed geezers were doing without. At least she could hear it all. Where was luscious Larry?

She'd found some Keds and fresh sweatpants to put on by the time the Dog Patrol types knocked on her door to report that a house in the compound had been gutted by fire and the front gate blown off. "What do you want us to do?"

"Nothing. You are fired."

"Sorry, lady, but we got to talk to a Mr. Fiedler. He's the one hired us."

"What, you don't read the papers? He was murdered here a few days ago. The bombings and the fire are just the frosting on the cake. Besides a murderer and the bombers, we've had homicide, the bomb squad, and the fire department here. And now you show up. We've been paying you all these years, too. For what, I don't know. But you're still fired."

"Not our fault. Our computer broke down."

❖

The dog-guard people and their Dobermans had at least scared off one shadow, but Charlie, Larry, Maggie, and Betty Beesom all waited nervously for some hidden bomb to go off.

They sat in Charlie's breakfast nook drinking coffee and listening to what was left of the night.

The shadow Larry had been following in the courtyard was not the woman in the long coat. He swore it was a man. And that man had been inside the burned-out shell of Jeremy Fiedler's house. Larry had avoided the dog patrol by reclining on the backseat of Maggie's Subaru, which she had not locked, still lulled by the habit of relying on the idea of Jeremy's protected fortress.

"Any other neighborhood, people would have moved to a motel to wait this out," he offered languidly. "But never, do I think, has this been any other neighborhood."

"Motels are dangerous places. Read in the paper all the time about people getting murdered and raped and robbed in one. We're safer here." Betty had removed her nightcap but wore what she called a "duster" over her nightgown. It was pink and flowered and frilly but seriously machine washable. Charlie figured it must be called that because it was meant to be worn while you dusted your house before you took your morning shower. People who had to be on the road early to commute to work need not apply. If she lived long enough to retire, would Charlie wear a duster? Nah.

"His ghost," Betty said with certainty. "I been dreaming about him ever since he was murdered. That was no shadow.

126

He still lurks around here, wanting to tell us who killed him."

This late at night, with Betty's weepy red eyes magnified by her eyeglasses, and everyone's lack of sleep after the dog patrol and bombers and murder had invaded the sanctity of their haven—Charlie could believe in ghosts, almost.

Except that Jeremy was the least ghostly type person you'd ever met—a realist, an undramatic, dependable guy. But then, too, Charlie had been dreaming of him attending his own memorial service last night and driving a semi at her on the 405 before that.

They all sat very quiet for a while. Tuxedo on top of the refrigerator glared hatred down on Hairy Granger, who sat in Larry's lap, his furry coat rippling pleasurable trembles with every stroke of Larry's hand. Charlie squirmed only a tad.

"Bet the man you saw tonight was the man that left that spooky message on Jeremy's answering machine when we broke into his house." Betty changed her mind. "Bet he was the one who killed Jeremy, too. 'I'm on to you and I'm going to blow your sick little world to pieces,' he said."

"You broke into Fiedler's house?"

"Before they blew it up, we all did," the old lady assured him. "That nice Detective Amuller said it was all right we did that, Charlie. Won't get us in any trouble. Wanted to know if I knew the voice of the caller. But I didn't."

"You told Amuller we broke into Jeremy's house? All evidence of that's been destroyed by the bomber and the fire department." Maggie Stutzman, in sweats to cover her sleepwear, scratched embarrassing places, ran her fingers through dark hair. Her hair was thick and luscious and wavy instead of curly and unruly like Charlie's. "Now he knows anyway."

"When did you talk to him?" Charlie had this drowning feeling.

"This afternoon. He was asking all about you, Charlie. I told

127

him about how I didn't care that much for you at first when you moved in, but how I'd come to see you in a Christian light."

Larry moaned and Tuxedo sat up on his ass on top of the refrigerator.

"I don't want to get your hopes up, Charlie. But I think that young man might be interested in you."

"Oh great, Mrs. Beesom. What kind of a Christian are you to want me to be suspected in Jeremy's murder? Jesus, what else did you tell him?"

"I don't mean in that way, Charlie dear. I mean it's possible he could be interested in you romantically. I just told him about you being all alone with a child to raise and how you worked so hard and lived so hard—you could sure use a rest. And how you came home from Las Vegas last fall and could still do your work and see to your mother and your daughter after all those people dying. Just take up your life like it hadn't happened. You're so strong to carry on like that after nine dead bodies . . . Charlie? I told him how I'd come to trust you after all that. What's the matter? Did I say something wrong?"

CHAPTER 21

O FFICER MASON ARRIVED while they were eating breakfast. She thought the idea of a memorial service for Jeremy was a good one. "Be interesting to see if anybody shows
up. I'll see if I can't pull some strings and get notification of it
in the morning's *P-T*."

"He must have known somebody outside these walls. I'll
post a sign on the wall out front. Maybe one on the back wall,
too. Hold it tomorrow down at the beach walk."

"That's a little soon to get a minister lined up, isn't it?"

"Larry can officiate. He's an actor. Can't you, Larry? Betty
and Maggie and I'll write you a script."

Right now Larry looked more like a handsome derelict in
need of a shower and a shave. But he set down his bowl of rice
with cinnamon, sugar, and milk, turned his palms toward the
ceiling, and shrugged at Officer Mary Maggie.

She shrugged back. "No law against it, I guess."

Charlie had poured the broth off the rest of the Mamas'
chicken soup to heat separately in a cup in the microwave and
poached an egg on top of the chicken and noodles. Still made
her thirsty, but she felt better. Betty and Maggie had gone home
to breakfast and Maggie was driving off to work late when
Officer Mason and Charlie stepped out onto the patio. Charlie
described the recent attack of the dog-protection folks and

129

Larry's following a shadow in the darkened courtyard just before that.

"Without police backup, those home-guard things are a rip-off. And house burglaries are not top priority at the Long Beach PD, but we still get there before most private security agencies. Was this shadow the mysterious woman in the long coat you keep telling us about?"

"Larry swears it was a man. And he'd been inside Jeremy's bombed house."

"So why are you in such a hurry to have a memorial service?"

"I have the gut feeling the longer I'm the only suspect, the deeper the shit I'm standing in. Betty told me about talking to Amuller yesterday."

"Your gut has good instincts. You're playing games with us and the doctors about your hearing. And you have Mitch Hilsten. And you just spent the night with your hunk secretary. You don't come off exactly like Snow White, you know."

"What I know is Amuller's after me. But I thought you had some sense of fairness. You're beginning to sound like Kenneth Starr, too."

Officer Mason flinched as if she'd been slapped. "That's the nastiest—how—don't you ever compare me to that—cops have feelings, too."

Officer Mason, in a huff, passed Detective Amuller as she and her car roared out of the wide-open-ended compound. And, of course, J. S. was sitting in Charlie's living room when her hunk secretary stepped out of the bathroom shaved and showered.

"I'm going to run into the office. I'll be back tonight and bring something to wear to the memorial service."

"Don't wear robes," Charlie told him.

"Uh, right." He paused on his way across the room to ponder that with a knitted brow, gave the homicide detective a nasty scowl, and left. He'd thoughtfully folded up his bedding and stashed it somewhere so it looked like he had slept upstairs last night and would again tonight.

The homicide cop shook his head and sighed like a man twice his age. "You're certainly a busy single mother, I'll say that for you. Officer Mason told me about Mitch Hilsten."

What she didn't tell you, because she didn't know, was that I have been celibate and happy to be so since Las Vegas last October, which is probably more than you can say. What's more, I plan to remain celibate the rest of my life. Besides, my gorgeous Larry's gay. "Detective Amuller, this is not what it looks like. Larry worries about me being alone after murder and bombings and fire here."

"Oh, I'll bet he does. Where do you stash your kid on nights like last night? She's at a pretty dangerous age, you ask me."

"She spent the night with a friend."

"Your millionaire friend, the president of Esterhazie Cement? Or his son?"

Charlie tightened up somewhere inside as she had with that unsympathetic doctor at the hospital. She could hear the defiance and resentment in her voice. "It's concrete."

Careful Greene, you know how much trouble you can get into when you let yourself hate someone. He's just doing his job.

"He's never been a deaf single mom."

"It's hearing-impaired these days, lady. You seem to have this impairment intermittently, when it's convenient. And I'm never going to be a mom. But I am a cop, lady, with a job to do. And I don't care who you sleep with, I'm going to do that job. I assume, with all the trouble you've been in, you have a lawyer. But I suggest, since you aren't charged with anything, you don't call him in just yet. You noticed what happened to the Ramseys in Boulder. Since you were born and raised there, you must have sat home and watched the play-by-play on television."

"I work. I don't sit home. I don't watch daytime television." Again, that dangerous growl in her already growly voice scared her. She knew she was highly vulnerable as a mere citizen and a woman, but her taxes helped pay this guy's salary and he had no right to judge her on what he considered her profile or her noncriminal-related morals.

Don't get mad, Charlie. Get cool. And then get even.

"So why would I want a lawyer? I didn't kill Jeremy or blow up things around the compound."

Detective J. S. Amuller had been intimidated and insulted by Charlie and Maggie's take on Jeremy's house and their lack of involvement with him as a neighbor. But Maggie had that man, the married Mel, as an airtight alibi, and Betty Beesom, the only other known candidate for suspect, was a frail eighty-three-year-old. Charlie could think of only one other ploy to disrupt the cop's headlong course toward the easy way out.

"Somebody has been searching my computer files at work since you probably told them I was home watching daytime TV. I have the feeling the Feds are more interested in how someone could disappear electronically than—"

"That's their problem. Mine is who killed a man outside your back door. Even if his identity was erased from data files everywhere. They've got the computer problem. I've got the body. We all have a job to do, Ms. Greene."

His grin appeared more malevolent than silly now.

That's just your fear talking. Ever since your "intermittent" handicap you've felt more vulnerable. Charlie's inner self was ever trying to impose sanity on insane situations, when it should be panicking.

"And right now, you have everything going for you." He

132

settled more comfortably into her couch, his long legs bent at the knees like a grasshopper's, and grinned with his lips together for the first time Charlie could remember seeing. They were going to have a nice long chat with no Maggie Stutzman to interrupt with talk about menopause. "Where there's smoke, there's fire. And you've been involved in a lot of homicide cases."

"But in every one the killer was identified as someone else."

"The right people are not always brought to justice, but the wrong people always slip up some time. And I'm a patient man."

"That's nice, but I'm still not following you."

"You had motive, a nubile daughter in contact with a predator. Mother nature teaches us that there is no more dangerous animal than a mother protecting her young. And when he dies, you get his cleaning lady. You had the trust of and ready access to the victim. Were at the scene of the crime. People are most often murdered by someone they know. Plus you had the victim's blood on your sweatshirt. And you want to know the most damning thing against you? In all those investigations in the last three to four years of your highly questionable history, you were instrumental in solving many of those murder cases. No professional training for it, either, no education or experience in professional law enforcement. Lady, you stand out like a red light here, a sore thumb. What better way to escape a murder trial than to pin the murder on someone else? Plus, you exhibit no sorrow over the violent death of a man who was your neighbor, and according to your own words a valuable handyman and resource person in this woman's commune. Anyone fits the profile, lady, it's you."

It seemed everybody was looking for a profile these days—a way to group people. Millions and millions of individual people were too much even for computers, which could supposedly do math in the gadzillions squared, could sort out the individ-ual intricacies of genetic codes—and even play chess. But peo-ple had to fit a profile—fit into a group to be understood. Used to be called *type*, and then *category*, and now *profile*.

With the commercial use of information on the Internet, telemarketers could target individuals who fit a profile—who bought types of stocks, gave to types of charities. They prob-ably knew which geezers used Viagra so they could target their sex mates with K-Y Jelly. Medical histories could be passed on to health insurers who wouldn't want to deal with people who might actually get sick, let alone those who already were. Is this why Jeremy wanted to lose himself in cyberspace?

CHAPTER 22

◆

CHARLIE SHOWERED AND dressed in a cream-colored pants suit, green blouse, matching scarf tying her hair back, emerald stud earrings, and knee-highs with green slings. She made up announcements for the memorial the next day and taped them on the front and back walls of the compound.

Then, leaving a note for Libby and with her inner voice throwing a royal hissy fit, Charlie drove the gray Toyota out of the ruined gate and headed for Beverly Hills.

After Detective J. S. had convinced her she possessed every known reason for killing Jeremy Fiedler, so why waste time looking for another killer, the hearing specialist's nurse had called to remind her she needed to come in to determine if "appliances" could help with her problem. Apparently Charlie had made an appointment. Maybe they'd written her a note to that effect and she'd stuffed it in a pocket with the used Kleenex yesterday when Larry Mann had held her while she cried. Odd, the nurse didn't seem surprised that she and Charlie were carrying on normally over the phone. She couldn't remember the conversation now exactly. Maybe the nurse thought she was talking to Charlie's caregiver. Modern life was one big disconnect.

Anyway, after Amuller, that call from the Ear, Head, and

Neck Clinic set off a growing rage Charlie wasn't sure either she or her inner voice could control.

I'm your common sense.

"Oh, bugger off."

Charlie had either to take charge of something or lose her mind. So she took charge of the Toyota, and it felt good. What she would do was drop into the clinic and inform Dr. R. Rodney where he could stick his hearing aids. Then she'd drop into the agency, find out if there was anybody in the office next to hers and how come the authorities were allowed into her computer files. Then she'd go somewhere for a nice lunch.

The wind blew in off the Pacific and made a hole in the smog that lasted from Inglewood to the Santa Monica Freeway, letting the sun shine through. Charlie rolled down her window and wished she'd learned how to whistle. The wind mussed her hair but she didn't care. She even stuck her elbow out the window.

The hours of her life she'd spent on the 405, and never once had she been pulled over. Jeremy could drive without car registration for a long time, without a driver's license. But how could he get license plates for it—or them? You couldn't always keep old plates covered with mud. Most of Southern California was covered with concrete.

Speaking of which, another thing she could do, she decided now that she felt she had some control over her life, for the moment at least, was to further enlist the aid of Ed Esterhazie. The man was no fool. She needed to talk this out with someone like him. Who else could she turn to now? Bounce ideas off of?

Several years ago when the office receptionist was murdered, Charlie had met David Dalrymple of the Beverly Hills PD. One day soon, if she had one, Charlie should get in touch with him.

He thought she had psychic powers then, but he'd probably gotten over that. Yes, there were positive things Charlie could do and not just let her anger play into an inexperienced cop's daydreams of an open-and-shut case.

For once, Charlie's inner common-sense voice remained silent. Did that mean the two Charlies agreed? Or that even her inner hearing had disappeared itself again, like Jeremy did his identity?

Charlie listened to the wind and road noise and bleating of domesticated car horns and relaxed. Relaxed, sort of. This handicap threat at a gut level was almost worse than being accused of murder.

At the Ear, Head, and Neck Clinic Charlie was told that she'd been a bad girl by hiding the fact that her hearing loss was intermittent rather than total, that she'd wasted the valuable time of real important people who could have been dealing with her problem in a different way or dealing with someone who had total hearing loss.

After Detective J. S. Amuller of the Long Beach PD, Charlie didn't bat a guilty eyelash. She was kind of proud of herself. Did this mean a real live woman could outgrow guilt? Even one under suspicion in a murder investigation? Nah.

Dr. R. Rodney looked in her ears again with the icy little light probe, coldly asked her about unusual sounds, tingling, itching, pain then sent her to a technician across the hall who played a succession of silly sounds through earphones and asked her to evaluate sharpness, volume, and the register of each one.

What was it Art Granger had said about his brother who'd fallen off a tractor back in Iowa? His hearing came and went for a week, then was gone? "Deaf as a post the rest of his life."

At Congdon & Morse Representation, Inc, no one bothered to conceal their surprise at seeing Charlie.

"What the hell you doing back at the office dressed for work? You're on vacation. Your next-door neighbor gets murdered, his house burned, somebody blew your gate in and you standing so close you're deaf as a post half the time." Richard Morse accosted her, and in the agency lobby on her way in before she'd even closed the door. He stood there blinking his bulging eyes for a moment and shrugged. "Guess maybe I wouldn't wanna stay home either."

In his office (which was even more spacious than her's—he had one of those mahogany Admiralty desks you could serve the President's cabinet a seven-course dinner on—the smaller the man, the bigger the desk in good old Hollywood) Charlie accosted him back. "Richard, how could you allow the police access to my computer files without a court-ordered search warrant?" Or whatever the hell they're supposed to have.

"They had one, Charlie, and besides, it wasn't the police." He sat in the giant leather chair that accompanied the giant mahogany desk and disappeared. Why can't guys ever see themselves from the vantage point of those on the other side of their desks? Just next door sat Larry Mann, who had to be six-two if he was an inch—he lifted weights so he could be a he-man in beer commercials—dwarfing the cubicle and narrow ledge that held his computer and all the filing cabinets and shelves spilling over with the written dreams of hopefuls neither he nor Charlie could get through in a decade. Sort of like Charlie's dining room table before the magical Kate Gonzales walked through the door. Charlie wondered if Kate did offices.

"Charlie, can't you hear me now?"

138

"What? Oh, no, I'm sorry, just thinking instead of listening. What did you say?"

"I SAID—"

"DON'T YELL—I mean, don't yell. I had no idea how much crap deaf people have to put up with."

"YEAH, WELL, I mean, yeah, well, it ain't that easy for the rest of us either, babe. But what I said was, because of that little problem Evan Black got us into last October with the invasion of Area 51 and all the loot looted from Vegas, the Feds are after our balls. They wrangled an investigative search warrant into the agency's files and, working at the agency, you were meat, too, you know?"

"How? Is the agency being charged with anything?"

"No, but Evan is, and we represent him."

Evan Black, an incredibly talented producer/director/writer and pathological troublemaker, was wrapping up the filming in Spain of a media baby starring Mitch Hilsten and Deena Gotmor, financed with money made in Vegas on the wager of the century. Suffice it to say he'd infiltrated the secret sanctity of the unacknowledged air base known as Area 51 and made the military almost as much of a laughing stock as Kenneth Starr did the U.S. Congress.

"And they're also interested in how Jeremy Fiedler could erase his identity by using cyberspace."

"That's how I figure it, kid. But you don't have any stuff on him at work here?"

"No, but this rookie homicide critter is lining up merit badges by convincing himself and me that I killed Jeremy because I fit the profile while a murderer's busy erasing his involvement with every passing minute—which is tightening the noose around my neck."

"Jeesh," Charlie's boss said, "even our boy Monroe in Folsom couldn't write something this weird."

"I need your help, Richard."

"You got it."

"I do?" Usually he told her she was imagining things.

"Babe, with your luck, even I may not be enough." He sounded like he couldn't believe that, either.

"I wondered about contacting Lieutenant Dalrymple. Remember him?"

"Remember? Charlie, he was one of the locals escorting the Feds in here to look over your files."

If Charlie weren't already so suspicious she could play Mitch Hilsten's stalker in *Satan's Sadists*, his next-to-shoot film according to *Variety*—she would have decided it was a joke when Dalrymple agreed to a meet for lunch at the Celebrity Pit in an hour. She handed Richard back his phone. "That was too easy. Something big's happening. Is it Jeremy or Evan Black or Detective J. S. Amuller?"

"Got me, kid. I'll ask around if the industry knows anything they'll tell an agency who's files are being searched by the Feds. Charlie, you be careful, hear?"

"Okay, but I have one more question."

"Shoot."

If he only knew. "Richard, is Michael Congdon back in his office?"

"Let me give you some advice, Charlie." He tipped back his giant chair so he could put his little feet up on his gargantuan desk and did something with his eyes that demanded a mustache and a cigar. Sort of the Godfather meets Groucho. "You got enough trouble now. I know—God, do I know—how good you are at trouble, but trust me. Leave that one alone."

"That one what?"

"That last question you asked me."

Almost back to her own office, Larry Mann, dwarfing his

cubicle, stopped Charlie with another telephone and mouthed, "Your mother."

It wasn't so much his message as his amusement that made Charlie want to lob a loaded file cabinet at him. Instead she grimaced an I'll-get-even-and-you-will-suffer-boy look, reaching for his phone rather than going to her own in the plush digs next door.

"Glad to know you're not dead. You haven't answered your e-mail so I had to call," is how Edwina Greene answered Charlie's, "Hello, Mom?"

"You, as I remembered, wanted me to get e-mail. I got e-mail. Did you say 'Mom'? How thoughtful. Well, it's about time. But it's too late."

If Evan Black, writer/producer/director, was a pathological troublemaker, Edwina Greene, professor/biologist/widow/mother/grandmother, was a pathological mystery. She thought Kenneth Starr was cool. And that was only the beginning.

"Too late for what?" Oh please, Edwina, my trouble-quotient glass runneth over.

"Just wanted to let you know, so you could explain it to my granddaughter."

How does she know when I'm the most vulnerable? "What now?"

"Oh, 'what now'? As if I'm the trouble in this so-called family."

"Edwina, please, I know you're busy, but—" Over the phone Edwina Greene hit Charlie up the side of the head. At her expression, Larry grabbed the receiver and started talking to Charlie's mother and Libby's grandmother and Charlie couldn't even hear the crickets in her ears. She sat in the visitor's chair crowded into the almost nonexistent space between the door and this towering drop-leaf file cabinet whose doors would not close even when hell froze over.

When he finally hung up, Charlie was crying. He wrote out a note, walked around his computer ledge—he was even bigger when she was helpless and handicapped—and handed her the note. "Your mom has a boyfriend. She thought you should know."

CHAPTER 23

◆

D AVID DALRYMPLE ROSE to meet Charlie when the
Sharon Stone lookalike hostess showed her to his table.
"You haven't changed a bit."

He had. The semicircle of hair cupping his baldness had
shrunk to a ring around the edges and grayed, the lines in his
face multiplied and deepened. His jowls sagged. But the biggest
difference was the absence of eyeglasses.

He smiled at her surprise and lost twenty years. "Laser surgery. It's miraculous. I still need reading glasses for fine print
and if I become too studious. But it's been a wondrous im-
provement, and my sinus condition, allergy, whatever disappeared with the eyeglasses constricting my nose. How about
you? I notice you're not wearing those stiletto heels."

"Out of fashion except with spaghetti straps." Fashion de-
signers from the East Coast and their hauteur masters from
Europe still had their models wear them down the ramp and
they were big in sex sitcoms, but clumpy squares had caught
on and insisted on staying in. Besides, it was the frigging pantyhose that drove Charlie nuts.

Larry had chased Charlie through the hall and then the
lobby, catching her at the elevator just as her hearing returned.
She saw him see her recoil when it hit her up the side of the
head.

"I have a luncheon appointment," she'd told her secretary. "I'll see you back in Long Beach."

"Charlie, you can't just wander around on your own never knowing when it's going to happen again."

"Well, maybe I'm going to have to. Maybe I'm not going to let it louse up my life. Hell, I'm probably going to end up in prison for a murder I didn't commit anyway. I don't have as much to lose as you think." Besides, my mother has a boyfriend.

"Hi, I'm Tom." The Tom Hanks lookalike handed them menus and smiled way down at them. "I'll be your server today. Can I bring you something to drink while you decide on your order?"

Charlie realized she was turning her head toward the speaker because only one ear was hearing. She couldn't remember if that was the ear hit up the side of or not. Edwina had been a widow since Charlie was sixteen and pregnant with Libby. She had a profession and menopause. What could she want with a boyfriend?

Without even consulting Charlie, David Dalrymple ordered a bottle of Beaujolais.

"I'm off duty," he answered her blink. Soft-spoken, gentle, thoughtful, deliberate, he reminded Charlie more of a kindly professor than a cop. Made you want to confide in him, trust him.

Careful, Charlie.

I know.

Why did she even come once she knew he was in on the search of the office? Because she wanted to get away from the office and her secretary's pity. Because even though the man across the table was no longer a disinterested party, she might learn something she needed to know. Because he was so different from Detective J. S. Amuller. Because Edwina had a boyfriend? "I just remembered. Didn't I read somewhere that you'd retired?"

"I have, but I do part-time consulting. My wife couldn't stand my pacing the house all day." The skin crinkled around his eyes with the self-deprecating smile, but the watchful Dalrymple watched her from within those eyes—so small now without the bifocals.

The wine arrived for his approval and Tom Hanks poured them each a glass. Charlie's companion told her, "I remembered your preference for red in the days when white wine was so politically correct."

They both ordered the salad special that came with soup and hot rolls. David Dalrymple raised his glass. "To our meeting once again. Under less stressful circumstances this time, I hope. I've thought of you often."

They talked of their daughters and his granddaughter, circling the important stuff for now. Even the bus girl/water pourer/coffee refiller was an almost dead ringer for Deena Gotmor. Makeup, disguise, and impersonation had made giant strides since last Charlie'd noticed. You put the real Mel Gibson down there behind the bar with the bartender and you could probably tell the difference, but right now that guy looked and acted and smirked like Mel Gibson. And was that Charlton Heston or a plant at the table by the window?

The Celebrity Pit only recently opened just off Wilshire. Intended to lure tourists, it had become a campy destination for real Hollywood celebrities to appear and confound the commoners. It was an easy walk from the agency and Charlie'd been been here once before. The bar formed the center of the pit part surrounded by an expanse of stage where the likes of the Beatles, Liberace, Elvis, and the Herbicides cavorted for the diners in the evenings. A walkway under the pit allowed the drink waiters access to Mel or whoever was bartending that night—Arnold Schwarzenegger, the last time Charlie was here—without walking across the stage when the fake performers performed.

The people might be fake but the food was excellent: The salad special today was hot grilled portobello mushroom strips on a bed of icy lettuce leaves with grilled red, yellow, and orange peppers; the soup a creamy puree of squash spiced, according to Tom Hanks, with nutmeg and tumeric. The crusty french rolls steamed when you split them to spread whipped butter.

A woman appeared suddenly at their table and pointed at Charlie. "Wait, don't tell me—"

"What?"

"I know who you are. The name just won't—Jesus, I took my gingko this morning, too. It'll come to me. But then I won't know if you're the real one or not, will I?"

Charlie's bad ear ticked, buzzed, hurt, and then opened up for business. "I'm the fake."

"The fake who? Don't tell me. I'm so close. It just pisses me off when this happens." She walked to a table with several other women seated about a quarter of the way around this level of the graduated rings that surrounded the pit, each higher than the one below.

"Is it just me or is—"

"The world's getting crazier by the minute," Dalrymple finished for her, nodding, and refilled their glasses before Tom could do it for him.

"This is wonderful. I didn't realize how hungry I was."

"My pleasure. Like I said, it's good to see you again. And see you looking so well. I pulled you up on the computer the other day. A lot has happened to you since last we met."

Charlie couldn't remember the last time she'd cleaned up her plate unless it was eggs. But the salad and the soup and the bread disappeared as she told him about Jeremy Fiedler. Hell, he'd probably only seen Amuller's take on his computer. They had rich, strong coffee with the last of the wine. He ordered a chocolate dessert of some kind she refused even a bite of.

"It's interesting that so much of your life is on the computer, when your deceased neighbor isn't there at all."

"Jeremy's disappearance in cyberspace is more than interesting, it's impossible."

"I don't know, Charlie, I'm beginning to think nothing's impossible these days. You can't believe the squads of people it took to explain to me how to call you up on that goddamned computer."

"Just click CA for criminal activity at the top of your screen."

"You're computer literate on the law-enforcement channel or whatever?"

Charlie had to laugh at the helpless cast of his expression. She feared him but she liked him. She relented finally and explained Officer Mason explaining the procedure to Amuller. "He thinks because of my 'history' that I run around convincing law enforcement wherever I go that somebody else committed my murders. I have a life. A busy one. What he's talking about takes a cunning and time for planning I don't have. But he's so busy building a case against me he's not looking for the murderer."

"You have to admit that your encounters with death and destruction are bound to raise suspicions."

"Yeah, but look at Kinsey Millhone and V. I. Warshawski and—"

"They are fictional creatures, Charlie."

"Oh, well, okay but—"

"You"—the lady with the pointy finger was back in Charlie's face—"are Mitch Hilsten's fake girlfriend. I can't remember your name, but I know who you are. God, I feel so much better. I thought I was going crazy." She and her friends left the Celebrity Pit with a wave and a smile. They were all different ages, all appeared related and relieved.

Charlie and Dalrymple watched them leave, looked at each other, and then into space, trying to remember what they'd been talking about.

Dalrymple recovered first. "That's another thing, your notoriety. The police are going to look at that when your name pops up on the computer repeatedly—and Mitch Hilsten is not small potatoes."

Charlie was back on the 405 regretting all the wine and coffee. This was one long commute, and you get off on an off-ramp this close to rush hour—you could disappear in cyberspace, even.

We have an idea here.

No, we don't. We have a bladder here.

Put all this day together, all the things we've heard—the answer to Jeremy's murder is there. Somewhere.

It was at this point that Charlemagne Catherine Greene realized she was hearing her stupid inner voice and that was all. No crickets in her ears. No tickling. No NPR on the radio. No traffic on the 405.

She began watching traffic and the speedometer. Jeremy Fiedler might be able to beat the odds out here in the real world but Charlie, with this constant reminder of the end of her life as she wanted to live with it, did not feel so lucky. Not that being murdered was lucky, but her mysterious neighbor had gotten away with the impossible for years apparently.

The answer's there. Somewhere. In your last thought.

Now stop that.

Charlie didn't hear the siren—just noticed suddenly the flashing lights coming up behind her.

"Excuse me, officer, but I can't hear you. I'm handicapped."

"I don't see that on your license."

"I'm new at this. I didn't know you had to put it on your license." (Was it under height, weight, hair color, eye color? Probably under CA for criminal activity.)

But by the time Charlie had slowed enough to pull off onto the no-drive lane, the CHIPY had roared past her. Now she could hear her heart pounding blood in both ears. But that was all.

CHAPTER 24

———◆———

*C*HARLIE, FANTASIZING ABOUT all the horrible things
that would happen to her in prison if she couldn't hear,
drove the speed limit, pissing off the drivers behind her. And
she'd thought the hospital was a scary place under those con-
ditions. She sat so straight and tight her fingers and arms tin-
gled. Funny how different her mood was now, driving back
home, from her sunny attitude on the way up the 405 this
morning.

David Dalrymple had promised he'd do what he could to
find ways for her to clear herself. "The best thing would be to
remember some clue about Mr. Fiedler that would explain how
he disappeared from computers, figure out how he could op-
erate in the real world that way, talk to your neighbors again,
and to Libby, to see if they can come up with details they've
forgotten about him. And maybe trust your psychic instincts,
listen to them. You may know more about all this than you
realize. I'll keep in touch."

And about the investigation of the agency and her files.
"Evan Black is in serious trouble with the federal government,
Charlie, and has some very unsavory and questionable friends.
Your agency has been pulled into the mess and, I'm afraid,
your boyfriend, too."

"Mitch Hilsten is just a friend." Who, damn him, knows

how to work my monthly clock. "And film making is big bucks. You know as well as I do that where there're big bucks, there're questionable and unsavory people. And Evan's always been in trouble with the government and the courts. They're making him famous. You can't tell me this wasn't also a good excuse to look into Jeremy Fiedler's cyber disappearance as well. Let's face it, if you can erase your electronic identity, all government and business is at risk, big risk. The opportunities for attaining great wealth illegally is mind-boggling."

Dalrymple had just crinkled his eyes and watched her.

Maybe they had separate wings in prison for handicapped people. Maybe Edwina came up with this boyfriend idea because Charlie hadn't called her in a while. Maybe there was no boyfriend. Maybe Charlie's mom just wanted some attention. Edwina was a biology professor at the University of Colorado in Boulder, and certainly busy enough. Was the boyfriend another professor?

Could Charlie or her neighbors or Libby really know something they'd forgotten? Charlie's undependable hearing returned to one ear with a gurgle when she drove the gray Toyota safely into her disabled fortress at last. There truly was no place like home, even if portions of it had been blown up. By the time she'd changed back into comfortable clothes, the other ear had come on line.

❖

Mrs. Beesom, Maggie, Libby, and Charlie sat in the breakfast nook in Charlie's kitchen and concentrated. The formal dining room table was too formal for the tight neighborhood grouping, even now when you could see it. Larry was out picking up Italian carryout.

"Maybe if we hold hands and close our eyes," Libby suggested.

Everyone looked at the kid like she was nuts, but reached across the table and joined hands anyway.

"Mom, you're peeking. Now let's repeat 'Jeremy Fiedler' a lot of times and then be quiet for a while. See what happens."

"Where do you get this stuff?" Charlie asked her daughter.

"Watched Rudy Ferris this afternoon after school. He had two whole segments on concentrating and remembering buried memories."

"I thought you thought he was gross."

"Gross grows on you. Now get with the frame here."

They repeated 'Jeremy Fiedler' a lot of times and then were silent for a while.

Gross grows on you? Gross.

Shut up and concentrate. Jeremy, you out there?

"Does this 'marinara' sauce have hamburger in it? I like meat sauce on my spaghetti."

"Jeremy?"

"Mom, did he speak to you?"

"Didn't anybody else hear it? He said he didn't like marinara sauce on his spaghetti if it didn't have hamburger in it."

"Mom, Jeremy ate pasta, not spaghetti."

"Charlie, he never ate hamburger. A hundred percent no-fat ground sirloin of buffalo once or twice a year, maybe, but that doesn't sound like Jeremy at all. That sounds like—"

"Sounds like me, because I said it. I mean, I thought it." Betty looked frightened. "I didn't know I said it."

"You didn't," Maggie and Libby said almost in unison.

Everybody stared at Charlie now, everybody except Tuxedo on top of the fridge, who began washing the Stinky Slimy Salmon Supper Stuff off his whiskers. At least the cat had some sense.

"Hey, we came up with something we didn't know on Jeremy anyway," Libby said. "I didn't know buffalo grew a hundred percent no-fat sirloin anything. Let's try again. And, Mom, if you can pick up on Mrs. Beesom's thought, what else could be out there?"

Yeah, like your grandmother's boyfriend. But Charlie joined back into the ritual.

"Grandma's got a boyfriend? She's too old. She's a grandma."

Now everybody was looking at Libby. Everybody but Charlie, who as a mother did not like the idea of the kid picking up on her thoughts.

"Edwina has a boyfriend?" Maggie said. "When did this happen?"

"I don't know. It just popped into my head," Libby said.

They tried again. And just as Larry Mann walked in the door with Mrs. Beesom's least-favorite spaghetti sauce, Jeremy spoke to them all, and it freaked Tuxedo of the salmon breath right off the refrigerator and onto the middle of the table.

"Okay." The gay hunk set dinner plates and silverware in front of four shaken females and parceled out spaghetti pasta, garlic bread, and Caesar salad. He set the remaining marinara and Parmesan in the center of the table, poured Libby some milk and Betty some water, and uncorked a bottle of Chianti for the rest of them, pulling Jeremy's chair in from the dining room to sit on the end. "Now what is this about Jeremy saying something?"

"We all heard it—it even scared the cat," Betty said, wide-eyed and breathless.

"But what exactly did he say?"

"Said to watch out for Hairy." She tried to get her mouth

around a loaded fork and all the spaghetti decided to straighten out and slip off back to her plate slinging blood-colored droplets, one of which ended up on her bifocals.

"Hairy the cat?"

"Yes." Betty Beesom practically buried her face in her dinner. Her palsy, or whatever made her quiver, was especially evident tonight.

Charlie, Libby, and Maggie sat with their food suspended somewhere between their plates and their faces. Libby mouthed, "Hairy?"

That's not what Charlie'd heard, either. She thought she'd heard, "Watch out for the 405."

"I thought he'd said 'Watch out for Rory Torkelsen,' " Libby got up the nerve to confess.

"Who is Rory Torkelsen?" her mother asked.

"Oh, some jerk at school who came over one day when you were gone. Jeremy didn't like him—made him leave. It was nothing. What did you hear, Maggie?"

Maggie shook her head and crunched Romaine lettuce into minute molecules, finally flushed it down with a gulp of Chianti, and began the crunching ceremony all over with toasted garlic bread.

"He said, 'Watch out for Mel,' didn't he?" Charlie dared, and was answered with an ominous silence from her best friend.

"So if you all heard something different it must have been an internal message, special for each of you." Larry caught Charlie rolling her eyes and sent her a warning look.

"Wonder what he told Tuxedo," Libby said. "Poor kitty looked like somebody stuck his tail in a hot socket. Maybe Tux saw who murdered him and Jeremy sent him a message to point out that person."

Mrs. Beesom, old and quivery or not, could put away a lot

of food fast. She lay down her fork and wiped marinara sauce off her glasses and chin and the front of her blouse with a napkin dipped in her drinking water. "Mr. Mann, you going to keep watch tonight?" she asked Larry without quite looking at him. "I know you must be sleepy but I'd feel better if you did."

"I'll take a cat nap while Charlie and Maggie keep first watch and then relieve them. You, lady, can sleep the night through in peace."

When they'd all finished eating, Maggie made coffee and they tried again, Larry encouraging them not to call Jeremy from the dead but to simply say the first thing about him that came to mind.

There were lots of unexpected responses, but Libby came up with one they'd all forgotten but reacted to now. "His limping. Was it a bum knee or what?"

"Sports injury," Maggie said. "Was it jogging or working out at the gym?"

"The gym," Charlie reminded her, "never heard of him." That's another positive thing Charlie could do—go down to Judy & Gym's Age Buster and look around, ask questions, if she could hear the answers by then. "And remember, the limp came and went."

"Like your ears, Mom," Libby said kindly.

"Sports injuries will do that," Maggie offered. "Not most hearing problems."

"And his hair," Libby said.

"Did Jeremy color his hair?" Maggie asked, surprised. "I hadn't noticed. At one time I thought he might have had a lift."

"Facelift?" Now it was Charlie's turn to be surprised. "When?"

"I don't think so," Betty Beesom took a sip of the insipid

decaf instant everyone kept on hand in case she dropped in, which everyone knew she would do at a moment's notice. "Jeremy was not a shallow man like that."

"Mrs. Beesom, would you like a Snickers bar for dessert?" Libby asked, totally out of context.

"Oh honey, I'd love one," the older lady said, getting weepy. "Young people don't eat dessert anymore. They drink wine and strong coffee instead."

Libby was back in a minute with a candy bar for Betty and one for herself to feed her zits and monthly cycle. Charlie figured Betty was feeding her extended stomach. But life was short, especially at eighty-three. Let her enjoy.

"You are so lucky to have her, Charlie," Betty said. "And your mother is so lucky to have you. You are blessed, you know." Betty on a Snickers was like everybody else Charlie knew on a martini or three.

"Okay, ladies," Larry said, "we have a limp and bad hair days. What else?"

"Sometimes Jeremy liked Tuxedo and sometimes he didn't," Libby offered, "and shut up, Mom, you never liked Tux."

"Yeah? Who paid for all the frigging shots? Not Jeremy Fiedler," Charlie protested. "This is getting us nowhere. Let's—what's that noise?"

It sounded like a helicopter.

CHAPTER 25

◆

CHARLIE AND MAGGIE kept the first watch in the ruined courtyard. Larry and Betty were, they hoped, sleeping. Libby had just roared off in the Jeep Wrangler to spend the night in the Esterhazie mansion, no one willing to risk the kid to the jollies of a crazy bomber at night. Libby pointed out that the first bomb went off about noon, but didn't fuss too much. Maybe there was hope for droopy Doug.

Tuxedo prowled the courtyard, sniffing at everything as if this weren't his home, probably just waiting for Hairy Granger to come over so he could clean the old boy's clock.

The Wrangler roared back into the compound and Libby got out, her arms full of Hairy. "He keeps doing this. I don't even know he's in there until I'm two blocks away. Here, hold on to him until I can get out of here."

It had been a news helicopter flying over them, chasing other news this time probably. They could still hear it somewhere, but it wasn't close.

"Larry thinks I should get a lawyer. What do you think?" Charlie kicked at Tuxedo, who was slinking up on her and the cat on her lap.

"Charlie."

"You obviously never had a cat climb your head. I've still got that scratch on my cheek from Hairy."

157

"You haven't been charged with anything. Calling a lawyer makes you seem guilty. Look what happened to the Ramseys in Boulder when they got preemptive."

"Yeah, but look what really happened to them."

"Jeremy wasn't your kid. It's different."

"Was it 'watch out for Mel' you heard tonight?"

"You never liked Mel, did you?"

"Neither did Jeremy. You know, if we all heard different things we were probably doing it to ourselves and I think we know now why Hairy here was in Jeremy's car. He likes to go for rides. Tuxedo hates the car."

"But why did Tuxedo leap off the refrigerator like that if we were all doing that to ourselves? And Mrs. Beesom was lying about what she heard to watch out for. You can tell when she lies, bless her heart. She's so bad at it. Does Edwina really have a boyfriend?"

"That's what she told Larry on the phone. She was mad because I hadn't answered her e-mail. Hell, I left the damn computer at work. Even my cellular. I thought I was going to have a vacation."

The night was very still and very dark. Fog fingers crept into the compound as if hesitant to get involved. Charlie didn't blame them. Traffic noises, the helicopter thumping, a distant ship's horn, Tuxedo's low moan. "Put a sock in it, dufus. Hairy can sit here as long as he wants."

Charlie took in the smell of her lemon tree and Jeremy's burn-soaked house. "I don't hate Mel, I just worry about you."

"Not all of us have a Mitch Hilsten drop by now and then to relieve the hornies. Not all of us have a Libby to take care of us when we're as old as Betty Beesom. Don't you judge me, Charlie."

"I won't. You're right and I'm sorry."

"I worry about you, too."

"That's because we're buds."

A long silence as two best friends worked on forgiving because they needed each other.

"Your mother has every right to have a boyfriend if she wants to."

"Maggie, I said I was sorry."

Another longer silence. "I'm sorry, too. With your hearing problem and lack of an alibi and all, I don't have to pick on you now."

"Why is it so dark?" Charlie sat up, Tuxedo sprang, Hairy flew, and the chase was on. "The sky has the city-light glow, the fog is still patchy, the light's on over my door and yours and Betty's—"

"We don't have the lights on the parking lattices or the ones on the gates or the muted ones on the side walls anymore, Charlie. We haven't since Jeremy's house burned inside."

"He controlled all that, too?"

"When you think about it, we let him control an awful lot around here."

"Because it made us feel safe."

"Right. You ever notice his hair changing color?"

"He was vain enough to work out and get that body, why wouldn't he color his hair? But no, I didn't notice it. Why do you suppose he felt he had to disappear?"

"Somebody was after him? He was in trouble with the law? An ex-wife was after his money? He wanted to avoid taxes? He wanted to come back as somebody else—reinvent himself? He—"

"Where do you get that stuff?"

"Charlie, I'm an attorney."

"Not that kind of attorney."

"Wait a minute. I have all these clients trying to get out of paying almost all they own to inheritance tax or nursing homes instead of leaving their wealth to their children and grandchildren."

"There's nursing-home insurance now."

"It doesn't begin to pay expenses for long-term care—your heirs get screwed by taxes and long-term care insurance, too. You can live twenty years with Alzheimer's and not even know you've got heirs—or toenails, for that matter. And the costs per week are humongous for changing diapers on an adult."

"Jeremy never mentioned a family to me. But he wouldn't if he was trying to disappear. That would be a way to trace a past he intended to cancel."

"I kind of felt we were his family. I miss him, Charlie."

"Kind of awful to realize you don't realize you need someone till they're dead. Almost like being widowed. And I've never been married."

"Yeah. And whatever he was running from, I liked my world better when he controlled it. And I don't even like to hear myself saying it, independent female that I am."

"What are we going to do with Mrs. Beesom, now that Jeremy's gone?" Why couldn't life leave Charlie alone to enjoy her kid, her work?

"I don't know. We really were like a family here in a way, weren't we? And he was the sacrificial daughter. And you and I could work and Betty could snoop. But Betty's talking about rebuilding Jeremy's house and renting it to a nice young man 'like Jeremy.' "

"She told Larry and me that, too. She's even feeding Jeremy's pet seagull."

"Why would he leave his house to her, and how could she not know it? It doesn't play, Charlie."

"Since there was no loan involved, there would be no bank involved and no title deed or something, according to Ed. But

160

I still can't believe she didn't know, either. Tell me some of the stuff you and Jeremy talked about over morning coffee besides his travels and workout and your job."

"You're jealous."

"Tell me anyway."

"Charlie, have you checked in with your special sense? Now don't get mad but I believe in it more than you do, and if you really are my friend you'll tell me what it's saying."

"You sound like Dalrymple. But this afternoon coming back on the 405, it told me I already had the answer to Jeremy's murder and that I'd gotten it while talking to Dalrymple at the Celebrity Pit. All I got there was Tom Hanks for a waitperson and a marvelous lunch and a totally strange woman who accused me of being Mitch Hilsten's fake girlfriend. Maggie, what if I go to prison and can't hear someone sneaking up behind me?"

Hairy Granger stopped running and turned on Tuxedo Greene not far from where Jeremy Fiedler's blood had straggled downhill toward the drain as Charlie's inner voice or intuition or whatever kicked in again with.

That's it, we've got it all now. The answer to Jeremy's death and this whole thing. It all came together today.

Swell, so what's the answer?

The cats were dark humps with glowing eyes trading threatening moans that grew in graduations of fanatic urgency and decibels.

I don't know, I just sense it—it's so tantalizingly close to the tip of my—

Oh, knock it off.

"Who, me or the cats?" They were sitting on the picnic table with their feet resting on chairs, much like Charlie and Ed Esterhazie had the night before last, and Maggie leaned over

161

to bump Charlie's shoulder with hers. The gesture said, I know you talk to yourself and it embarrasses you but I think it's endearing.

But in real life Maggie said, "I have something to say, and I want you to be patient and hear me out, okay? I know you don't like to talk about it."

"After that wonderful lead-in, how could I refuse? I don't like to talk about what?"

"About your intermittent hearing problem."

"What, you consulted Kate Gonzales, the cleaning-lady doctor? We're supposed to be keeping watch, right?"

It seems that Maggie Stutzman had consulted the *Harvard Women's Health Watch,* a monthly publication she subscribed to. "And it had a section on hearing loss recently. Charlie, your problem doesn't exist."

"That means it'll go away, right? I can live with that."

"No, it means that what you are experiencing is impossible—apparently."

"Like my ulcer that apparently doesn't respond to antibiotics. Can I get a second opinion from the cleaning lady?"

"Hearing doesn't return. Your exceptional hearing going from nothing to normal and back again because of trauma doesn't play."

"And if the Long Beach PD gets a hold of that information, they'll interpret it as just another example of how my veracity cannot be trusted. Maggie, how do you know when Betty Beesom is lying? You said she was so obvious."

Like her common sense, Charlie was beginning to feel tantalizingly close to something, too. But like life itself, there was always a distraction that wiped out the sense of the progression of things or reality.

"Now don't change the subject. As I understand it, we hear because of little hairs way deep in our ears, and the hair cells are often gradually destroyed with aging and hearing diminishes in stages. But traumas like auto accidents and explosions that cause complete hearing loss suddenly mean that the trauma has destroyed those hair cells. The only time you lose hearing completely and it returns is with ear infections. Your type of hearing loss doesn't exist."

"Oh yeah? Well, tell that to Art Granger's brother. He fell off a tractor and hit his head, and heard on and off for a week."

"Then what?"

"Never heard another thing again."

CHAPTER 26

❖

JEREMY FIEDLER'S MEMORIAL service was a real bust. But it wasn't because Larry Mann didn't perform. He even used Mrs. Beesom's Bible, mostly as a stage prop, but since he couldn't wear robes—"Feareth not, for I am the only chance you got, sayeth the Lord. Isaiah—words and numbers."

Wherever possible these days, an ocean beach protected by a breakwater, natural or manmade, or a sea wall to shelter it from the surf, sports a paved walking, running, biking, skating, baby-stroller, dog-walking path. Long Beach was no exception.

The memorial ceremony could not have been more different from the one in Charlie's dream. There was no cliff, no torrey pine, no rock for Mrs. Beesom to sit on (she'd brought a small, webbed aluminum lawn chair), no Jeremy Fiedler looking on approvingly. There were lots of seagulls and enough wind to tatter the fog remnants and send sand runnels across the paved beach path. There were mothers running behind high-tech strollers, a lean gray-haired gentleman loping along with a cel-lular to his ear, the inevitable dog walkers with pooch-poop bags in the hand not holding the leash, and the golden-years couples—holding hands, walking briskly, he looking somewhat shell-shocked, she doing all the talking.

Spandex, sweats, jackets—no swimsuits this afternoon.

The scent of sea sort of welled up—salty, fishy, decaying.

The lingering fog wisps carried the scent, too, but with a cooling freshness.

Larry and Charlie had somehow ended up on one side of the beach walk and Jeremy's few mourners on the other. Everybody else out today passed between them, looking a bit uneasy about the ceremony.

This location had been a mistake, Charlie knew immediately, and wondered if it was the dream that had formed her decision. There were too many people here. Who could tell if any of them knew Jeremy? Officer Mary Maggie had dressed in a long dress, sandals with white socks, and a stretched-out sweater with a matching knit hat. She certainly didn't look like a cop.

Charlie and Maggie Stutzman had spent half of Larry's watch last night making up his eulogy or whatever, which Larry wasn't following at all. Libby and Doug Esterhazie and Lori had taken off from school to attend—any excuse welcome there. Art and Wilma Granger came to stand by Betty's chair. Even good-time Mel had accompanied Charlie's best friend. And just when she thought that was it, Ed Esterhazie sauntered into view, and not long after that so did David Dalrymple and Detective J. S. Amuller. Charlie didn't know if they were all together, but they all had dressed in spandex and jackets and running shoes to blend in.

They stuck out like rollerskaters in a buffalo herd.

"And God shall smite ye down with Jerry Falwell."

A few people stopped and stared. A couple stooped to scoop poop with plastic covered hands while runners and bikers too pooped to notice nearly ran down young mothers and baby strollers and dogs trying to sniff out the scene. There was something of a traffic jam on the beach path where Jeremy Fiedler's memorial service took place.

Car horns from inland, ship's horns from seaward, sounds

of seabirds. The chatter of the retiree wives seemed sort of nervous passing here.

"As ye sew, so shall ye sleep."

And Charlie'd thought her dream surreal. If the woman in the long coat had come, she wasn't wearing her coat. What else could Charlie identify her by? She'd had the sense that though the woman could outrun Charlie, the only people who couldn't were in wheelchairs, and not all of them qualified, she was not young. Somewhere in middle age, maybe. And Charlie decided that sense came from the way the woman moved. She'd seemed slenderish, and her hair was shoulder length—it had swung about when she ran. She was tallish and probably white. Not much to go on.

Larry finally mentioned Jeremy Fiedler and his tragic death. How horrible that it should be by another human's hand. His voice sonorous and rich, his vulnerability and defiance barely masked by slick cynicism—ever the protection of those who don't quite fit in. Even though more of them slowed down and didn't even pretend not to notice, the passersby were giving him a wide berth. People who preach on the beach are gonna be suspect—get used to it.

The three rollerskaters in the buffalo herd garnered quite a few looks, too. Sort of reminded Charlie of Secret Service dudes in disguise. They moved their eyes and not their heads— they missed nothing, except the man who'd crossed the beach and behind them from the street access. Ed Esterhazie, tall and distinguished, Detective J. S. Amuller, even taller and determined, and David Dalrymple, smaller but professional.

"Weep ye not—all ye need fear is fear itself."

Officer Mary Maggie stuck a stick of gum in her mouth and pushed her glasses back up her nose. She was watching Betty Beesom.

Betty did not look good. She had her hand over her heart.

Since Charlie was the only mourner on Larry's side of the walk and people kept walking between her and the others, she worried she'd lose even more control of the sermon on the sand. She was afraid to leave Larry on his own but he ignored her gestures to move across the path to the people who came to hear him. He was playing to a bigger crowd where he was.

Mel watched two Spandex blonds in swinging ponytails and running shoes bounce by. And then Maggie and Libby noticed the burly tanned guy in Levi's and a flannel shirt open over his T-shirt standing behind the three pseudo–Secret Service dudes.

". . . and the Lord shall impeach thee."

Charlie, on her way to Betty, was nearly creamed by a high-tech running stroller for twins with a St. Bernard tied to the handlebars beside a Spandex mom. She emerged safely (with a rude remark from the mom) to find Maggie and Libby looking at her while pointing to the burly guy in the flannel shirt. But when she reached Mrs. Beesom, he was not the problem.

"I saw him. Knew I shouldn't of come." Betty stood up and clutched Charlie. "I forgot he's still here. I get so confused sometimes, Charlie. I'm so sorry."

It was the guy in the flannel shirt who noticed Charlie's distress over Betty's distress first. Art and Wilma, held in shock by Larry's strange beach preaching, weren't far behind. Charlie felt she'd topple over herself trying to support the poor woman.

"And the Lord said, Let there be Might, and behold there was Genghis Kahn and elephants, too. And Hitler and—"

Shit, people on the path were beginning to congregate, hurl questions, congest traffic. A Monty Python Horror Picture Show—story of Charlie's life.

"And the Taliban," somebody from the beach-path audience yelled. "Cover up those women and shame them—ignore their needs and lame them."

"You need help here?" Flannel Shirt asked unnecessarily. Art and Wilma and both Maggies were attempting to fan air in Betty's face, eight hands waving between Charlie and the guy suddenly holding Mrs. Beesom up by the armpits.

"Betty, who did you see?"

"Hairy."

"Hairy Granger? He never strays this far from home."

"Jeremy warned me," the old lady said before her eyes rolled up under swollen lids and Flannel Shirt picked her up in both arms.

"Didn't seem like a very proper service," Ed Esterhazie complained as they strolled to Manic Mechanics, in no hurry because they wanted to get there after J. S. Amuller and David Dalrymple left. "Was your assistant on something?"

"No, he's just an actor who can't help but entertain people."

"I thought they were going to stone him there for a minute. Is he . . . ?"

"Yes. And it's a good thing there weren't any stones available."

Betty Beesom had revived before Maggie Stutzman and Officer Mary Maggie loaded her in a squad car to rush her to Urgent Care. Her heartbeat had settled down and she refused to explain to Charlie what she'd been apologizing so profusely for except that it wasn't for talking about Charlie with that "nice Detective Amuller."

"That poor old lady's lying about something, Ed, and it's got her tied in knots. At her age she doesn't need that, but what do you do?"

"You don't think she could have had anything to do with Fiedler's murder?"

"Jeremy's death is hard on all of us, but her most of all. She had the most to lose by his death."

"Except his house. It's hers now."

"But she didn't know that—she says."

"That poor old lady is rolling in Sara Lee, Johnson & Johnson, and Exxon."

"Are they good?"

"They pay dividends. Get enough of it and live at her standard of living and you don't even have to worry about cashing in shares to live on—since she doesn't have anyone to leave it to, anyway. She's got no worries."

Charlie stopped and considered him. They were on a street corner she didn't think she'd ever driven through. Now, the 405 and the 10 she knew by heart. The street signs had been destroyed but she was pretty sure they were somewhere in the vicinity of Wilson, Libby's school. He wanted to walk and she wanted to talk to him. "How do you know this, Ed?"

"I checked her out on the Internet. Or rather, Doug did. It's scary how far he's into this computer stuff. How comfortable he is with it, when it drives me to madness."

Charlie's extraspecial, nonexistent other sense was perking up again. No, it was common sense—she just wished it would tell her what was going on.

"Doug can just break into people's investment records? Mrs. Beesom doesn't invest by computer. She doesn't even own one. I mean, she doesn't use the library anymore because the card catalog is now a computer."

"But her broker does her transactions online. Her records are out there. Credit-card companies, and those wanting to target her for sales and I'm sure scams and—we're all of us Internet-accessible, Charlie." Ed was into yachting and had a deep tan and lots of dark hair that contrasted with the bandage on his forehead to give him a dashing appearance. "You, for instance, are heavy into Automatic Data and Stryker and Oracle. Doug looked you up, too. We're all an open book."

"Except for Jeremy. If he hadn't died, cyberspace wouldn't know he'd ever existed."

When they reached Manic Mechanics—a plain, one-story stucco with two car bays and a big window to write the name of the shop and the hours on—Joe Manic was leaning against the storefront window, smoking a cigarette. He was the burly man in the plaid shirt. More importantly, he had introduced himself as Jeremy Fiedler's mechanic.

CHAPTER 27

◆

I NSIDE, MANIC MECHANICS looked a lot like old-fashioned filling stations did before they were conglomed into convenience stores with gas pumps. Joe replaced the cigarette he'd stubbed out on the sidewalk with a toothpick. He had a bowl of wrapped, flavored toothpicks and offered it to his visitors like you would candy.

"I didn't catch much of it, but that was some sermon your preacher was dishing out down at the bay. What religion is that?"

"He's an actor," Ed explained. "When he's not a secretary."

"Actor, right. Should have known." Joe shrugged a this-is-Southern-California shrug and rolled the toothpick over to the other side of his mouth. "You another cop?" He gestured toward Ed's tailored sweatsuit and spanking-new running shoes—like Amuller's and David Dalrymple's, none of which looked like they'd ever seen dirt, let alone sweat.

"I was a friend and neighbor of Jeremy Fiedler's, and I just wondered what you knew about him. Ed's a friend of mine."

"Ed Esterhazie." The two men shook hands, ignoring her.

"Concrete—Esterhazie Concrete?"

"That's right. Do you work on Porsches?"

Charlie looked around while they talked guy stuff. A TV up in one corner of the shop played Rudy Ferris's talk show with-

171

out sound. If you had to watch Rudy, that was the way to do it. It must be a repeat—he was usually on later in the afternoon. He was standing in the audience aisle berating some poor guy on the stage. Rudy would have looked better in black and white. His thin hair was a sickly orange, his suit a bright blue, his shirt yellow, his bow tie a bright red, and his mustache brown. Why didn't he dye his mustache to match his dyed hair, or get a rug to match his mustache? A kid in overalls rolled out from under a fancy SUV, flashed gleaming teeth from a grimied face, and headed for the soda machine.

"Well, all I can tell you is what I told the cops. I came to the funny memorial service because I recognized the picture of the dead man in the paper. Worked on his Trailblazer and the Ferrari, too."

"Did you get to know him well?" Charlie asked.

"Not at all. He didn't spend any time chatting. But I was real curious about him. Figured he was trouble, so I didn't ask questions."

"That why you didn't get ahold of the police right away when you saw the picture?"

"Yeah, and the name was wrong. And the license plates changed a lot, and he always paid in cash." He raised his eyebrows and grimaced so hard he broke the toothpick. "But I guess now that he's dead I don't have to worry about somebody coming after me if I talk about his business. What was his business?"

"He was a landscape architect, or so he said. What did you mean, his name was wrong? He wasn't Jeremy Fiedler to you?"

"Jonathan Phillips was the name he gave me. I'd show you his signature, but the cops took the few records I have on him. That's what was on his car registration, but if you can gin up false plates you can probably do it with the registration, too."

"Hey Joe," the kid with the soda can and grease-stained

overalls said, "don't forget the limp." And then he turned to Charlie. "You're Libby's mom, right? Somebody pointed you out at a football game last fall at Wilson. You were cheering the cheerleaders. You got the same eyes as her. I'm Pepe."

Pepe, too, had noticed sometimes this Jonathan limped and sometimes he didn't.

"He was a jogger, had injuries," Joe Manic said. "I can't understand people jogging but I sure can see how it would give them injuries. It's the two names and paying in cash for fixing a Ferrari, for chrissake, and different license plates with different numbers—now that's what's suspicious."

Ed Esterhazie and Charlie were at the Esterhazie mansion being spoiled by Mrs. McDougal and waiting for Doug to get home from school. Libby had diner duty after school today and Charlie was pretty sure Lori Schantz had some kind of singing club practice. When the housekeeper learned Charlie and Ed had had no lunch, she put her hand to her chest and expressed an "oh my" without speaking. A bottle of red wine, a carafe of strong coffee, and a plate of orange segments and another of pâté with crackers appeared on the small patio table on the west lawn as they sat on lounges in the sun protected from the breeze by gorgeous plantings everywhere, and of course here the flowers in boxes and on bushes and in ground beds were splendiferous.

And if you'd come from Boulder or, even worse, New York, all this floral splendor in March seemed decadent somehow. Charlie was in Dockers and a jacket today but she took a sip of wine, turned her face to the sun, dipped a cracker in the pâté, and sighed, lifting her glass to Ed Esterhazie Concrete. "Here's to decadence."

"I'll drink to that. When do we start?"

"Start? Have you smelled that coffee?" Charlie poured herself a mug but inhaled the fumes before taking a sip. "How do you keep your figure?"

"Liposuction," he answered. "Better go slow. Mrs. McDougal is not used to having anyone home for lunch on a weekday, and I saw that gleam in her eye when she saw you."

"She didn't like Dorothy." The coffee had a nutty flavor as deep as Ed's voice. The wine had a fruity flavor. The pâté was not, Charlie thought, goose-based. There was cucumber in it somewhere.

"Dorothy was controlling."

"And I'm not?"

"You're not interested in controlling household matters."

"I wouldn't be home for lunch on weekdays. Would have no time to interfere with anything."

"You'd be too busy to care about what she cares about most. Charlie, I have a confession to make—"

"Oh, please don't. This is the first time in my vacation that I almost feel like I'm on vacation."

"Okay. What did you have for breakfast today?"

"Half an onion bagel and one cup of coffee. Why?"

"Mrs. McDougal knows your weakness for eggs. I'm dating again, and you're the solution again. What do you say to that, Ms. Hollywood Agent?"

"Congratulations, and can I get a doggy box?"

❖

Douglas Esterhazie was allowed to finish off the orange slices, pâté, and crackers plus an enormous sandwich and two glasses of milk before Charlie and his father led him to the study. Charlie's huge doggy box of creamed hard-boiled eggs with firm asparagus and pearl onions in a paper-thin pastry crust was tightly secured in the fridge for her to take home.

Charlie stood behind Doug with another cup of that wonderful coffee not understanding a thing she saw on the fast-changing computer screens as Doug smoothly moved from mouse to keyboard, often playing each with one hand at the same time.

Edward Esterhazie's study was a rectangular room that probably wouldn't fit in the first floor of Charlie's house even if you removed all the walls and added the patio. Two walls had French doors and mullioned windows interspersed with floor-to-ceiling bookcases and lighted art niches. The desk was in the center of the room where you could sit and look out at the lovely plantings and swimming pool, but there were no blinds and no bars—anybody could see you sitting in here, too. You couldn't pay Charlie to live in the open like this, and you couldn't pay Kate Gonzales to clean it.

"Do you have to hack into every brokerage firm to find somebody? How'd you find Betty Beesom?"

"There's a general listing of all investors and their preferences and amounts invested," Doug said. The screen kept flashing "access denied," "improper coding," and "subscribe now."

"Do you have to have a password or something?"

"They keep changing everything to keep people out who haven't paid up—brokerages and direct marketers and stuff. You just have to diddle around for a while and you can get through."

"Doug, who taught you to do this?"

"I learned some from my friends and most on my own, just—"

"Diddling around."

"Yeah, and computer games teach you more than you think—how systems work, stuff happens—you know. And if you know where to find them, there's places on the Web that can walk you through a lot of this. They come and go pretty quick, but the word gets out. Okay, here we go."

There was no Jeremy Fiedler.

"Try Harry Fiedler."

"Who's that?" Ed asked from one of the leather sofas where he'd been pretending not to be snoozing.

"I don't know, but Mrs. Beesom keeps talking about a Harry and I keep thinking she means Hairy Granger, the cat. But she knows something she's not sharing, with me anyway."

"No Harry Fiedler."

"Try Jonathan Phillips." While Doug diddled around, Charlie lapsed into a fantasy of standing in a reception line after a garden wedding outside those windows and—

"Four of them—none in this area."

"Try Harry Phillips." And Charlie stood next to Libby, who wore a gorgeous wedding dress and no zits, and next to her was a handsome, rich Doug who'd grown into his bones and—

"Two in L.A., three in Sacramento, none in Orange County, one in Long Beach but not Belmont Shore."

And this well-dressed woman took Libby's white-gloved hand and said, "And where is your father, dear?" And—

"There was a Fiedler Enterprises back there. Companies invest."

"That's it." Charlie said. "That's where Kate the cleaning lady got her checks from. And try Beach Enterprises, too."

And Libby said, "Oh, I'm a bastard—and here's my mom."

Ed and Charlie were both breathing down Doug's neck now.

"Out of business or bankruptcy or NA as of last Friday, both of them. I don't know what all these letters mean."

"And Jeremy died that night."

CHAPTER 28

CHARLIE AND ED Esterhazie were walking again, this time to Judy & Gym's Age Buster Health Club where no one had ever heard of or seen Jeremy Fiedler. Ed should never have bought those running shoes—they were like foot Viagra. Doug would pick up Ed at Charlie's house by six and deliver Charlie's precious doggy box. Ed promised to take his son to the diner for meatloaf if he promised not to touch the boiled egg and asparagus concoction.

"Do you really keep your trim figure by liposuction? I mean I can see laser surgery to get rid of eyeglasses—well, almost— but suck out fat?"

"Actually, I did it once on the gut and it wasn't that big a deal. Does that disgust you, Charlie? It did Mrs. McDougal."

"Did I tell you my mom's got a boyfriend?" Charlie wished she hadn't gotten into this conversation.

"Edwina? Good for her. She's been alone too many years. Have you met him?"

"No, she just called and told me, no details yet. And she's not alone. She has a job—I mean a profession."

"Poor Charlie, you still don't get it, do you?"

"Get what?"

"When Libby leaves home—what if you lose your job? What if no one wants to hire you in your profession? All you'll have left is Mitch Hilsten, whom you claim not to want, and if that's true he'll have wandered off by then. What will you do with yourself?"

"Ed, I should worry? I'll be in prison for murdering Jeremy and won't be able to hear anybody coming up behind me."

At Judy & Gym's Age Buster Club the wind met them at the door. You'd have to step outside to get away from it. Some of it had to be the music and the clapping. If one butterfly spreading its wings can cause a tornado somewhere around the globe, this place must be destroying whole planets in space. People rode bikes that went nowhere so fast their temple vessels bulged. Others kicked and boxed at air and jumped like maniacs bent on destroying evil and the rest of life as we know it. And all in sync with the music. Three incredibly pregnant women, butts elevated, bicycled their legs and breathed in and out with so much sweat you expected an infant to explode through the seams of the Spandex crotches.

Charlie, who was tone deaf and detested most music, started to cry when it disappeared.

Edward Esterhazie put an arm around her and she could feel him talking by his chest vibrations to the man who'd come up to them. Probably Gym. Charlie would not know what they discussed until Ed wrote it down for her at home. The walk there was silent and humbling.

Charlie knew how uncomfortable Ed must be, suddenly unable to communicate with someone he'd been talking to half the day. She would have felt the same had the situations been reversed. And she'd gone just as suddenly from a normal, functional, reasonably good-looking, vital, important, necessary, respected member of society (if you didn't listen to Detective J. S.) to a dependent, struck dumb and helpless, ugly lost soul of no use to anyone, a burden on friends and society. Someone she, as a busy important professional, would have pitied but shunned, because her patience and sympathy cup had long been drained.

Charlie's common uncommon sense was down in the dumps, too. It suggested she could survive by sneaking around LAX with a little written card that, because she was a deaf-mute and had no income, begged a dollar or five from travelers who looked like they came from the Midwest or the South or Texas.

❖

Larry had picked up a whopping salad of greens, mixed sweet peppers, and fresh mushrooms at Salads R Us. And they toasted leftover garlic bread from last night to put the creamed egg and asparagus concoction on. It was a wonderful dinner even for a hearing-impaired, devastated ex-person.

Charlie's secretary reached across the table in the breakfast nook and stroked the back of her hand as she reached for her glass of milk. They both had tears in their eyes, which made him look wavy.

Larry mouthed, How about some tea for dessert?

She'd nodded before she realized she'd read his lips through tear-film. They'd communicated without even any crickets in her ears. Charlie finished her milk, cleaned the last of the creamed egg off her fork, and used her napkin to blow her nose. Still the tears kept coming. She hated being weak enough to cry.

Suddenly she was nose-to-nose with Libby's damned cat, who'd managed to do his top-of-the-refrigerator-to-the-top-of-the-table-fly-through-the-air-and-land act without overturning any plates or glasses. She couldn't hear him purr but she knew he did—he had all the power now. He sniffed her face, her tears, her mouth, and slid himself between her middle and the tabletop, and then under the table to curl up, warm and vibrating, on her lap.

Charlie sat stone still. The creature had found her vulnerable and was planning a diabolical attack—which everyone would blame her for, because she reacted inappropriately or was insensitive to the higher intelligence of animals or some such nonsense.

Larry stuck the cups with the tea bags into the microwave and came over to check out Charlie's lap. Tuxedo was kneading it through her Dockers. *He prefers you helpless.*

He's planning to bite me.

Try petting him.

He'll bite me.

Try anyway.

It was strange how slowly you talk when you think someone has to read your lips and how slowly you answer when you can't hear your own voice, but they were communicating. Albeit at a subhuman level. Charlie couldn't hear herself speak, but she could feel the vibrations of it in her throat somewhere.

Go on, Tickle him under the chin, too.

Charlie dared a hand on the cat's head and then ran it down his back. She was surprised that he enjoyed it so much he rolled over on his back and raised his chin. She scratched under his chin and was sort of beginning to feel better until she petted the proffered tummy. He curled up in an instant and grabbed her wrist with his front claws, bit her hand savagely, and raked her forearm with his back claws. Then he was off on a scramble around the kitchen and into the living room on one of his demented Grand Prix binges—usually reserved for after a colossal dump in the litter box.

And the most beautiful man in the world sat on Charlie's kitchen floor laughing so hard she thought his head would fall off.

So what's so goddamned funny? she vibrated.

Charlie, that means he accepts you. He doesn't hate you.

He doesn't love you. That's asking too much of a cat. That's how he would accept another cat.

Charlie sucked blood from an injured hand and counted to twenty.

Ed Esterhazie had written to Charlie, before he left to take Doug to the diner, that he had a physician friend at the Yacht Club and was going to ask him who the best specialist was to consult on Charlie's problem. Almost as an afterthought he'd added that Judy and Gym Malakevich still had never heard of Jeremy Fiedler, that he'd never worked out at their health club.

She'd written back that they'd forgotten to ask Joe Manic the mechanic if he'd ever seen the woman in the long coat.

She and Larry were sipping tea, Libby's cat once again lording it from his refrigerator throne, when Larry stood suddenly and Tuxedo looked down at the door. Larry opened it to Detective Amuller and Officer Mason. Oh, swell.

Once was, anybody came to the back door it was one of her condo neighbors. Now that the gate was dead anybody could get personal. Charlie hated it.

The three of them stood in the middle of Charlie's kitchen, talking, gesturing, the cops occasionally turning toward Charlie but in the middle of a word or something, talking too fast, not facing her. Amuller directed a few pointed remarks at her—he didn't believe she'd lost her hearing. Charlie *really* hated this.

Then Larry looked up, seemed confused for a moment, and left the room. When he returned he had the cordless and was talking to it but gesturing toward Charlie. Both members of the Long Beach Police Department and the cat on the refrigerator glared down at Charlie through squints of suspicion, Detective J. S. with a satisfied smirk as well. What the hell was going on?

Larry knelt to mouth words at her with exaggerated lip, teeth, and tongue movements. *It's your mother. She wants to tell you about her new boyfriend. She thinks you're avoiding her.*

Doesn't believe you can't hear. They (and he tilted his head back at the cops) *don't either.*

Amuller was rolling his eyes by now, Mary Maggie shaking her head sadly as if to say she couldn't believe Charlie could be so stupid. Tuxedo yawned.

Charlie sat in an interrogation room being interrogated by people she couldn't hear. Big guys gesturing and leaning threateningly, giving her tough looks. Pounding on the table. A weary Mary Maggie Mason sat at a table in the corner.

Charlie lay in a fringed hammock hung between two coconut palms, a paperback mystery by Marlys Millhiser in one hand and a rum drink with a skewered piece of pineapple and a paper umbrella in the other. The day was hot but the soft caressing breeze off the ocean and the fact that she was nearly naked made the temperature just right. No shoes, no hose, nothing more confining than a coating of beach sand on her feet and a bikini barely covering what she refused to shave and her-hardly-there-anyway breasts.

She considered a gorgeous young native man to rock the hammock and offer to fetch some grilled morsels of shellfish on toothpicks and maybe a massage later—but J. S. Amuller was suddenly in her face and she thought better of it. He was shouting, she knew, because he'd recently eaten some raw onion and she had to wipe away traces of spittle. But she could tell he was pretending to mouth words like Larry but didn't have the knack even when pretending. It was possible he thought he was talking about "your mother's boyfriend."

Now Charlie really, really hated this. She even considered going ahead with the massage on the beach.

Edwina had begun to date a man twenty years her junior, which wasn't all that young. He'd come to her house to repair the kitchen and bathroom tile and stayed to visit a while. Jesus.

The tough-guy flailing of arms and pointing of fingers and condescending sneers and gestures that came just short of striking her finally came to an end.

Just as Officer Mary Maggie Mason led Charlie out of the room, Charlie flinched when somebody said behind her, ". . . lawyer."

And good old J. S. Amuller answered, "Don't worry. A little jail time and she'll break. We'll have a confession by breakfast."

CHAPTER 29

CHARLIE STOOD BENT with her hands out against the coldest concrete wall in creation while Mary Maggie did a cursory search. "You might as well give it up, Charlie. We checked with a specialist, Dr. Rasmasen. Hearing loss from an explosion doesn't come and go. Hearing loss from an explosion is gone. Period."

Of course, now Charlie couldn't admit she could hear. The cop sighed when there was no answer. "Suit yourself. But he's willing to testify in court."

Moments later, Charlie sat on a hard cot, her back against another cold concrete wall. Two other detained females watched her as suspiciously as she watched them. One finally approached her with a confident hello-sister-let-me-tell-you-what-it's-like-in-the-real-world look. Charlie gave her a Hollywood-agent look and the woman backed off.

If her hearing went out again, she'd be vulnerable again and at the woman's mercy. She would have to hide her terror—wasn't sure she could. Larry had vowed to get her a lawyer. He was going to ask Maggie Stutzman and Ed Esterhazie for help.

Charlie could not continue in her work as a Hollywood literary agent and have this handicap happening to her and the sudden vulnerability it caused—it would be like swimming with

184

sharks when you're menstruating. If they didn't put her away forever for a murder she didn't commit, what else could she do for a living? She'd had her fill of the dole while getting an education and raising a kid. Once off the Edwina dole, she sure didn't want to get on the public dole, lose power over her own life and happiness.

Charlie was determined to stay awake all night and not use the commode in full view in the corner. Her cell mates looked just as determined, sort of a three-way distrust mode. They'd seemed ready to gang up on Charlie until her dead silence and literary-agent tough had quelled that idea. One was black, the other white—a few down-and-dirty curse words that registered no effect on her left them silent, too. After raising Libby Abigail Greene, any shock value in their obscene renditions were more familiar than threatening. She knew these women could be suspected of murder, too—might even be guilty. One or both could also be shills.

Actually, Charlie wasn't as afraid of them as she knew she should be. She was angry enough to want to hurt them if she could, to take her anger out on anybody. How dare Amuller assume her guilt in the murder of Jeremy Fiedler because she was the most likely or available candidate for the hangman? His problem was really that he knew nothing about the victim, only the circumstances of his death—much of which Charlie didn't know so she couldn't fight back until forced into court as the one charged with the deed.

She would have loved to return to the soft, balmy air of the beach and shell out for a massage, but knew she'd better concentrate on staying awake against her cell mates and plan a strategy for her defense. She'd simply overlook her more immediate problems—PMS, her contact lenses, and her ulcer.

When a strange woman cop awakened Charlie, her mouth was dry and her eyes even more so. She could taste blood, and there was some on the pillow she'd vowed not to touch with her head. Her stomach screamed for something soothing that antibiotics couldn't deliver. She could hear, though—crickets in her ears and the disgusted and weary breaths of the uniformed woman leading her down the hall.

And the stench of a human zoo. Charlie vowed to fight Amuller to the death to not spend her life in it, hearing-impaired or no. She thought she was being led back to the interrogation room to be given another chance to confess, but instead was presented with her watch (it was four A.M.) and what had been in her pockets—two Kleenex, a key to the back door, and a twenty. Amuller had given her no time to grab her purse and then was totally perturbed when she couldn't remember her Social Security number or produce her driver's license. She could see that even when deaf as a doorknob.

Without sound, the dire threats about her never driving again or whatever seemed like the dentist demanding she brush and floss morning, noon, and night and after snacks. In other words, totally out of the reality frame.

A small television over in one corner was playing a Rudy Ferris show. What was going on here?

But the real news was Charlie had a lawyer—Ernesto Seligman. A sleepy, grumpy, totally bald man in a knit sport shirt and sweater over rumpled chinos and tennis shoes. He was a well-known Long Beach attorney who had a reputation for tackling the tough cases. Great—although innocent, Charlie was now a tough case. Old Detective J. S. would make hay with that. She waited until they were in the lawyer's car to speak. "I have to get home right away, then I'll talk to you."

"Charlie, why?" Maggie Stutzman said from the backseat.

Larry had gone on in Ed Esterhazie's Porsche. "You're in real trouble here."

"Because I wouldn't use the stool sitting out in the open in that cell, and I'm in really real trouble. Here." Ernesto Seligman and his brand-new Lincoln Town Car had Charlie home in record time.

"I made no statements, confessions, nor did I answer any questions," Charlie told her new tough-case attorney. She, Ed, Larry, and Maggie gathered in the kitchen because Libby and Doug and Tuxedo were sacked out in the living room—Libby on the couch, Doug on the floor with his feet on the ottoman, and the cat on his chest. "Simply because I couldn't hear what they were asking until just as I was leaving the interrogation room. And then Detective Amuller was saying that with a little jail time, I'd confess before morning."

It was curious that both kids snored. Tuxedo wandered in, stretched, had some breath-enhancing food, and slipped out the cat door to kill birds, bugs, other cats, whatever. How could he sneak up on his prey with breath like a vulture?

"Well, he obviously didn't know you have friends." Seligman had the rasp of a sick crocodile. Medication? She didn't remember the total baldness from his pictures, either. Chemotherapy?

"Oh, he knows—that's the black mark on my character. He thinks I'm sleeping with Ed here, Larry, and Mitch Hilsten all at the same time."

"And are you?"

"Of course not," Charlie told her attorney. Jeesh.

"Mitch is in Spain," Maggie told Charlie's attorney.

"I haven't had the pleasure," Ed added. He didn't shrug, but you could almost hear one in his voice.

Larry clinched it. "I'm gay."

Attorney Seligman got on his cell phone while everyone but Charlie ate the McDonald's takeout breakfast, the civilian MREs that Ed and Larry had run out for. Charlie had a poached egg on milk toast with a glass of milk.

She'd taken out her contacts, put drops in her eyes, brushed her teeth, but she couldn't wait to hit that shower. The kids were chowing down on McMuffins and potato whatevers with Cokes, taking turns in the shower and getting ready for school. Charlie didn't know Libby ate breakfast, but then Charlie's commute took her out of town ever earlier. And now she could hear Rudy Ferris on the TV in the living room.

"What's happening? Is some network doing old Rudy Ferris shows back-to-back or something?"

"Haven't you heard? Your agency handles him," Maggie said on her way out to get ready for work herself. "He's doing a two-day marathon for ED."

"Next month he's doing one for breast cancer," Larry said, following her. "I'll be back tonight. You behave yourself."

"During the week? That's when people want to watch their soaps and the tabloid talk shows, like his. What's ED?"

"Erectile dysfunction," her lawyer told her solemnly. "Where you been, on Jupiter?"

"Oh, the Bob Dole thing—we have Jerry's Kids and now it'll be Rudy's Geezers."

"Yeah, I'm thinking of going back to Edward," Ed Ester-hazie said. "I'll leave you to talk to Ernie here. You can trust him, Charlie, tell him everything. I'll be at the office if either of you need me." And Edward was gone, too.

The kids passed through the kitchen all clean and sham-pooed and fresh. Charlie felt like the queen of grit. "It'll be okay, Mom, now you got a lawyer—the LBPD will have to stop harassing you."

Charlie was so relieved to be home. Still, she resented everybody going off to work or school but her and her attorney. It's godawfulnotfun to be unimportant. "Ernie?"

"If Ed can be Edward I can be Ernesto." He took a yellow legal pad out of his briefcase and looked as tired as she felt. "I want you to tell me everything from the minute you got home last Friday night until you walked out of that jail at four o'clock this morning. Feel free to stop at any time and go back and fill in. The important thing is that you not leave out a thing."

Charlie realized that this was Friday, too. The nightmare had begun only a week ago—it seemed like a month. But she began, "I will never take another vacation as long as I live, so help me God."

When she was through, they went out to look at Jeremy's fire-gutted house and the bombed gate.

"Blood on a pillow. You sure nobody hit you at any time during that questioning?"

"I told you I have an ulcer—and no, antibiotics won't help it. Amuller may know nothing about Jeremy Fiedler, but he can accuse me. I know nothing about Jeremy's death. How can I defend myself with no information on how he died?"

"He was murdered."

"I know that. But how? Why won't they tell me anything?"

"They assume you know. They assume you did it." Charlie's attorney looked at Charlie like she was handicapped, pitiable.

He opened his car door and leaned against the Lincoln with his fist on the roof, chewed on a knuckle. "I'm going to want to talk to this Betty Beesom, but not until I've had some sleep. The Dr. Rasmusen Officer Mason referred to is Pete Rasmusen, friend of mine. Ed Esterhazie described your hearing problem to him and he gave Ed the same answer he gave homicide. The symptoms as described are not consistent with trauma due to an explosive sound. The trauma causing your apparent hearing loss might be more psychological than physical. Told Ed to

189

have you see a psychotherapist instead of him. Ed wanted me to tell you this because he thought you'd pop your cork and he didn't want to be around."

"In other words it's all in my head. Gee, where have I heard that before?"

"Yeah, I know. You women are always so misunderstood. Look, I took you on as a client because Ed is a special friend."

"So who needs a lawyer who thinks she's guilty?"

"And because I trust his judgment. Ed told me about witnessing your latest loss of hearing. Ed said you winced like you'd been slapped. And then the terror came into your eyes. And then the tears. 'Charlie doesn't cry,' Ed said. 'She's tougher than concrete. She wasn't faking it, Ernie.' Now that's not going to hold up against Rasmusen in court. But it got you the best defense attorney in all of South Cal."

He slid into the Town Car and smiled for the first time. It was the kind of smile that made you feel better. "Get some sleep, and don't attempt any Nancy Drew stuff. You'll really piss off police and prosecutors. And there're a few leaks about the case in today's *P-T* that might clear up some things for you."

"You read the paper already? It just got here—you've been here since before dawn."

"Nah, I heard about the leaks first." And Charlie's attorney backed out of the compound's blown-up gate.

CHAPTER 30

◆

CHARLIE THREW THE *P-T* on the dining room table because the table suddenly looked naked instead of clean.

She stripped off her clothes and took a long, hot shower, soaping and scrubbing from the tips of her hair to the tips of her toes twice and then again. She threw a perfectly good slacks outfit, from the underwear out, into the trash because it had been in jail.

She dared her ulcer with a mug of coffee and snuggled with it and the morning paper into the corner of the couch.

Sources, who asked not to be named, said that Jeremy Fiedler had died of a gunshot wound to the chest. The weapon had been in the car with him and though there was an attempt to make it look like a suicide there was a suspect in the case. Funny, Charlie didn't remember any smell of gun smoke when she opened the car door and Jeremy all but fell out and Hairy Granger flew into her arms. Police were confident that an arrest would be made soon but were still asking anyone who might know the man pictured above, a photo of the corpse this time and not an artist's drawing, to contact them at the number given below.

Oh, great. Charlie was just supposed to relax and rest up and let her attorney and J. S. Amuller take care of everything. Right. Hairy hadn't smelled like gun smoke, either. Now there was no mistaking Jeremy Fiedler's dead face and naked shoulders. Charlie grieved for him and for the security he had created in their fortress so wantonly destroyed with him. She didn't believe that little "leak." It was misinformation meant to frighten her. She didn't believe the homicide folks had much to go on but intuition. And she felt even angrier than last night on the hard cot facing down hard women.

So instead of getting some rest, Charlie got dressed—in an outfit that could go places instead of sweats—and took the Toyota to Manic Mechanics.

Joe had a toothpick hanging out one side of his mouth and an unlit cigarette out the other. He grinned when he saw Charlie and lost them both. "You can't afford me to fix this heap." He slapped the Toyota's hood. "Not that these babies ever wear out. Never forgive the Japanese for that."

"Actually, I came to ask you more about Jonathan Phillips. Do you know where he kept the Ferrari?"

"Never asked, he never said. But it was inside someplace. Figured he had a garage for it at home. Left the Trailblazer out. Could tell by the finishes on both. Or he kept it outside under a cloth cover. But that's asking to have it stolen. Pepe, you ever hear Phillips mention where he kept the Ferrari?"

"He never said anything to me," the kid with the grimy face and gleaming smile said, "but the lady who came to pick him up when he left it here told me he took better care of it than he did her. She was kidding, you know."

Charlie took a deep breath and leaned against her faithful Toyota. Ears, don't fail me now. "Did this lady have long hair?"

"Just to her shoulders, maybe. Brown hair with gray at the roots."

"How often did she come here?"

"I saw her maybe three, four times."

"Oh yeah, I forgot about her," Joe Manic said. "Must be

getting old. Never got a name, sort of thought she was Mrs. Jonathan Phillips."

"She wore skirts, not pants or shorts. Skirts with sneakers and socks, no sandals. I think I seen her at Von's once, too." Pepe stared at the empty TV screen, searching his memory. "I do remember something about Mr. Phillips, though. I forgot yesterday. His hair changed color. I think he had more than one rug, and they didn't match."

There it was again, Jeremy's hair. And her inner voice sort of alerted her again, like this was all part of what she already knew. But she didn't.

Charlie drove along the route she'd chased the woman in the long coat, trying to find the place she'd lost her. Now that she thought about it, the woman had not been wearing slacks that night under the coat. Pepe's skirts?

She parked the Toyota about where she thought the woman had disappeared on her and got out to walk. And to think.

This was still Belmont Shore. A series of modest homes added on to or pop-topped. No graffiti. Garages opening off alleys. The sound of a nearby bus on Xemino was muted somehow by big old trees and lush flower beds and the insulation of homes evenly spaced on small lots. No gates, a few grates at front doors and windows. One or two warnings of savage dogs on the premises. Charlie had never roamed her own neighborhood let alone those a few blocks out. There was a great deal of charm and good living going on here—in a world she'd assumed hostile and crime-ridden.

The old growth of nature and neighborhood and outwardly modest comfort on closer inspection revealed expensive cars, window coverings, landscaping, and concrete driveways. No faded or peeling paint, no broken roof tiles. One house's spiky plantings still held pieces of toilet paper that were too high to reach. Charlie's yard had been T-Peed three times, and Maggie's once—which everyone considered a mistake, teens thinking it was Libby's house. Anyway, this particular house also had spray-painted remarks on the sidewalk that had been painted over but not totally obliterated.

Charlie walked up and down the alleys looking in garage windows. In the third alley she found a red Ferrari. She walked around to the front door but no one answered, so she prowled around back to peek into the windows of a walk-out basement. One room held a huge array of exercise equipment, even one of those bicycles that tilted forward like those at Judy & Gym's.

At Judy & Gym's, she asked Judy Malakevich if a Jonathan Phillips was a member of the health club. He was not.

"We don't give out names of members, but I can tell you he isn't. I saw you here before. I know you're a neighbor of that poor guy who got shot in his car."

"I'm also looking for a woman, possibly middle-aged, shoulder-length brown hair with gray at the roots, who drives a red Ferrari and always wears skirts with anklets and sneakers instead of sandals—you don't have to give me a name, but can you at least tell me if you've seen someone like that?"

"Doesn't sound like anybody who'd come here—the Ferrari, maybe, but not the dress code. Is that the suspect the paper was talking about this morning?" Judy Malakevich leaned her hard, sleek, sweaty body closer in to Charlie. "We got a cop who works out here and he hinted the suspect was a woman."

Actually, I'm the woman they suspect. "Well, yes, she is. She often wears a long coat, too. We neighbors have noticed her hanging around a lot. You know?"

Charlie handed her a business card that nowhere mentioned the word agent and Judy promised to ask around about this mysterious woman in anklets.

Next, Charlie drove to Von's. She might be a prime suspect

in a murder investigation, but she was still the one who had to put food on the table. She bought a mixed salad in a bag and asparagus and artichokes, chicken and fish for the grill and in quantity, because she had no idea who-all would be eating at her house and because she kept imagining the horror of prison-food-eaten-in-the-human-zoo smell. She bought deli potato salad and macaroni salad and cole slaw and cooked barbecued ribs, french bread and cat food, toilet paper and Kleenex and dishwasher detergent.

Would Libby have to go live with Edwina and her boyfriend in Boulder if Charlie went to prison? She threw some Snickers bars into the cart for the poor kid.

We're not feeling sorry for ourselves one little bit?

Oh, yes, we are. I'm stopping at the Wine Merchant on the way home, too. So there.

Charlie had just finished piling everything in the Toyota and turned to stash the grocery cart in the provided stall when it started raining. Great, Jeremy's bombed-out house would smell like a wet fireplace again.

Look, droopy dumps—at least you know where the red Ferrari is.

I know where a red Ferrari is.

She'd half-hoped to see the woman with the swinging hair and anklets at Von's like Pepe had. But she saw her about a block away at the Wine Merchant instead. The woman was wearing a sweater today instead of a long coat and was just stepping out of a red Ferrari as Charlie stepped out of the wine store. She knew Charlie by sight because she slipped back into the car at first glance and tore off. By the time Charlie got back to her Toyota and headed after her, the Ferrari was lost somewhere in traffic and Charlie was left with little but the impression of a rather fragile and unhappy face.

Charlie drove slowly past the Ferrari's house again. Unlike

most of the houses in the neighborhood, it was not stucco or painted concrete block. It looked to be stained redwood with a wide deck on one side. Charlie pulled up to the curb and parked. The Ferrari wasn't home, but she punched the doorbell and then knocked. She peered in a window off the deck and saw a shadow duck behind a kitchen counter—the shadow of a man, not a woman with shoulder-length hair.

Back at the compound, which no longer was one, Betty Beesom wandered over to hold the back door open for Charlie as she carried in groceries. "That's an awful lot of food for two people."

"Two people live here, but it seems like there's usually more that eat here. And I never know. Larry's coming back tonight, will probably stay the weekend, and you know what happens if Doug Esterhazie drops by for a snack."

"Wish I could move that fast," the old lady said as Charlie whirled the food from bags to cupboard and refrigerator.

Charlie stopped to study her neighbor. "Mrs. Beesom, you don't look good."

"Well, I made up this wonderful chicken salad for sandwiches and was going to have Wilma and Art over for dinner— I mean lunch, and they weren't home and I was wondering if you'd had dinner—uh, lunch—yet. Made an awful lot for one old lady."

Charlie put the milk, butter, eggs, and fruit in the refrigerator. "Chicken salad sandwiches. On pasty white bread?"

"Well, it's white. I don't know if it's pasty."

Charlie checked to be sure the fresh asparagus and deli salads were in the fridge too. "With real potato chips and real mayonnaise?"

"They're regular—not baked or lowfat or no salt." Poor Betty began to sweat, and it was actually chilly now with the rain. "But there's chopped celery and onion and green peppers in the chicken salad. And lettuce to keep the juice out of the bread."

"Iceberg lettuce?" Charlie asked sternly.

"Well—"

Charlie put her arm around her neighbor's shoulders and guided her out the door. "Sounds marvelous, Mrs. Beesom. Let's eat."

There was even whole milk for Charlie's ulcer. It tasted like cream after the one percent at home. "What's wrong, Betty? I'm your friend. You can tell me."

"In the paper this morning, Charlie, it said the police had a suspect in Jeremy's murder. You and me was the only ones here. Nobody'd suspect you. You're somebody's mother."

"Oh, Betty." Charlie was facing the refrigerator door with the hummingbird magnets and yellowed picture of Mrs. Beesom's church's glorious gift of the sentry palm. Why hadn't Charlie ever wondered why Betty Beesom could overlook Jeremy's little girlfriends—considering her religious attitude about everything else? She obviously didn't approve, but she'd done nothing about it. Then again, she was the one most dependent on him here. And it was obvious that she liked him.

Hell, we all did.

"We can alibi each other, can't we? Even if we're women? And Detective Amuller is sweet on you. So that just leaves me."

"Betty, stop this. I'm the suspect here, not you. And he's not sweet on me, he used that to get information from you."

"Charlie, you got it all wrong. I talked to Lawyer Seligman himself this morning. He only works for murderers and bad people. I read about him all the time in the *P-T*. I'm just an old lady who didn't know what she was doing."

"You've got it all wrong. He's my lawyer. I spent most of last night in a jail cell. He got me out. Listen to me. They think I did it. You and I know neither of us did."

"Oh Charlie, I'm so sorry."

"For what? I know you are not telling the whole truth, Betty. I know God loves you, but I know you can lie. Now Detective Amuller is going to try to use what you told him to convict me of Jeremy's murder. And Ernesto Seligman is going to try to use what you told him to prove Amuller is wrong. Mrs. Beesom, I want you to tell me what you're so sorry about—what you really know about Jeremy, and your owning his house, and I want you to tell me about Harry."

"He's a cat."

"No, *Harry*. The man."

An astonished but miraculously recovered Betty Beesom rose to wrap the half of the sandwich Charlie couldn't eat in cellophane. "Don't worry, dear. I can't tell you about Harry, but I can say that he will take care of everything. It will all be just fine. I'm so relieved Mr. Seligman is not my lawyer. But Charlie, there's another problem. And it's much bigger. And I'm so sorry."

CHAPTER 31

C HARLIE GRILLED THE tuna steaks in a grill pan on the stove because the on-and-off rain turned into long and steady. They propped open the kitchen door to let the fresh smell of the rain join them for dinner. She coated the steaks with Captain Iam's Sinful Seafood Seasoning and served them with steamed asparagus, strawberries, macaroni salad, French bread, and wine. Not a bad meal for a little-interest, no-talent cook.

Charlie told Larry and Libby and Edward Esterhazie about the redwood house with a red Ferrari in the garage and a man who hid when she knocked on the door. "I'll bet you anything his name is Harry."

"Or Jonathan Phillips," Ed said.

"Pepe and Joe at Manic's remembered a woman who could be the one I chased before the bomb went off in Jeremy's house. She'd pick him up when he left off one of the cars for repair. And I saw her and the Ferrari at the Wine Merchant this morning, went back to the redwood house, the Ferrari was still gone and the man still there."

"You've been pretty busy for a woman who spent the night in jail," Edward said. He was too robust and distinguished for ED. "This tuna, by the way, is excellent. I didn't know you could cook."

"Yeah, Mom, the asparagus is even good. And it's green."

"A secret gourmet seasoning on the tuna and dill weed in the water under the steamer for the al dente asparagus," Charlie said smugly.

"And the macaroni salad has the classic taste of—" Larry kissed the ends of his fingers and then unpetaled them toward his fellow diners, in a burst of gastronomic pretension, "—could it be France—no, it is, I think, Hastings—Von's Deli, yes?"

"And a very good year for mayonnaise," Charlie agreed. "After spending the night in jail, I'm stocking up on good memories."

"Have you told Ernie Seligman about this redwood house and the woman at the Wine Merchant with Jeremy's car?" Edward wanted to know.

"My tough-case lawyer didn't want me snooping around and annoying Amuller even more. I was ordered to be a good girl and stay home and let him and the LBPD do the legwork. Seligman even questioned Mrs. Beesom. She was convinced she was the suspect reported in this morning's *P-T*."

"Tomorrow morning, first thing, I'll go with you to this redwood house and we'll find a way to make this guy answer the front door," Larry said and tore a piece off the crusty baguette.

"I have to take Betty to the eye doctor."

"Tomorrow's Saturday."

"He had a cancellation and is open on Saturday mornings and Wilma Granger still had his card I showed her and finagled an appointment for Betty and me, too."

Betty had thought that an even worse problem for Charlie than being the suspect in Jeremy's murder. "I told her she shouldn't bother you with that now, but Wilma's just a doer, Charlie."

"Mrs. Beesom's eyes have always been red, Mom. Does she need new glasses?"

"Charlie, far be it from me to criticize someone as altogether as you are, but have you checked the arrangement of your priorities here?" Edward asked.

"Betty Beesom knows something she's not telling and I'll have several lovely hours all alone with her on the 405 to L.A. and back to pry whatever it is from her. Trust me, it has to do with Jeremy's murder and, Libby, Mrs. Beesom has a cloudy film on her eyes called cataracts and they can be removed by laser surgery. And did you notice Edward here doesn't wear glasses anymore? Well, he had a different eye surgery that made that possible and that everyone thinks *I* should have. So Betty and I will go together to see Dr. Pearlman, and, Larry and Edward, you can visit the redwood house for me at the same time and we'll outsmart J. S. while looking innocent."

"When did Mr. Esterhazie become Edward instead of Ed?"

"This morning just before you left for school, as I remember," Charlie said.

Edward added, "It's one of those adult things you don't want to know about."

Libby studied Doug Esterhazie's dad with a squint and chewed on the last spear of fresh asparagus. "It's about sex?"

Actually it was, but nobody wanted to explain erectile disfunction to Libby Abigail Greene. Especially her mother.

When it was impossible to avoid doctors, Charlie tended to look up those closer to work than to home because she could schedule them during their mutual working hours. So this was an L.A. doctor, and Charlie and Betty headed out on the 405 early the next morning. Charlie stopped at the drive-through for her latte and bagel just like it was a work day. Betty refused anything—she'd had her All-Bran and decaf.

"Does your mother really have a boyfriend, Charlie?"

"Apparently."

"Well, she should. My Nathan died late enough in my life I didn't have the energy to deal with anyone else. But she was widowed awful young, too young to have to be alone."

Apparently not as young as her boyfriend.

The fog was thick this morning after the rain last night, and even on Saturday the smoke from cars on the 405 added to it to form smog. Charlie drove with headlights on, the strong coffee gradually clearing the fog of sleep from her head.

"Oh, she's lucky to have you, Charlie. And you're lucky to have Libby. I don't have anybody. Never really wanted children. They always seemed messy and cranky and demanding, but now I know what I probably really knew then, if I'd bothered to pay attention. Children grow up to be responsible and dependable as you grow old and messy. They need you and all that attention early on, but you're going to need them and attention later on. I know it's been obvious since Jesus was born but when Jeremy came he promised he'd look after me in my old age because he didn't have a mother or children, either. And I thought everything would be all right. Then I got too nosy and the problems started. Charlie, old people can get scared and desperate, too. And the other night when you put your arm around me and said I was your friend, I felt so good. And then we found Jeremy dead."

"What problems started, Betty, when you got nosy?"

"Nathan, he had a boy by an earlier marriage. He was quite a bit older than me—Nathan. The boy died young and Nathan split up with the mother. He didn't want another child. So here I am—old and alone."

"You didn't answer my question, Mrs. Beesom. And who is Harry, the man?"

"Oh, there's no man, just Hairy the cat."

"You said yesterday he would take care of everything. A cat can't do that."

"Don't pay no attention to the ramblings of an old woman."

"Who did you see at the memorial for Jeremy that upset you so you had to go to the hospital? Betty, I'm not just being nosy—the police think *I* killed Jeremy."

"Have they searched your house for the gun that shot him?"

"Not that I know of."

"Well, see, they don't really suspect you. Taking you to the jail was just to worry me into a confession."

"Did they search your house for a gun?" This conversation was growing more strange than informative and Charlie had been concentrating on it and navigating the thick fog smog and not spilling her latte so she didn't register right away that the low little car passing her could have been red in the thick gray engulfing them, that it had the possible shape of a Ferrari and a smeared-to-indiscernible license plate, until the car disappeared into soupy air ahead. A monumental double semi passed next and demanded all her attention.

"Charlie, what happens if your hearing goes out again in this traffic and fog?"

Charlie didn't answer Betty Beesom as Betty hadn't answered her. Hardball seemed to be the only solution to the impasse here. And Charlie controlled the Toyota, if not the situation. She was reminded of her dream about the crash with the semi and Jeremy, Tuxedo and Hairy in the cab with him, when the Ferrari and the double semi appeared out of the fog soup ahead side-by-side yet again. But the car she imagined was the Ferrari pulled to the right with blinker flashing and disappeared on an off-ramp. Charlie relaxed some, finished her bagel, and took a last swig of latte.

"You know, Charlie, people younger and stronger than me take advantage of my weakness."

"You know, Mrs. Beesom, they do me, too. Younger people take advantage of my weakness and older people take advantage of my strength. You're just part of a larger world that doesn't have a clue, either."

"What a stupid thing to say."

Charlie led Betty Beesom to the elevators in the FFUCWB of P building and punched the button for the fifth floor.

"We're gonna be early. Maybe we should of stopped for pie and coffee first."

"This isn't the eye doctor's office. It's mine." *And you're not going to get pie on Wilshire this early in the day.*

"What'd we come here for?"

Charlie slid the pass card's magnetic strip through the slot on the agency's door to release the lock instead of answering the poor woman.

"Guess you're mad at me, huh?" Betty blinked helplessly but followed Charlie into the reception room of Congdon & Morse, Inc. rather than be left alone in the strange hallway.

"I don't like being lied to by a good Christian like yourself." Charlie hated playing hardball with a white-haired neighbor with cataracts. But as long as Betty could convince herself she was doing Charlie no harm, she wouldn't give up her secrets.

Sometimes agents came in to catch up on off hours, but the agency sounded empty this morning. Charlie hoped Dorian Black hadn't brought in a woman, the pig.

The intestinal distress of the tiny office refrigerator, the inexorable slow drip of the faucet above the sink next to it, the huffing of the ventilation system, Mrs. Beesom's worried sniff—all made Charlie so aware of how she depended on her over-achieving hearing system. Was it still that acute, or did it just seem like it compared to the unwelcome periods of total silence?

Ruby Dillon's desk was clean and perfect as usual. Charlie led Betty down the hall toward the front of the building, passing up Tracy Dewitt's cubicle and the other agents' offices to throw open Richard Morse's door and let Betty gape at the two walls of windows on the corner office, the huge desk, and leather furniture. "This is Richard's office. Mine is right next door."

And she showed Betty into Larry's cubicle.

"Oh, this is very nice, Charlie." The older woman tried to sound impressed. "Now we'd better get ourselves over to that doctor."

"This is Larry's office—mine's right through here." Charlie's message light was flashing and she thought she could smell cigarette smoke. The message was from Keegan Monroe, her most valuable client, a screenwriter with incredible credits—still in demand at thirty-five. And unfortunately in Folsom Prison. He wanted to know what she thought of the new screenplay and wanted her to know he was to appear before the parole board on Monday morning.

Great, her most valuable client was just about to get out of prison and she was just about to get into one. Charlie left Betty to be impressed by Charlie's position in the world because of her impressive office and went back to Larry's cubicle to search for Keegan's screenplay. Larry had loved it, and hidden it when the cops and Feds or whoever came to look into her computer files. Charlie knew where he hid things he didn't want found.

In the towering drop-leaf file cabinet stuffed with stuff they'd probably never get to, she looked under *M*. It was in the first folder. The working title—no producer in the world would refuse to look at a full screenplay by Keegan without the usual pitch first, but rarely would they use his title, either— was *Open and Shut*.

Charlie tucked it under her arm and tried the door of the office next to hers. To her astonishment, it opened. The air here reeked of cigarette smoke and the hole drilled through the wall this office shared with hers was much larger than a peephole now. It was large enough to stick a hand through and move A. E. Mous's poster aside. But the office of the mysterious silent partner, Daniel Congdon, was empty.

CHAPTER 32

◆

I HAD NO idea you were such an important person, Charlie. Your office is so grand. And you don't even have to do Mr. Morse's typewriting and answer his phone."

The whole idea of taking Betty to the office had been to force her to face the fact that Charlie had a real-world job, and Betty's hiding the truth from herself away in her age-cocoon wouldn't work in the real world. Or something like that.

After Dr. Pearlman had assured them both their vision could be restored by the magic laser, Betty began to revert into her self-protective fantasy self again, so Charlie decided to blow Betty away with a lunch at the Celebrity Pit. Shake her up again.

Well, the poor woman's stomach was growling and she'd had no pie for a snack this morning. It had been a long time since her All-Bran and, as Charlie understood it, the purpose of that breakfast was that it passed through rather quickly.

Mrs. Beesom sat speechless over her iced tea—a large glass, it had taken five sugar packets to make it potable. The poor woman was puffing—too much walking for her age bracket here, even though so far most of it had been down stairs because the escalator had brought them up.

Charlie ordered herself the special and Betty the crêpes— the closest thing to pie here. And herself a glass of wine.

"Oh, do you think you should? You have to drive us all the way to Long—is that Charlton Heston up there?"

"I think he's a plant."

"No, the man sitting in front of that window. He's talking to the woman across the table. Plants can't talk."

Betty's first course was a crêpe filled with steamed vegetables, but saved by a rich hollandaise sauce. Betty was not overly fond of vegetables, but cooked beat raw any day. Warmed-up canned was even better. Charlie's first course was a leafy salad. And the French bread with real butter didn't hurt, either, but the crust was too hard for Betty to chew.

"You know, I don't think Jeremy was shot at all," Charlie said to get the conversation back to the particulars.

"But all that blood, Charlie."

"Could have been a stab wound. I never saw him when he was turned over."

"But from the picture of him in the paper—it was Jeremy."

"Oh yes, but if he'd been shot we'd have smelled it in the car and probably on Hairy. And they'd have checked both of us for gun-powder residue on our hands."

"So what are they up to, do you think?"

"Trying to get me to slip up, probably." Like I'd like to get you to. "What do you suppose Jeremy meant by warning you to 'watch out for Harry,' Mrs. Beesom, when he warned us all of something different the other night?"

"Probably thought the cat fights in the middle of the night would startle me into a heart attack."

The second course for Betty was two turkey-and-potato crêpes with another rich sauce even Charlie couldn't pronounce but Betty was astonished to find could not have a Campbell's Soup base.

"You lied about not knowing you owned Jeremy's house, didn't you, Betty?"

"Told me once he'd take care of me. Guess that's what he meant. Wasn't what I meant."

"Do you also know where he kept his money?"

"In a bank, I suppose, like everybody else."

"So he was paying taxes on the house for you and you didn't know it."

"It was sort of a trust. But the trust could pay the taxes. The designated payee doesn't have to be the owner—like the bills on a rental are sent to the landlord's address."

Charlie had no idea if this was possible without Betty signing something. But this whole thing seemed so illegal and screwed up she wouldn't doubt it.

Betty's dessert crêpes were stuffed with cherries and blueberries in a crème she described as a burnt-sugar custard. Charlie was getting stuffed watching her eat it. How could someone that small, who mostly sat, eat all that rich food? Charlie hadn't been able to finish the dinner salad and artichoke soup.

When the imposter coffee-pourer automatically poured them each a cup of coffee, Charlie was about to warn Betty it wasn't decaf but Betty interrupted with, "My dear Jesus, Charlie, it's him, Mitch Hilsten, your—"

"No, it's not. And Betty, that coffee isn't—"

"Yes, it is—him," the lookalike said and handed Charlie the check with a wink. He was fairly convincing, but too young—his teeth perfect because of an orthodontist instead of capped, and his blue eyes were just blue, not powder blue.

"Things is so bad he's waiting tables? You said he was doing very good."

"Betty, this whole place is a setup—a campy—these-people-are-all-fakes-pretending-to-be—Betty?"

"What, Charlie? You're looking pale all of a sudden—must be the wine. It's not your ears again, is it? We got to get home somehow." Betty was so frightened she looked pale, too, drank down all the coffee, and didn't even notice the famous heart-throb, Mitch Hilsten, refilling her cup before he picked up Charlie's credit card.

"No, it's—I think I've figured out what I've been trying to tell myself half the week. Why do I never listen to me?"

By the time Charlie excused herself for a run to the bath-room and Betty Beesom had downed a third cup of very strong, rich coffee, Charlie'd formed a strategy for their trip home. She just hoped the poor Toyota could handle it.

"Charlie, dear, I'm so happy my eyes can be fixed."

"I am, too, Betty. Are you feeling all right?"

"Oh yes, it was a wonderful dinner. Lunch. Lunch is what I meant—oh you're driving too fast, aren't you? And too close to that truck?"

"Settle down. I got you here, didn't I? I'll get you home. You're so jumpy. Tell me more about Jeremy. Where did you say you met him?"

"Wish you hadn't had that glass of wine. It's not safe for you to be driving now, Charlie."

Charlie swerved suddenly, not to frighten the old woman as she'd meant to but because at that moment she noticed the red Ferrari behind them. No fog or smog or double semi to give her doubts this time. How long had it been following them?

"Jeremy came over to take the second house finished on my lot—I had rights on the first."

"Is that when you learned he would care for you in your old age and that his house would be yours when he died?" It was *a* red Ferrari, not necessarily *the* red Ferrari.

"That's why the police think I killed him, and not that you did."

"And when did the trouble start because of your nosiness?"

"I didn't like him having those snotty young girls sleeping at his house. I told him so, too. That's when the trouble started."

"Betty, you didn't have to be nosy to notice he had young girls at his house."

"Charlie, I have to find a bathroom. And soon."

It was clear and warm that evening and Charlie warmed up the deli ribs for them to eat outside. She sent Doug for beans at the diner. Libby worked tonight, so it was the Esterhazies and Larry and Maggie. Maggie brought the salad greens and strawberries, Charlie put out the deli potato salad. They sat outside talking low so as not to disturb a very disturbed eighty-three-year-old woman with cataracts and some serious secrets.

Larry and Edward had found the redwood house, but no red Ferrari and no man. There had been a female figure lurking, ducking, and hiding inside this time. Obviously reluctant to answer the door.

"That could be because the Ferrari was following us," Charlie said, "and there's only one way its driver could have known our destination. I think he was thrown off by our route, which was a problem with his source."

"Mrs. Beesom?" Maggie Stutzman shook her head. "I'm sorry, Charlie, but I've known her longer than you have. Longer than I've known you—and I have a problem believing that old woman would—"

"Did she really pee in your car?" Doug Esterhazie didn't seem convinced, either.

"Doug, you've never had coffee at the Celebrity Pit and then gotten on the 405. Trust me."

"And she talked?" Larry asked.

"She talked some. And the red Ferrari turned off to go to

211

Dr. Pearlman's, unaware that I was going to the office first. But he picked us up again there and followed us to the Pit and all the way here until we turned off the 405 because the driver knew where we lived."

"Went home to the redwood house and the woman with the socks."

"Exactly."

"Did you get a look at the driver?"

"No, but I'm assuming it's the guy who lives in the redwood house—Harry or Jonathon, especially since you saw the woman there today. But I suppose it's possible that more than two people live in that house with Jeremy's Ferrari."

"I suggest we have coffee and wait awhile before revisiting that house," Edward said.

"Larry, I took Betty to the agency and picked up Keegan's script. I wanted to show her I had a real life beyond her impression of my life here."

"You wanted her to know you were an important person who had much to lose if she didn't give up her secrets."

"Right. But the door to Daniel Congdon's office was unlocked and the room reeked of cigarette smoke."

"Sounds like *The X-Files,*" Maggie said.

"Charlie's life so often does," Edward Concrete pointed out.

"That's true."

"And when I asked Richard about it the other day," Charlie ignored them, "he essentially said, 'You don't want to go there.' What do you think's going on?"

"Sounds like the Evan Black project, *Paranoia Will Destroy Ya.*"

"The one Mitch Hilsten's making in Spain—where they blow up Las Vegas?" Maggie managed to grab a remaining strawberry before Doug noticed it.

Larry nodded. "Made with big money smuggled out of the

country with no deductions by the IRS. Therefore funny money. Because the agency handles Black, our records have been looked into most carefully. Especially Charlie's. And I heard *Paranoia* has wrapped."

"They're also desperate to find out how Jeremy could disappear in cyberspace."

"Oh, I almost forgot," Doug said, finishing up the last of the leftovers. "I got to diddling around on the computer this afternoon again and came up with four accounts closed out to a Jeremy Beesom, one to a Nathan Beesom, and two to a Harry Beesom. All closed out the same day as Fiedler Enterprises and Beach Enterprises—the day Fiedler died over there."

The sea breeze clicked the sword fronds of Betty Beesom's sentry palm in the quiet that settled abruptly on this tiny portion of Belmont Shore.

"You almost forgot?" Charlie rasped finally.

"Yeah, see last time I stopped at Betty Beesom and didn't go on with the Beesoms because I was looking for a Phillips and a Fiedler. Oh, there was also a Jonathan Beesom, closed three accounts the same day. All with different brokerages. If I understand the abbreviations, these were all cashed in for cash. Wouldn't the IRS be looking for these guys? Those accounts were all way over ten thousand. Of course it all takes a while to work through the system."

"It could have been going on longer than just the last few days," Charlie said thoughtfully. "There must be a lot of it, a whole lot. But what made you look under Beesom?"

"I didn't, but I thought why not do a search on just Jeremy—one word? That's when I came up with Beesom, so I did a search on just Beesom. Duh."

CHAPTER 33

❖

THERE WAS NO one home at the redwood house, not even the Ferrari. Charlie, Ed, and Larry snooped around the best they could hoping they wouldn't alert neighbors to call them in as prowlers. A dim lamp lit one bedroom enough to expose signs of some serious packing going on.

"It's Saturday night. Maybe they went out to dinner," Larry whispered. "We could park up the street and wait for a car to pull in here."

"Maggie's out with Mel and Doug's meeting friends. That leaves Betty home alone. I don't like it. I've got a hunch we could find the Ferrari faster at my place."

"Why is it when I have a whole idea and you just have a hunch, we act on your hunch?" Larry asked as they hurried back to his Bronco. They'd decided Ed's Porsche would stand out, and Charlie's Toyota had been hanging around this neighborhood too much already.

But when they reached the compound it was not a red Ferrari that greeted them. Instead, an ambulance with all lights flashing backed into the street.

"Ohmygod, another bomb. Please, not poor Betty this time." Charlie was the first to reach Clayton Melbourne, who was bringing a shaking hand with a shaking cigarette to his face. He leaned against Maggie's Subaru, his car parked in Jeremy's place. "What's happened now? Is Betty all right?"

"It's Maggie. Oh, Charlie, I'm so glad you're here. I can't tolerate hospitals. You have to go to her. She's at Memorial."

He and Maggie were on their way to his apartment when Maggie insisted on returning home for something she'd forgotten. He'd parked and she'd run in. When she came out, she was clutching her chest. "She's had a heart attack, Charlie."

Charlie asked Larry and Edward to check on Mrs. Beesom, grabbed Maggie's purse out of Mel's car, and ran into her own house for Keegan Monroe's script. This looked to be a long night.

The frantic staff in the emergency room as much as told Charlie to go climb a tree, until she found someone who would stand still or stay off the phone long enough for her to explain she had the insurance information for a Margaret Mildred Stutzman who'd just been delivered by ambulance.

"They've taken her to cardiac. Paramedics thought some guy would be following the ambulance in with her stuff."

"Mel can't stand hospitals. Poor baby."

When she'd filled out most of Maggie's history so she could be sick legally, Charlie sat outside the cardiac unit reading *Open and Shut* until a young Dr. Jenkins came to sit beside her. He looked gray with exhaustion. "Your friend is in a great deal of trouble, I'm afraid. We'll stabilize her overnight and may do surgery tomorrow. Why people never learn I don't know. Women are succumbing to this younger and younger."

"Are you talking bypass or angioplasty? Maggie?"

"If people don't straighten up their acts, we'll all be dead by thirty-five. And the very first thing she has to do is throw away those damned cigarettes."

"Maggie doesn't smoke. Far as I know she never did."

"She reeked of cigarettes when she came in here."

"Her boyfriend smokes. She probably reeked of Mel." And Charlie explained Kate Gonzales's theory of estrogen deprivation and how it causes irregular heartbeats and fear takes it from there.

"This is an emergency situation, your friend's life is in danger, and you want us to treat her illness on the basis of pop medicine from some women's magazine?"

Actually it's from the cleaning lady. But Charlie didn't have the nerve to say so aloud. This poor guy was under a lot of stress.

"Women cannot go on hiding behind PMS, menopause, and hormones—they're going to have to take control of their lives and their diets. Caffeine, alcohol, stress, and a fatty diet—"

"She had two glasses of red wine with dinner at my house and Maggie eats more fresh fruits and vegetables than anyone I know." Charlie failed to mention her friend's taste for strong coffee and the barbecued ribs and deli potato salad she'd also had for dinner. "I'd be real sure it's a heart attack before I'd do bypass if I were you. My friend's a practicing attorney of long standing in this town."

He looked unconvinced. "Well, she certainly doesn't look like one now."

Open and Shut was chilling and funny as hell, the title a double entendre concerning a cop bent on proving a famous chef guilty of killing his obese wife by poisoning her with excess and his fabulous cooking. (She could see a studio ruining half the fun and half the macabre by titling it something bland like *Killing with Kindness*. A lot of the fun of Charlie's job was getting to experience the truly creative talents in the industry, which the industry often watered down for the common man.)

The wife had become so heavy she couldn't bend in the middle and the gifted chef had had a double-wide recliner made for her, and then a triple-wide. Their apartment was above the restaurant and he would have his minions take up morsels of his best work to keep her happy until he was through in the kitchen and then would bring up the best of everything to share with her.

This, of course, was in a series of flashbacks as chef and staff and around-the-clock male orderlies were questioned—male orderlies because of the lifting required to see to her hygiene—by the cop who Charlie pictured as J. S. Amuller. The first scene, behind the front credits, was this young homicide detective viewing the triple-wide recliner and its contents. The chef's wife had passed over with a smile on her lips and vomit all down her front. The deceased eater was tested for poisoning, but never once did our clever cop suspect that. He came to the conclusion that, since the orderlies were encouraged to go down to the kitchen to enjoy their own dinner, during that precious two or three hours that the couple had together to share their mutual love (food and wine), on this fateful night the chef reclined his helpless wife flat for a period of time so that when the rich meal came up, she choked on it.

Now the chilling part was that the chef had no alibi, had to admit he fed extravagantly rich food to an enormously over-weight wife, and yes, she had money he would now inherit.

The funny part was how the couple talked to each other as they dined late at night (both did most of their sleeping during the day). The description—it was one of those script experiences where you're reading it, hearing it, seeing it, and casting it, even if you're only an agent. While Charlie grew ravenous at the couple's descriptions of the food and its taste and texture and color and odor, she grew fearful for the poor chef who must have loved the woman to slave for her so. (Hollywood would throw in a young blond for him to sleep with and wreck the whole thing—but that's the biz). She laughed at the play going on between the orderlies downstairs and the gofer cooks, the departing patrons exclaiming over the wondrous, exotic, fragrant ambrosia they'd experienced inside. It made *mouthwatering* such a tame expression you wanted to ban it from the language. Jesus, this is going to play in Europe even.

But you not only watch the food cooked, described, pictured in color, and shared descriptions between chef and wife and staff and customers—suffice it to say that the huge Mrs. Chef experiences multiple spontaneous orgasms every night at dinner.

Okay, Keegan's a guy who learned about women from *Playboy* and other totally clueless, out-of-the-frame sources. But the point was that's Hollywood, which is male, and Charlie was terrified for the poor chef while tingling all over with that wonderful we-got-something-here-or-what? agent feeling.

I can sell this.

Hell, anybody could sell this. It's Keegan Monroe, for godsakes. Get ahold of Keegan ASAP. With your luck he's looking for another agent because you haven't told him how wonderful the script and he are.

I'm talking holding up big studios for really big money up front. I'm talking the deal of the century.

You should be talking staying out of prison first.

"Are you Mel, Melody?" a woman asked softly and handed Charlie a packet of nose tissues.

"No, I'm Charlie Greene. Here for Margaret Stutzman." Charlie realized her crying and laughing and joy for poor Keegan had not gone unnoticed in the waiting room of the cardiac unit. And then she noticed there were only four other people there left.

"Miss Stutzman has been moved to a semiprivate and is asking for Mel."

"I told them you are a local practicing attorney and not to rush to judgment about surgery here."

Jenkins was right about one thing—Maggie sure didn't look like an attorney. She was always pale but now her glorious hair was limp and she had funny red spots on her cheeks that weren't blush. The blue eyes had lost their snap.

"I was finally stabilized enough to remember the name of my gynecologist. Thanks, Greene, but wasn't Mel at my bedside?"

"He can't handle hospitals. And I'd have been there but they wouldn't let me in. Isn't there a blood test that proves or disproves whether or not you had a heart attack?"

"A guy at my office went around for two years being treated for a bad heart until they took out his gallbladder. Heart's been fine ever since. My doctor will be here in the morning. I promised to sue if they did anything surgical without her approval."

"Last time this happened, Detective Amuller upset you in Jeremy's living room. What set it off this time? Mel said you just ran back out of the house holding your chest."

"Sometimes it doesn't take anything. I can just be sitting in a chair. One time I was moving a heavy load of files from my desk to a table in my office. But this time it was Jeremy. I saw him in the house."

"Jeremy's dead."

"It was his ghost, Charlie."

Out in the hospital parking lot, Charlie found her Toyota the center of attention, particularly to the biggest black labrador Charlie had ever seen. He had a cop attached to his leash.

Another cop stopped her. "That your car, ma'am?"

"Yes, what's happening?" But Charlie had a pretty good idea and another thing kachunked into place.

"Mind telling me what you were doing in the hospital?"

"Visiting a friend in the cardiac unit. Margaret Mildred Stutzman. My name is Charlie Greene."

He checked this out with admissions on his cellular. Charlie didn't even blink when the bomb squad arrived. She'd seen that weird truck before.

"We had a bomb scare tonight and they found nothing until the officer walked his dog past your car on the way to his car. That dog's decided there's bomb makings somewhere under your car or in the trunk."

It was after midnight when Charlie came home in a black-and-white to find Libby and Larry snacking in the kitchen. There'd been a bomb device attached to the underside of the Toyota. It wouldn't detonate but the bomb squad would keep the car and return it after a thorough search.

"Larry, don't let me forget to call Keegan tomorrow. *Open and Shut* is a winner. I'm exhausted. Maggie will live—we'll talk tomorrow, okay?" The wonderful thing about the title was that while the cop hero knew he had an open-and-shut case, the chief suspect—the chef—had to hand-feed his wife, and he would say "open," and spoon in some devilishly wonderful food, and he would say "shut," and she would close her mouth and chew while he took a bite. And then they would describe the taste, texture, seasoning, even the mood of the food in a truly sensuous way. It was brilliant. It even made Charlie horny and it wasn't her estrus time.

She crawled into bed to find some wet green stuff on her pillow. Goddamned cat. She threw the pillow to the floor and grabbed the other. It wasn't until morning that she found other chewed green things around the room and could identify them as hundred dollar bills.

CHAPTER 34

◆

L ARRY SCRAMBLED EGGS the next morning and Betty brought over her sinful cinnamon rolls, hot out of the oven. One of the long-standing mysteries of the compound was solved when Larry asked her how she did it. "I just called to invite you, couldn't have been a half hour ago."

"Oh, I don't make them, dear. Have a freezerful. They're Sara Lee and I own stock in the company. Just doing my part, you know. Take them out of the freezer and warm them up. I take them out of the aluminum pan and put them in this Pyrex one to bake. This here's two boxes' worth."

Libby was still asleep. Charlie would go to the hospital to Maggie. Ed would come by and pick up Larry. The guys intended to get to the bottom of the couple with the red Ferrari in the redwood house who looked to be planning on leaving town. Charlie was fairly certain she already had figured it out, but wouldn't mind a little corroboration.

"Do you want to come with me to see Maggie, Mrs. Beesom? We could take your car since mine is still with the bomb unit."

"Oh no, dear, but you can take my car. Two places I don't go except under force—hospitals and nursing homes. You two won't understand until you get to be my age."

Charlie wasn't about to touch that one so she turned to

Larry. "*Open and Shut*'s got everything. You were right. I was laughing and crying in the waiting room and making a total ass of myself. I wish Keegan would call again before I go to Maggie."

"I never imagined anything so erotic. And from a couple married what, thirty, thirty-five years and she unable to bend in the middle? And so sad and so funny, too. Making love with food isn't new, but Stew's going to love it."

"They weren't really making love with food, Mrs. Beesom," Charlie told the woman threatening to hyperventilate while chewing. Once started, Betty wouldn't pause while eating if Jesus Christ walked up and asked directions.

"How can Monroe be such a genius and so unimpressive to look at? And was there really a bomb attached to your Toyota?" Larry wanted to know. "Who could predict Maggie would have a heart attack and you'd drive it to the hospital where they could attach it? Or is there a random bomber following you around?"

"That labrador was sure convinced, practically mounted the tailpipe—that's just an expression, Mrs. Beesom, he didn't really. I just wonder if the bomb had been there for a while and didn't go off like it was supposed to. The makings of a dud might smell the same to a dog." That could also have been why the red Ferrari followed them to the eye doctor yesterday—to punch a detonator at the right time or to witness the success of the planting of the bomb.

"You mean there could have been a bomb on the back of your car when we drove to Dr. Pearlman's and all over the city yesterday?" Betty slowed the lifting of her fork.

"I think it's a real possibility that whoever was following us in a Ferrari like Jeremy's wanted us dead—both of us. You too. And Maggie claims that what set off her heart problem last night was seeing Jeremy's ghost in her house when she returned unexpectedly for something she'd forgotten—and, Mrs. Beesom, no one who lives here and knew Jeremy is safe."

"Charlie," Larry said, studying the old woman with concern, "careful here. Her heart's a lot older than Maggie's."

"She's not safe, Larry. Nobody who lives here is safe without Jeremy. And, Betty, if I have to choose between you and Libby in a dangerous situation, how would you imagine that scene would play?"

"Jeremy's ghost," Betty said.

"It wasn't Jeremy's ghost, was it, Mrs. Beesom?"

Betty was saved answering that embarrassing question by Maggie Stutzman walking in the back door without waiting for an invitation. "Tell me you haven't eaten all the cinnamon rolls."

Maggie, replete with the rest of the cinnamon rolls, took Charlie over to her house for serious coffee. She didn't want to go alone. And Dr. Jenkins warned her she was lucky this time but if she didn't give up cigarettes, caffeine, alcohol, red meat, and dessert, she'd be back again fast. "And don't think you can blame everything on hormones because you're female," he said.

Her gynecologist had arrived to look over the stats, see to her release, and drive her home. "Blood tests aren't conclusive, but we're not rushing into surgery here even though I was supposedly at death's door less than twelve hours ago. Paramedics scared me worse than Jeremy's ghost."

Larry had gone off with Edward Esterhazie to investigate the redwood house and its occupants, Betty off to church with Wilma and Art Granger.

Charlie and Maggie snuggled bare feet under the center cushion of the couch and raised their lattes in a toast.

"Cheers. And thanks for being there for me, Greene."

"Seems to me you were there for me not many days ago, Stutzman. Good friends can be a pain in the butt, but hard to find."

"Give up caffeine and desserts." Maggie's coloring was back to normal and the red on her face was clearly anger this time. "And I maybe smoked two cigarettes in my whole life—well, tobacco ones. Where does that doctor get off anyway?"

"Same as my nonexistent hearing loss, but in reverse. Certain minds get made up before problems occur." Charlie wiggled her toes under the cushion and sipped the strong, fragrant coffee with pleasure. She'd miss these moments if she went to prison or if Mel moved in here. And for a moment she didn't want to talk about the harsh reality their lives had become, so she told Maggie about *Open and Shut.*

"I love Keegan's stuff—any possibility you could give a poor heart-attack victim a sneak peek? I promise I won't tell a soul. I want to read it at your house, though." Maggie looked around at her own house with a shiver.

"See what I can do. I have to go home and call Keegan anyway."

"Can I shower over there, too?"

"Sure. Let's enjoy our coffee first."

When the ritual ended and Maggie took the cups to the sink, Charlie told her friend about the bomb attached to her car.

"I hadn't even noticed the Toyota wasn't here. Did it blow up in the hospital parking lot? I saw the local news on TV this morning and that wasn't mentioned."

"I figure the bomb had been attached for a day or two and hadn't gone off. It was a dud."

"Our bouquet bomber?"

"Probably. So where was this ghost of Jeremy when you walked in unexpectedly last night?"

"I know you don't believe in ghosts, Charlie, but I saw him. Now I know why Tuxedo and Hairy have been acting so wild. Animals are very sensitive to the supernatural. What do you mean 'unexpectedly'?"

"Well, you left with your boyfriend, presumably for at least the evening, and then were all of a sudden back again."

"Ghosts don't care about that—but then, I suppose you can surprise a ghost. He was just sort of drifting down the stairs when I walked in the door. And he stopped when he saw me and I stopped when I saw him and my heart suddenly went into this wild overdrive."

"You didn't tell Dr. Jenkins about this ghost?"

"I'm not that dumb, Greene. What are you holding? Spinach?"

"A hundred-dollar bill after a cat attack. Let's go upstairs and get you a change of clothes and your shampoo and stuff. Better bring your own towel. Libby goes through ours so fast, I've been known to dry off with the shower mat."

"Why don't you just buy more towels?"

"You've seen Doug Esterhazie eat, and you've never said, 'Why don't you just buy more food?' "

Keegan Monroe finally called Charlie at home and was so happy and relieved to hear what his agent thought of his script, he cried. And boy did Charlie feel like a rat. "I thought the story was so awful, you didn't even write. You had time."

"Keegan, it's the best original you've ever done." Then again his greatest hits had been based on the novels of other envied writers lucky enough to get published in New York and worth a fraction of what he was. "It's the greatest script I have ever read from you or anyone."

"You're not going to trivialize it by offering it to cable?"

"Absolutely no way." Her book writers would have substituted OPB, or original paperback, for cable. OPB was the fate of more and more authors this glorious nut she represented envied. And they were the lucky ones. Other previously published writers were now having to publish their own works and try to sell them on the Internet, where a whole new species of shark lurked to exploit them.

But Keegan's best news was his lawyer's certainty that the decision at the parole hearing tomorrow would be positive. Charlie didn't want to douse his hopefulness with the news that she might well be his replacement. She hung up with the promise that come the morrow she would be leaking the fact that the latest Monroe script would cost the earth and be worth every penny of it.

Charlie also didn't mention that would be if she still had her hearing, could get to work, etc. This hungry, but rich writer didn't need to hear her troubles.

Keegan had spent several years in Folsom for manslaughter in the death of a novelist whose book he was turning into a screenplay. They'd been drinking vodka on a beach and he became too drunk to save her when she'd gunned her car into the water instead of backing it up. Keegan left the scene without reporting what happened.

Charlie searched her own house while her best friend showered. She found two regurgitated hairballs, a poor little bird's wing minus the bird, and another bill with Ben Franklin's face all tooth-pocked.

Tuxedo napped in the sun, sprawled on the picnic table on the patio, unconcerned that cat burglars and loose dogs could now venture into the compound with ease. She waved the hundred in front of his nose. He opened his eyes to slits and reached out to grab it from her. Still lying on his side, closing his eyes against the sun, he chewed and tore at it.

"What is it you have against money, cat?" Charlie rescued Ben Franklin at great risk to herself. "More importantly, where did you find this?"

Cat yawned, stretched, and sauntered across the compound and through the back gate to the alley.

While her best friend curled up in Charlie's living room to read Keegan Monroe's screenplay, Charlie went over to her house and searched it. Then she walked around the outsides of both houses and the wall.

When Charlie went inside, Maggie giggled and sniffed over *Open and Shut*. Libby was in the shower. She had to be at the diner by eleven.

Larry Mann and Edward returned—deep laughter, camaraderie—just two guys on a mission, Charlie thought when they came in the kitchen. They were of different generations, different preferences, different dress codes—but both tall, well built, lots of hair, and handsome in different ways. The Ferrari was home in the redwood house, as were the couple, but they refused to answer the door. They'd been breakfasting on the deck and left their dishes and the Sunday paper outside, locked the doors, and closed the drapes.

"I think it's time to tell the police about these folks," Larry said.

"At least Ernie Seligman," Edward added. "We actually came up with a few ideas on how to smoke them out, but figured we'd end up in jail with you, Charlie."

"Talking about smoke—Mom, can't you do something with that cat?"

"He's your cat."

"Yeah, well, he got soot and stuff all over my sheets. Smells like a wet fireplace."

Charlie stared at the wake of her departing beauty and again thought, *Kachunk*.

CHAPTER 35

*E*DWARD ESTERHAZIE, OUT on the patio, talked on his tiny pocket cellular. Larry and Maggie, in the living room, discussed Keegan's script in glowing terms. Charlie stood in the middle of the kitchen trying to decide what to do. She had to get to work tomorrow and start the buzz about *Open and Shut*. But things were moving too fast here. No one in her little community was safe. The dud bomb on the Toyota told her that. And the couple with a Ferrari like Jeremy's were readying to leave. The guys' visit this morning would no doubt accelerate that schedule.

Her heart pounded like Maggie's when it broke rhythm.

"Two messages," Edward said when he came in the kitchen. He bent to look in her face. "You okay? You are hearing still?"

"Yeah, what's the two messages?"

"Called Ernie. He's coming here this afternoon. Mrs. McDougal called me to say she's cooking up a lavish feast for battalions and will send it over with Doug between three and four. So don't eat lunch now." He bent to look in her face again. "So what is it, Charlie?"

"A feeling. A real helpless feeling. I'm scared, Ed—Edward. I just wish Jeremy was here."

Maggie and Larry and Tuxedo were suddenly in the kitchen with them.

"Who are you scared for?"

"Everybody who lives here or who happens to be visiting. I'm especially worried about Mrs. Beesom. Ed, could she stay at your house tonight, and Libby and Maggie, too? I've got this really bad feeling."

"Why not you?"

"I'm the one suspected of Jeremy's murder. I need to be here and not in jail, particularly tonight."

"What's going to happen tonight?"

"Something's got to. Time's running out."

"For whom?"

"For me and Betty Beesom and whoever knows about Jeremy's cash stash, but doesn't know where it is. Betty won't go to a motel."

"You expect more bombs?"

"I don't know what to expect." But Charlie knew there was no time to wait around and find out. Even a dumb cat could find the stash. This compound was a dangerous place.

By three in the afternoon she got Larry in a private corner and brainstormed the buzz leak for *Open and Shut*. By four, when the Sunday feast arrived, five casual phone calls had been made. Three people actually picked up when they heard Charlie's name. The other two returned her calls during dinner.

Charlie and her secretary made several contingency plans to get out of town early the next morning, and by different routes than usual.

They carried Mrs. Beesom's picnic table over to Charlie's patio and Betty invited the Grangers from across the alley. Charlie's lawyer, Ernie Seligman, joined them for roast beef in wine sauce with little red potatoes, a steamed and herbed vegetable medley, a fruit compote of berries and mango, and dinner rolls.

Good thing Doug stayed to eat with them. "Mrs. McDougal

229

said you and Libby would have plenty of leftovers for next week."

Betty and Wilma Granger talked of Betty's coming laser surgery and wanted to know if Charlie planned to have her eyes "fixed," too.

"It's hard to make any plans right now," Charlie told them with a purposeful glance at her hotshot lawyer. "My future's sort of up in the air here."

And, of course, Mrs. Beesom didn't think to tumble to what Charlie meant by that until after Detective Amuller arrived.

Ed and Larry had explained the problem of the redwood house to Ernie Seligman. Charlie was having problems with this Edward-and-Ernest thing. She never expected anyone to call her Charlemagne. Just because your name is Ed doesn't mean you can't get it up.

Besides the wine sauce it was soused with, the roast beef came with a wondrous creamed horseradish—reminding Charlie of Keegan Monroe's film script about the couple who made love with food. "I don't know who you're dating, Ed, but don't piss off Mrs. McDougal. Her, you can't replace."

"He's dating Cynthia," Doug managed to say with more than a hint of scorn and around a mouthful.

Ernie snorted and buttered a dinner roll. A flavored whipped butter, of course. "An irreplaceable treasure—Mrs. McDougal, I mean."

"Cynthia," Ed told Charlie, "is thirty years old and has no plans to make me over."

"Doesn't mean she doesn't have plans," Ernie said. "Be sure you got your kids set up in your will so she can't share your wealth with her boyfriend when you're gone or unable to manage your own affairs." Doug's sister lived with their mother in Florida.

Charlie had brought her cellular home with her after the

last trip to the office and her first call back came just as she was enjoying a little potato in its skin, rich in flavors of olive oil and dill and at least two other things Charlie might have tasted at some world-class restaurant. "Well, you are a special friend, Donnie, and I hated to go public tomorrow without warning you first. . . . Not a chance, darling. This is not only Monroe but bigger than anything he's ever done. Ever. And he's getting out. . . . All I can say now, sweetie, is sensual beyond belief. Bye."

Everyone at the table was looking at Charlie except Larry, who gave his approval with a wink before diving back into the best meal served at this house since Jeremy Fiedler was murdered, or maybe ever.

The Toyota came back with the bomb squad's blessing shortly before Detective Amuller swept in with an unmarked Crown Victoria and without his raincoat. His attitude, however, was familiar, and well in place. He and Charlie's hard-case lawyer exchanged nods. J. S. made a point of noting the presence of Ed Esterhazie Concrete and luscious Larry Mann. "So where's Mitch Hilsten?" he asked Charlie. "Run away with your daughter?"

To give the men present their due, they studied their food instead of taking the bait offered for Charlie's nomination as the catch of the day. Betty Beesom, however, swallowed the sinker.

"Well, I think you should know that neither Charlie or me are going to stand for you holding us up as murderers to everybody in town by that article in the paper about a suspect. Charlie is smart enough to point out to me there was no smell of gun smoke in poor Jeremy's car when she opened the door, and none on Hairy Granger when he jumped out of the car and into her arms. So we know you lied. Charlie says Jeremy was stabbed and not shot. So there, Mr. Big-Deal Policeman."

Betty took another slice of the roast and nodded her triumph at Charlie and Lawyer Seligman. "Charlie's a good and smart woman and shame on you for leading her on with your romancing. God will see to you, young man, and Jesus, too."

Ernest Seligman pushed his plate away so he could bury his head in his arms. His voice came muffled but audible. "With friends like yours, Charlie Greene, you might look into religion yourself. If only for revenge."

Charlie lost her appetite, too, when Detective Amuller beamed triumph. "Now, what a coincidence. That's exactly how Mr. Fiedler died, and who could know better than the person who stabbed him?"

"The person who found him first. And Charlie's been around murder often enough to know there would be the smell of gun smoke if he'd been shot," Ed said smugly and poured wine all around.

"As Charlie's attorney, I request that all her well-meaning friends shut up as of now. If you love her, you will speak to me and no one else. Detective Amuller, I think you should know that what may well be Jeremy Fiedler's red Ferrari now resides at this address, and you might want to question the people who are driving it."

Amuller took the slip of paper Seligman handed him, looked at it with tired skepticism, and then at Charlie with purpose. "Don't leave town." And to Seligman, "See you in court, Ernie."

The homicide detective drove off looking happier than Charlie had ever seen him. Open and shut case—he had her now.

"I can leave town anytime I want to."

"Cops watch too much TV and they think you do, too," Ernie agreed. "But as your lawyer I suggest you follow his suggestion."

Her cellular bleeped again. "Hey, Maury . . . oh, you've heard. Well, I tried to get to you earliest. I know how much you love Keegan's work—honest—yeah, I've never read anything like it and I've read everything he's ever written. And I see it before anybody. This will be the biggest deal I've ever handled. Couldn't leave you out. No, we're going for up-front and major. Line up your money and get out your checkbook, sweetie. Monroe's one writer you can't diddle down—because he's got a damn good agent. That's why. Get back to you."

Maggie and Larry gave her a thumbs-up. Larry said, "Turn it over to voicemail, boss, or they'll be hounding us all night."

"You talking about Keegan Monroe, the screenwriter?" Charlie's lawyer squinted at her like he'd never seen her before. "He's in Folsom for manslaughter."

"Lots of time to write there." Charlie took a sip of wine and dared relax a little. Why did the good times always get mixed up with the bad?

"Oh Jesus, I forgot." Larry slapped his forehead and the Grangers, who'd been at Jeremy's memorial and had been watching him with suspicion throughout the meal, straightened their spines to red alert. "Rudy's people wanted to set up a meet for lunch at the Pit and I forgot to have you return his call. Well—murder's hectic, you know? Sorry, Charlie."

"See if you can salvage tomorrow, Tuesday at the latest. It's perfect."

"Rudy Ferris takes calls on weekends?" Maggie said.

"His people do," Larry answered and added cryptically, "and Charlie's people make them." He went off to converse with his own cellular.

"Beverly Hills is not the town Amuller is talking about, Charlie," Ernie Seligman reminded her. "I don't care how many celebrities you know." Now his cellular bleeped. "Right. On

233

my way. Come on, Ed, it's Amuller. We'll have dessert when we get back."

"Maggie, can I help you make coffee?" Charlie and her best friend went off to the house across the concrete courtyard, leaving Doug and Betty and the Grangers chomping merrily away. Forget Mrs. McDougal's leftovers for a week.

❖

Mrs. Beesom and Maggie Stutzman refused to go to the Esterhazie mansion for the night, but Betty did condescend to cross the alley to the Grangers, and Maggie insisted on going to Mel's apartment instead.

"What if you have to go to the hospital again?" Charlie worried.

"Don't mommy me, Greene, I'm older than you are. I can take care of myself. Have a great time not leaving town tomorrow."

Amuller had dutifully gone to the redwood house and found the Ferrari and the couple living there gone, on vacation according to neighbors. Furniture still in the house—nothing suspicious. Except their names were Gladys and Jonathan Phillips.

Charlie, Ed, and Larry were out in the alley hammering holes in the back of the late Jeremy Fiedler's house when Officer Mary Maggie Mason and her silly smile showed up. She'd come in the open front way and peered through the back gate at them. "Now what are you all doing? You're just hanging poor Charlie by doing anything. The more you mess around, the deeper you bury her. And this case is still under investigation and you're tampering with a crime scene. Now get away from that wall."

Larry had already moved his Bronco and Charlie's Toyota to street parking some blocks away, which would be safe until the neighborhoods noticed—but Ed would ferry them there to pick up their cars too early for that.

No one planned on sleeping tonight.

Including Officer Mason, apparently. She planted herself and her black-and-white in the middle of the courtyard. From Charlie's kitchen window, the conspirators watched her settle in to protect the crime scene.

With a cop car protecting the place and keeping them from searching further, they decided Charlie and Larry should get some sleep and be ready for the big day tomorrow. Ed would stay awake, get them up in time to shower, and rush them out the front door to his car and then to theirs.

But before they gratefully took him up on the offer, he asked, "So if this cash stash is so big somebody's willing to commit murder and blow up neighbors for it—I'm assuming we're talking about all the stock cashed in under assumed Beesom names and various Enterprises Doug found on the Internet—why are you so sure the couple in the redwood house with Jeremy's Ferrari haven't already found it and aren't off to Switzerland with suitcases of hundred-dollar bills right now?"

Charlie knelt to pick up a chewed Ben Franklin from under the table in the breakfast nook, smelled it, and handed it to Ed. "Because Tuxedo's still finding them."

CHAPTER 36

❖

*R*UDY FERRIS AND half the Hollywood tabloid press (read half the Hollywood press) greeted Charlie and her boss, Richard Morse, at the Celebrity Pit when they stepped off the elevator.

"Jeez, what's Rudy got going I didn't know about?" Richard side-mouthed to Charlie. "You know what this is? They don't turn out like this for telethons."

"Remember what you told me about not questioning what went on in Daniel Congdon's office? 'You don't want to go there,' I think is what you said."

"That's what I'm still saying. I still want to know the reason for the coverage here, and why the press is looking at you and not me. You know?"

"Relax, Richard, and smile. Enjoy the coverage. Wait for my cues."

"Charlie, this is the first time you haven't leveled with me. What's going on?"

They were talking through smiles for the cameras.

"This isn't the first time you haven't leveled with me. Heads up, here comes the *Reporter.*"

"Jesus, what do you have to know about Congdon?" Richard said through a particularly phony smile. "Charlie, don't leave me hanging out like this."

236

"Does he smoke?"

"Daniel? Not that I've ever seen. What's that got to do with the price of blubber? You're gettin' strange on me, kid. And this ain't a good time, if you know what I mean."

Rudy and his people had tables pushed together on the pit level cordoned off from the adoring riffraff. The press, however, had been invited. Rudy was not happy with the attention his new agency was getting. He sat next to Charlie and informed her that his next telethon would be on breast cancer, and he wanted to have her as one of his guests because she was a survivor.

"My mother had a mastectomy last year. Maybe that's what you heard. I've never had cancer and I don't want it."

"How old is she?"

"Fiftysomething."

"Too old. Demographics. All the press you're getting today, it would have been great. You know any twenty- or thirty-something survivors?"

"They don't usually survive, Rudy."

"Crap—I got this set up already. I need young breast-cancer survivors. We air in a couple months."

His people had apparently not done their homework. "You had old guys up there on your erectile dysfunction telethon."

"Young guys don't have that problem," he said patiently. "Nobody wants to see old women on my show, unless they're running for president."

"Any news on when Keegan Monroe will get out of prison?" the reporter from the *Reporter* asked Charlie from across the table.

Richard made a whiny sound on one side of her and Rudy sucked his teeth on the other.

"He's meeting with the parole board right now," Charlie said.

"How come you didn't tell me that?" Richard whispered.

"So when are we going to get back to breast cancer?" poor Rudy, the man picking up the tab for all this—including the bar bill, which looked to be getting extensive—wanted to know under his breath.

Theirs was a campy lunch of grilled prawns and raw vegetables with various dipping sauces served with garlic mashers and roasted leeks.

When Charlie's cellular chimed faintly, she excused herself and took the gadget to the edge of the stage. Wouldn't you know, Mitch Hilsten was tending bar. It was Larry on the phone. He'd had various inquiries as to the sensuous Monroe script. They had already decided who would see it this round, and Charlie was confident this round would do it.

But she pretended to be making a selection from prospects as he ticked them off. This was all a setup and Charlie couldn't believe the press didn't know that, but she knew the reporter from *The Hollywood Reporter* had followed her from the table and there may have been others. "Only the majors, Larry, and send copies of the full script by runner."

"You doing this like a book auction?" the *Reporter* reporter asked. Several of his colleagues had joined him. "Isn't that a little unusual?"

"Yes." Charlie excused herself again to rejoin Rudy Ferris and his quest for young breast-cancer survivors.

She knew she was taking incredible chances here, betting the ranch by adding puff to the buzz early. But she was strapped for time.

Ed had driven Charlie and Larry to their cars by circuitous routes before dawn. He'd wanted them to take the same car for safety reasons but they'd both thought they might have to go their separate ways during all the excitement they hoped to stir up today—cover for each other, who knew what? Charlie was not about to leave Keegan Monroe hanging just because the Long Beach PD was on the verge of bringing murder charges against her. She'd have things so far along even Richard could carry on if she was jailed—with Larry, of course, doing the real work in the background. She'd have the major ducks lined up and quacking before that.

Mary Maggie had been snoozing in her car in the middle of the compound that morning and they'd snuck out the front door as planned without anyone noticing. They hoped. Officer Mason had kept them from looking for Jeremy's stash, but she'd probably kept anyone else from doing so, too. No bombs had gone off in the night. Why the officer hadn't noticed fewer cars in the compound, Charlie didn't know. They'd slipped Libby's Wrangler into the Toyota's space next to Mrs. Beesom's Olds 88, but that was it.

Anyway, Charlie expected to be arrested at any moment, so she wasn't surprised when David Dalrymple appeared in the wings and Mitch Hilsten left the bar long enough to deliver a sealed note. Everyone at her table waited for her reaction, but she didn't. The lookalike's wink wasn't bad, but his smile was wrong.

"So," Rudy said, trying to regain the limelight, "breast cancer is as much of a scourge to women as prostate cancer is to men, and we're going to raise hell and money to fight it with a—"

"I believe," a woman of the press said, pausing to swallow a bite of prawn, "that breast cancer strikes and kills and maims far more women than prostate cancer does men."

"Okay, heart attacks then."

Charlie enjoyed another prawn, too. They were so good they didn't need dipping. But then she thought of years of prison food and Keegan's script and dipped it in drawn butter bubbling over a flame anyway.

The note said, "When you get a minute—Dalrymple."

Charlie savored two more of the succulent prawns before taking her leave of the argument waging around the table, the naughty butter still coating her tongue.

"I have a job, David. A career. Responsibilities. I can't just drop everything and stay home when big things are happening to people who depend on me just because some self-righteous twerp of the law decides to nail me for something I didn't do. If you knew that you were going to die in a week and you had people you cared about, what would you do?"

"Get my affairs in order, I guess." He was driving her back to the agency where she could pick up what she needed to take home, and then he was to deliver her to Long Beach.

"Exactly. Do you know Detective Amuller thinks I have time to sit home and watch daytime television? 'Don't leave town' to him means I get to sleep in. Sleep in with Mitch Hilsten—"

"Was that him at the Pit?"

"No. Or sleep in with Esterhazie Cement who is divorced and dating a thirty-year-old. Or sleep in with my gay secretary. Or—if he discovers I have spoken to you several times—*you*. The man is out to get me because I'm an easy target."

"I think you feel victimized and therefore underestimate this Johann Sebastian Amuller, Charlie. He's a human, too. And in many ways as insecure as you are."

"Johann Sebastian. *Yes.* J. S.—I love it. David Dalrymple, I know you're a cop first and a friend second. And no, I'll never trust you completely, either, but thank you for that little piece of information."

"You really think it will help you with any of this?"

"No, but it solves one mystery in a life overrun with them."

"Now come the violins, Charlie? I watched you working that impressive crowd at the Celebrity Pit just now." He followed her up to her office at the FFUCWB of P, determined she wouldn't slip away.

"So what's happening, Larry?"

"So far it looks like your gamble paid off. Even got an offer sight-unseen from Allied Sharks."

"Did you tell them what the floor is?"

"Yeah, sputter, sputter, you gotta be crazy. That's why I hate agents, especially pushy broads. Monroe's just a goddamned writer for chrissake, sputter, sputter, hang up, bang." Larry leaned back in his chair with his arms crossed behind his head. "How sweet it is. Looks like our other scenario is about to shoot." He nodded at Dalrymple.

"You know the script."

"Right. Break a leg."

"Charlie." David Dalrymple followed her into her office and closed the door behind him, which elicited a guffaw or two from her secretary. "I strongly suggest you—"

"You smell something?"

"What?"

"I smell cigarette smoke. I even know where it's coming from." Charlie pushed A. E. Mous's *Dead Men Don't Need Jell-O* poster aside. This was the other scenario. The hole behind the poster now was almost the size of the poster.

"This is Daniel Congdon's office. He doesn't smoke. You want to stick your head in here and take a sniff?" Charlie watched David Dalrymple not move. "You don't have to, do you?"

"Charlie, trust me—"

241

"Why? I thought Feds who still smoke were only on the Fox Channel or in vintage films."

But it was down in the parking barn where things really came to a head. "No, let's take my car. Your secretary can bring yours."

"I need my car and Larry needs his. He has a life, you know."

"I insist. We need to talk."

"You can ride with me if you want. Find someone to bring you back into town—rent a car in Long Beach. Call a Fed."

"Charlie, I strongly suggest—"

"That's right, ex-Lieutenant Dalrymple. Because suggest is all you can do. Unless you've decided to work for a new organization, but I think you're too old for the Feds. And I have not yet been charged with Jeremy's murder and can't be ordered to stay at home in Long Beach."

"Your attorney—"

"—is very famous but human, and would probably love to see this case go to trial. I would if I were an attorney. If you want to talk with me, ride with me. Otherwise, I'll see you in Long Beach and we can talk there. Remember, I don't have to do this. Don't you just hate pushy women?"

But she was glad when he relented. Charlie intended to exceed the speed limit mightily and she could use some help when she reached Belmont Shore.

CHAPTER 37

◆

W HY ARE YOU coming back to Long Beach voluntarily
if you're so sure there's no law that says you have to
or that the LBPD or Attorney Seligman have any right to ask
it of such an important personage?" David Dalrymple asked
wryly as Charlie pulled onto the 10. He hadn't admitted she
was right in her assessment of his power to order her around
just now, but he hadn't denied it, either.

"Because I'm a pushy broad. Because I'm tired of being
expected to show blind obedience, allow others to make decisions for me that will affect them only a short time but could
affect my entire life, and my daughter's, forever. You don't just
hand your fate over to somebody because they tell you to. But
I'm rushing back to Long Beach right now mostly because I'm
very uneasy about Betty Beesom."

"You turn your fate over to someone else every time you
let a broker make an investment decision for you. Or a banker.
Or a doctor or a plumber or—"

"Yes, but I am willingly paying them for a service, not being
coerced into confessing to a crime I didn't commit, and poor
Betty—"

"You should be more concerned for your own well being,
Charlie, than your neighbor's. You are in a lot of trouble."

"And she is eighty-three and defenseless. And, other than

the murderer, I think I'm the only one who knows what's going on."

"If you have any information you think the police don't have, tell them right away before you get in deeper trouble."

"Not until I can prove it, so that information can't be used against me."

"Leave that to the experts. Crime solving is not your specialty."

"But manipulating people and information is. I know how it works. Now you know why I'm speeding back to Long Beach and I still don't know why there's all that stale cigarette smoke in Daniel Congdon's office and a master rat hole in the wall of mine."

"Explain to me first why you think the authorities will use information against you if you are not guilty of anything. Charlie, you're just not being rational."

Charlie explained that the fact she knew the report in the *P-T* that Jeremy Fiedler was killed by a gunshot was misinformation only proved to Amuller that she was the murderer. "Hairy the cat, and the Trailblazer, didn't smell like gun smoke."

"He could have been shot elsewhere and put into the car after."

"You know, I hadn't thought of that."

"See? Pushy broads don't know everything."

A gurgling and then a hot feeling in one ear. "Oh, shit."

"What?"

"Nothing." Charlie pressed Betty's number on her cellular and felt even worse when she got no answer.

"Charlie, I would like to serve, unofficially, as a mediator here. What do you say?"

I say I will not let this hearing thing get to me now. I will not. I will not. I just can't—"So what's with the hole in my office wall and the cigarette smoke?"

"Unofficially, there was some surveillance of your office and the agency."

"Jeremy's murder isn't half as exciting as how he disappeared electronically, huh? What did they expect to surveil if I was on vacation? They already had my files." Could he see her sweating?

"Most investigations strive to leave no stone unturned and this Daniel Congdon, the silent partner with an office, is a suspicious character."

"You're telling me. I've never laid eyes on him." And you're really not telling me anything I hadn't already guessed or even suggested to you, mediator.

"Now, what do you have for me?"

"Remember when we lunched at the Pit and you encouraged me to trust my special senses to learn about Jeremy, even maybe contact him? Well, I did. There were several of us there who tried, and he had a different message for everybody. Told me to watch out for the four-oh-five."

"That makes sense." Dalrymple put a hand out to the dashboard as she came up too fast on a gasoline tanker, pumping her brakes to warn the SUV behind her and flashing for a lane change. Hell, Charlie could do this while drying her hair.

She told him of everybody's warnings but Mrs. Beesom's. She didn't mention the old lady's presence at the silly pseudoseance in her breakfast nook. "And our cat really came unglued."

"Animals are very sensitive to supernatural phenomena."

Yeah, and to murder and smoky hundred-dollar bills, too.

By the time they reached Inglewood, she'd tried Betty again and again with no results. No gurgling in her head now, but there was still the odd heat. Within minutes her cellular played its stupid little tune—sort of like a muted Big Ben on Prozac.

It was a breathless Keegan. The parole board was about to spring him—he'd be home soon. He sounded joyous.

"That's the best news I've had in years. I just hope you can handle the press, pal. The buzz has been jumpstarted. This is going to be big."

When they hung up, he was crying—happy crying. Her cheeks weren't exactly dry.

"And Charlie, you have to admit Detective Amuller attended the memorial service and followed up those leads. It's not as if he doesn't listen to you," the ex-cop said out of context. "He mentioned something about a house with a car like Mr. Fiedler's you and your friends had apparently staked out."

"That's why I'm in such a hurry. I hope Libby went to the diner this afternoon. And, David, I hope you're armed."

❖

When the Toyota pulled into the compound, David Dalrymple was busy explaining that Jeremy's ability to obliterate his identity and still function in society and pursue the pursuit of happiness without paying taxes and leaving no "footprints" was a threat to everyone. This was such a national hazard that all stops had to be pulled. Extreme measures were justified. (Like blowing smoke through a hole in her wall.) Criminals could get hold of this method and ravage and pillage. Foreign spies and terrorists could disappear into the streets without trace.

Charlie thought that's what it was they did already, but she didn't say so. She was too worried about Betty and her own ears. Betty's old Olds sat in its proper place. Libby's Jeep Wrangler didn't—one good thing, anyway.

"Well, it seems I spent the better part of the afternoon on a long commute for nothing," Dalrymple told her.

"Probably told you more than you told me."

"Charlie, you need professional help here." He followed her to Betty's patio.

A seagull stood on Jeremy's picnic table scarfing up fish scraps off a newspaper. Betty must have had fish for lunch. "Hey, I got a renowned lawyer who tells me to stay home and do nothing."

"And that's sound advice."

"I'll let you know when I get the bill." But "sound" advice was suddenly of even less use to Charlie. The sharp pain in one ear was so sudden she might have been shot, but the hearing was gone from both ears. They stood at Betty's door, Charlie ready to pound on it. But her hands had volunteered to cover her ears instead. One of them came away bloodied.

Dalrymple was talking at her in a real panic mode, but when he saw the blood on her hand he lost it, pushed her to the ground facedown, and sprawled on top of her.

Charlie'd had a bleeding ulcer, fallen over cliffs, been injured in an explosion. She'd survived Mitch Hilsten in rut, a teenaged daughter, a menopausal mother, and a true raft of flirtatious Hollywood geezers—but this little escapade broke a rib. She felt it happen—and she'd thought her ear hurt.

"I can't hear you, but get off me," she couldn't hear herself say. "You broke something in my middle. You're killing me. I wasn't shot. My ear's bleeding—because of the explosion, I think. Please."

Charlie hurt so, she forgot to worry about Betty until her moderator rolled off her so she could turn over, and there was Mrs. Beesom standing above her, wringing her hands and crying behind her eyeglasses.

"Betty, I'm so glad you're all right. I was worried, tried to call. You've got to get out of here. Go over to Art and Wilma's. Anywhere, fast."

But Betty Beesom wasn't paying any attention to Charlie. Maybe Betty couldn't hear Charlie's voice, either.

"David, I really do need you now. There's no time to lose. You did bring a gun, right?"

He didn't even help her up. By the time Charlie got to her knees and, clutching her rib cage, finally to her feet, Dalrymple had his hands in the air with no gun in sight. He and Betty were looking over Charlie's shoulder.

She turned to face Jeremy Fiedler. He *had* brought a gun.

CHAPTER 38

◆

CHARLIE SAT ON the floor of Mrs. Beesom's dining room/ living room with her knees under her chin, her wrists taped together around those knees and, mercifully, up against Betty's soft recliner. She could lean into it and take the misery off her smashed rib when she breathed. Whenever she relaxed her back posture, the rib stabbed something that must be a vital organ because it took her breath away for lots of seconds. Charlie knew very little about her internal organs—other than her troublesome stomach, which was often shown to her in colorful drawings attached to examining room walls by helpful doctors. Mostly, she didn't want to know, you know?

Ex-Lieutenant Dalrymple, in much the same condition as she, leaned against a wall. He didn't have a broken rib but both his wrists and ankles were taped together. Betty, looking frail and scary, slumped without restraint in a cute little Swiss Chalet–type love seat on gliders. A woman whose name might be Gladys, in white anklets and Keds and a gathered shirtwaist you'd have trouble finding anywhere but on a black-and-white episode of *Lassie* on the Nick, was untethered, too. But she was one upset lady. And the man who was sometimes Jeremy Fiedler—now deceased—stood against a backdrop of Jesus on black velvet.

"Where's the Ferrari, Jeremy?" Charlie didn't hear herself

say, but felt the vibrations in her throat. Everyone but Jesus looked at her when she spoke this time.

Charlie would never say she was getting accustomed to her unpredictable handicap, but things were a little different now. She might have lost her hearing, but she'd be willing to bet she was the only person in the room who saw the whole picture. Betty thought she did, but she was mistaken.

Everyone but the woman in the anklets talked back to Charlie, but they didn't speak directly to her or exaggerate their lip movements. Jeremy gestured wildly at her and then at Betty. Unfortunately, so did the gun. Guns have little holes at the end that speak for themselves when you're eyeing them.

Somehow this little hole spoke for the man behind it who moved his lips incomprehensibly. It told her to get to her feet. With a totally pulverized rib, this wasn't as easy as it looked, but the little hole seemed to grow in proportion like there was a howitzer—whatever that was—motioning her upright.

There she stood on her feet and the Jeremy, behind the howitzer, mouthed terrifying threats he didn't know she couldn't hear but did a circular motion with his finger pointing down that intimated he wanted her to turn around. She did. The metal nudge in her back strongly insinuated she move forward. She did that, too, hoping if she and Jeremy and the gun made it out of the room, ex-Lieutenant Dalrymple might find a manly way to save the day and Betty Beesom.

As she stepped up to the dining-room level, she dared glance back to find Gladys of the anklets also holding a gun, holding it on David Dalrymple. So much for that little rescue scenario.

If the worst thing in the world could have happened to Charlie now, she would have said it was a toss-up between the feel of a bullet entering her spine and what actually happened.

She and her captor stepped out of Betty's kitchen door and then off her patio just as Libby Abigail Greene stepped out of her Wrangler. A rough hand on her shoulder stopped Charlie. Surprise and then shock stopped her daughter.

A hard metal poke in the back again sent Charlie moving forward toward Libby, who was talking and gesturing either to Charlie or to the man behind her. He would have to kill Libby now, too. There had to be something Charlie could do. Just giving him what he wanted would only ensure the slaughter of everyone in the compound and anyone who happened by. There could be no witnesses. There was too much at stake here.

But anything she did could endanger her daughter. Anything she *didn't* do could, too.

She watched Tuxedo jump onto the picnic table with a ravaged familiar piece of green and in desperation walked off toward the gate to the alley. Charlie gambled and did the unexpected with a man holding a gun, a man who had to kill once he got what he came for, a man who was between her and her child. Libby would be so distracted to find Jeremy alive she could hardly be expected to do anything rational. But what would the kid do? Charlie dared not think.

Charlie's plan was to separate herself from Libby so he'd have to decide which one to go after. Charlie hoped he'd chose her. She hung a right and angled toward the back gate of the compound and without a glance at or permission from her captor.

This is so dumb. He's gotten this far, he's obviously smart enough to force Libby with him into the alley and shoot you both there.

Not until he finds the money, he won't.

It took Charlie every ounce of will she owned to not look

over her shoulder. If there was a gunshot and Libby lay dead, she wouldn't have heard it. The gate wasn't locked. Why bother now?

In the alley, fluffy Hairy Granger tried to squeeze between her feet with every step and Charlie finally picked him up so she wouldn't trip on him. Cats had to be the most irritating animals on earth. Okay, next to murderers.

The holes in the stucco she and Larry and Ed had made in Jeremy's alley wall last night looked to have grown in size. For all of Officer Mason's threats, no crime-scene tape had gone up around that wall. In fact a seagull perched in one of those holes right now. He wasn't eating money and he wasn't eating fish scraps. He was sure eyeing Hairy Granger, though.

Charlie kept walking. She'd never wanted to know much about alley life—figured it would make her angry, disgusted, and guilty, and her plate was too full of that already. Besides, this alley was too close to home. But Hairy stiffened in her arms as they approached a pair of legs in scruffy pants and sandals sticking out from behind a storage unit for garbage cans.

The guy's feet and legs looked relaxed unto death, but when she and Hairy passed him his face looked euphoric unto a high just short of an overdose, and he had cigarettes and booze nearby for when he came off it. His eyes couldn't track and his nose was bleeding, but he winked at her. He was one happy fella. A stack of unopened pizza boxes sat innocently next to him. This man had everything but shelter. This man had money. This man had probably followed the seagull. This man was going to be dead meat in seconds.

Charlie, you may not hear him babbling at you. You can't even hear Hairy, whose vibrations could mean either purring or growling, but you must do something.

Screw the idiot, he's killing himself without my help, and this damn cat is making me feel sneezy.

But Hairy clung to her when she tried to put him down, so she faced the breathless inevitable by turning around with this overhaired burden hanging on her front to face the reality of what the armed creep might have done to Libby. Charlie could not only not hear, she couldn't breathe. Her options were minuscule, her time frame destroyed.

She had seen that look in Jeremy's eyes before but had denied it as reality because she needed him. It was the Jeremy who could throw rocks at Hairy one day and entice Tuxedo onto his lap by merely sitting down the next. The Jeremy who fed the seagull his dinner scraps and then chased it off with curses. There was insanity here. To believe she'd allowed her Libby to live so near this danger all these years made her sick now.

Hairy climbed up on her shoulder, taking the pressure off her rib, and Charlie sucked air into her lungs.

Libby Abigail Greene lay sprawled at his feet. Jeremy had the gun in both hands extended out and aimed at Charlie, but was looking sideways at the seagull sitting in the hole in the ruins of the house he'd deeded over to Betty Beesom. His mouth looked as if he was shouting—maybe raving, who knows?

And Art and Wilma Granger were sneaking up behind him, motioning for Charlie to hit the deck before the good-sized plank in Art's hands contacted Jeremy's skull. In front of him at his feet, Libby raised her head and made a thumbs-up motion. Thank God she wasn't dead.

But it was too late for Charlie. Jeremy pulled the trigger.

CHAPTER 39

◆

THE LAST TIME Charlie was dead, she couldn't hear. This time she could. And she'd thought *life* was interesting.

The problem was, the sound she could hear was deafening.

Are you never satisfied?

"Will you shut up?"

"Mom?"

"Oh, honey, I didn't mean you. I was talking to the buzz in my head."

"She's got a buzz in her head," Libby told some guy who looked suspiciously like a paramedic. The two of them bent over her.

"Don't let them resuscitate me, Libby. I've already got a broken rib, forgodsake."

"It's your head that's bleeding," the paramedic said. "And we don't normally resuscitate people who can talk."

"Actually, that's from a different trauma. I did the rib by accident when I thought she'd been shot because of the bleeding ear. This woman has been greatly mistreated, but I think not shot in the head." David Dalrymple looked down on her now, too. "She's been totally deaf for the last two hours."

"I can hear now. Don't let them take me to the hospital, David. Libby—what's happened to Jeremy? I heard the gun go off and it was aimed at me. Tell me Mrs. Beesom's okay."

"Trauma injuries to the ear don't work that way," the paramedic assured the ex-lieutenant. "Bleeding from anywhere in the head is serious—no matter how or when it happens."

"Art hit him over the head with a piece of two-by-four, but I saw you go down about when the gun went off." Wilma Granger had that smile on her lips but fear in her eyes. How'd she do that? "You sure you ain't been shot, Charlie?"

Actually, Charlie wasn't sure of anything. One ear was sore and her head felt bruised where she'd hit the alley going down. Gladys, if that was her real name, had turned over her weapon and untaped Dalrymple, who spirited both women out of the house. She'd kept saying, "Help me, please? Hurry, he'll kill us all."

"You just can't stay out of trouble, can you, Ms. Greene?" Detective Amuller's joined the faces above her.

"Johann Sebastian," Charlie greeted him with glee and then passed out. Most probably from the needle prick in her arm.

Charlie was treated in the emergency room—X-rayed, analyzed, lab-tested, checked for balance problems, and released. She had no bullet wounds, only some dried blood in one ear. It was strongly suggested she must have passed out from the fear of being shot by a man pointing a gun at her or by the pain as her hearing returned.

Her lawyer arrived. So did Amuller.

Her rib wasn't broken, merely cracked. There isn't anything you can do for a cracked rib but learn to move in the least painful ways and to avoid lifting. Sort of roll off the front of a chair instead of leaning on your arms to rise. Never twist your body entering or leaving an automobile. Avoid jarring of any kind and roll your legs over the edge of the bed allowing gravity to work for you while transferring most of your weight to your legs and feet before somehow getting your upper body upright, and never, never breathe shallowly, even when asleep. Because you'll get pneumonia.

Otherwise, piece of cake, no problem, nobody ever died of a cracked rib, well hardly nobody, and you'll feel totally normal in six to eight weeks.

"Six to eight weeks—that's two months. I can't—"

"Sure seems to be hearing fine now," Johann Sebastian Amuller shouted for everyone in the emergency room. "I suppose you're going to tell me Jeremy Fiedler killed Jeremy Fiedler and Gladys Phillips. I got Fiedler on a slab and I'll soon have the man who shot Gladys. I think you should know I'm not convinced that I don't have two murders and two murderers."

Everyone seemed to be shouting. Charlie heard too well. Seemed better even than before the bouquet bomber blew away her self-confidence and the safety of her fortress. God, she missed Jeremy.

The Jeremy with the gun escaped from the alley attack after Art hit him with the two-by-four only to find Gladys on Betty's patio with Betty and Dalrymple, so he shot Gladys dead on the spot. Betty would have been next but Dalrymple knocked her to the ground, stood in front of her, and aimed Gladys's gun at Jeremy when Art and his two-by-four charged again, this time into the compound and Jeremy took off out the front destroyed gate. It all happened in a matter of seconds and Dalrymple would have shot the fleeing murderer in the back but discovered too late that poor Gladys's weapon was not loaded.

Art Granger lobbed the two-by-four after him but it fell short. Jeremy was gone again, leaving more murder in his wake.

No sign of hearing loss or major damage to the little hairs deep in her ears could be detected. Dr. Peter Rasmusen, Long

Beach's renowned hearing specialist, was highly recommended by the staff in the ER to look into any problems that might crop up.

Johann Sebastian gave Ernesto Seligman a thumbs-up, Charlie a wink, and repeated himself. "See you in court."

Attorney Seligman turned to David Dalrymple. "You're positive she wasn't hearing for at least two hours this afternoon?"

"Tried to tell Amuller I'd swear to it in court. I will, that's a promise. He won't listen. You know, Charlie, you may be right about him. We need good young men like that in law enforcement desperately. I can't understand his mindset here."

❖

"It's *Good Cops, Bad Guys,* David. Unfortunately it's easier to learn about people from it and movies than actually observing reality."

"So you saw Charlie flinch and go wimpy, too, when her hearing shut down?" Ed Esterhazie asked Dalrymple. "Sorry, Charlie—but that look you get when you suddenly can't hear isn't any I've ever experienced."

They and Ernesto Seligman were helping Charlie and Libby search for loot in the ruin of the fortress.

"So which man was Jeremy Fiedler, the dead man in the Trailblazer or the one holding you all hostage?" the attorney asked.

"They both were, or neither. There have been two Jeremys all along. But nobody noticed, except Mrs. Beesom. She notices everything."

"That is way weird," Libby said. "That's why sometimes he limped and sometimes he didn't. Why sometimes his hair looked different, and one day Tuxedo would jump on his lap and another day hiss at Jeremy."

"We see what we expect to see, not always what's really in front of our eyes." Evening light was fading to night dark and even flashlights didn't reveal much inside the holes in Jeremy's house. They had to take their chances. Charlie had insisted Libby go to the Esterhazie's or to Lori Schantz's but the kid was getting fed up with this.

"I'll leave if you will," had been her reply.

Life sucks when your teen can make such pronouncements while having to bend over to look you in the face. "I have the feeling it was Harry who Tuxedo didn't like," Charlie said now. "The man who was holding a gun on us this afternoon. He even had the nerve to attend Jeremy's memorial. That's why Betty Beesom practically went into shock at the beach that day. She knew there were two of them. She didn't trust Harry for some reason, and especially not with Jeremy dead. But Harry got to her before our little trip to the eye doctor and convinced her somehow that he'd see to it everything was all right for her. And since she ended up owning Jeremy's house, maybe she decided that meant Harry, too, would look after her—if she didn't give him away, that is."

"Exactly when did you figure all this out?" Dalrymple wanted to know.

"Like I told you, I was beginning to tumble that day we lunched at the Pit. All those lookalikes, the clever impersonations and disguises, makeup—probably surgery even—to look like someone you aren't, and so convincingly. On the way home on the 405 I kept feeling I was on the cusp of what was going on here, just almost there, and then my ears did their thing and I couldn't concentrate on anything else. And Mrs. Beesom kept saying she meant Hairy the cat when she'd slip and say 'Harry.' And then Doug came across all those Beesom brokerage accounts that had been cashed in, and Tuxedo started dragging tortured hundred-dollar bills into the house instead of poor birds and bugs. It all came together. And the redwood house and the red Ferrari."

"What would that have to do with someone methodically destroying his identity electronically?" Dalrymple pulled a chunk of wall away to make a hole bigger and Ed pointed a flashlight down it to disclose stacks of bills, neatly piled. These holes were cut into unusual cavities between the inner and outer wall, and there had been less damage to wall and cash down that far. "Oh, all this money."

"Right. Maggie told me her retired clients in their estate planning are desperate to avoid inheritance tax and long-term care costs—to leave their money to their heirs, not the government or nursing homes. The two Jeremys got a lot of money somewhere and invested it to make more. And they wanted to take it with them. In cash—tax free. But only one of them knew where it was hidden. The dead one. That's why the guy over there behind the garbage cans is so stoned and pizza-fed. He found some of it. But not all. The Jeremy who was Harry saw this hole with a seagull in it before he shot at me. He'll be back, and soon, for the rest and for Betty and anybody who gets in his way."

"Especially—I would think—you, Libby, and Maggie," Ed said solemnly.

"Where do you get all this shit?" Attorney Seligman was holding out a black plastic Hefty Cinch Sak with a yellow drawstring. "You just make assumptions all around, upside down and right and left—and why didn't you share all this with me yesterday?"

"There wasn't time then, and there isn't time now. And you wouldn't have believed me anyway. You want to spread that bag open wider for more 'assumptions'?"

"You'd have to disappear electronically to make so many huge cash transactions in so short a time," Dalrymple said.

"Even on multiple accounts supposedly in several different names."

"This had been planned for a long time." Charlie had to swivel from the hips up to get to the bills and then get them to the plastic Hefty bag. "At least since the condos on the alley had their doors and windows boarded up. I'd be willing to bet the art niches were configured somehow to open and allow money to be stashed. But only the one Jeremy knew about it. The mastermind. He could have been stashing it away for years."

"Do you think Mrs. Beesom's niches were used to stash money, too?" Libby asked.

"Yeah, we'd better finish here and get back to her. Art and Wilma are in danger, too, just being there. And Jeremy had the key to Betty's house, so it wouldn't take much to slip in while she was at church or the beauty parlor and stuff money in her walls, too."

"We really should leave the money in the wall, let the authorities remove it," the lawyer with the garbage bag said. "We're just bagging it for the murderer—make it easier for him to haul it off."

"And let every drunk and druggie walk off with handfuls instead?" Charlie turned to point at the homeless man they'd been ignoring. He was moaning now, and she was, too. He coming out of his chemically induced slumber, and she'd remembered too late never to twist her torso. The paramedics and then Amuller's men had tried to question him but he'd been too incoherent to make sense, so everybody gave up on him. Charlie was glad to see he was alive, but the other Jeremy would shoot him for sure if he stayed so close to the holes in the alley wall.

But she needn't have worried. The man who staggered to his feet from behind the garage can *was* the other Jeremy, and he was still armed. The homeless man was too hopeless and embarrassing to look at, so they hadn't. The other Jeremy lifted the can's lid to reveal the bum stuffed inside it, part of the back of his head all over the back of his T-shirt. "Finish putting my money in the Hefty, folks, and then we'll go next door for the rest."

CHAPTER 40

◆

Y OU SAID YOU'D take care of me in my old age," Betty
complained while Charlie pretended to look for some device in the old lady's art niches that would release the entry to
a stash hole.

"Oh, I intend to, Betty love," the man with the gun said in
Jeremy's voice. "You won't have to worry about a thing again
ever."

"But I didn't mean the house or money. I meant . . . looking
after."

"Were you two twins?" Charlie played for time. Ed had
called Amuller on his tiny cellular before they went into the
alley, telling him what they planned to do and that they expected the murderer to be back for the loot any minute. Of
course, he'd had to leave that message on the detective's voicemail.

"Just brothers. And I suggest you hurry, Charlie. I'm getting
nervous." This brother's hair was redder and not as thin as the
other's.

Great, now you notice.

"Why? You'll just kill us all anyway."

"Oh, I think I'll take lovely Libby with me. Just for snug-
gles. That ought to frost your huevos, huh?"

"So was Gladys your girl or your brother's? Or both?"

"Cousin, actually. The third heir. You can see why she had to die. I just didn't realize she knew that was in the plan."

"Well, once you killed your brother, she might have guessed."

"She was stupid. Who knew what she would guess? Now get moving or I'll pistol-whip your precious blond bombshell in front of your eyes."

He grabbed Libby just as Charlie inadvertently touched a spot of extra plaster in the niche and the bottom flapped down on hinges, hidden until the flap released to reveal them. The picture of the Last Supper slipped into the hole half its length, stopped by, she was sure, more hundred-dollar bills.

But she had no time to look because Libby decided to be fed up again. Just when Jeremy's brother noticed the Last Supper slipping but after he'd grabbed Charlie's daughter from behind, Charlie's daughter performed a catapult.

It was something she'd learned in cheerleading. It did not involve a somersault or leap on her part but was used as a method of hurling one of the smaller, lighter girls from behind her in a somersault over her head to the top of a pyramid, a spectacular maneuver they were not allowed to use since a girl on an opposing team had broken her neck at cheerleader camp when it went wrong. But Libby and Lori Schantz thought it was wonderful and practiced it endlessly last year, Lori flying through the air, catapulted by Libby, often caught by Doug.

Much heavier and caught unaware and unwilling, the other Jeremy didn't fly through the air but landed on the stairs between the dining and living room areas and Libby, unable to control her angst, jumped hard on the middle of his back where it spanned the two stairs. His bones cracked instead of the pistol in his hand. It went flying.

"Well, he just made me *soooo* mad," Libby had said at the time, not the least in need then of Officer Mary Maggie's counseling on guilt because she'd almost certainly caused a man to become a paraplegic. And no more so now, two weeks later.

It was a Saturday morning and they all crowded into Charlie's breakfast nook to look at the preliminary plans Mrs. Beesom spread on the table. The plans to rebuild Jeremy's house. Officer Mason had stopped by to check on the survivors.

"It's going to be just like before." Maggie Stutzman was the first to notice.

"That's right, except there won't be no holes in the walls on the alley. I'm even thinking we should all go together and have the gates rebuilt."

"I agree," Maggie said. "I liked it better here when we had gates."

Officer Maggie gasped heavenward. "But this is Belmont Shore, or have you people noticed? The reason the gates were here was not to protect you but to protect the money the Jeremy brothers and their cousin didn't want to pay taxes on. The real danger was here inside the walls with you."

But the glances among the other four women in the room were in solid agreement. Even Libby-the-rebel Greene's.

"And," Betty went on with a certain aplomb, "we'll find a nice young man to live in it who knows how to fix things and knows who to call if he doesn't."

"But who isn't about to inherit a huge amount of money," Charlie added.

"And who is only one of him," Libby said, garbled, but they all knew what she was saying.

"Hear ye, hear ye," Maggie the lawyer pounded the table, "let it be known the women of the compound do hereby agree. And you, Officer, are our witness."

Officer Mason pushed her glasses back up on her nose,

tucked her hair behind her ears, and shook her head. She reached to the top of the refrigerator to scratch Tuxedo under the chin and reached for the door out. "Oh and Charlie, two things. We finally traced the phone that was used to report Jeremy's death. A cellular belonging to the people in the redwood house."

"Probably the Jeremy named Harry stabbed his brother and put him in the car while I was putting groceries away and then he called in the murder on his way home. Maybe they had a fight because the Jeremy we liked wouldn't tell him where the money was and might have suspected his brother might commit murder to get all the money. So, what's the second thing?"

Mary Maggie Mason's sloppy grin was back suddenly. "I just heard on the radio this morning that Mitch Hilsten and Deena Gotmor are engaged. Thought you'd like to know. Not that I can make much sense of anything in this place."

Libby cheered the news with a whoop when the police woman had left, and added, "Poor Deena."

"Oh, Charlie, I'm sorry." Betty blinked red eyes, one cleared by surgery already and the other scheduled.

"So what do you think, Greene?" Maggie Stutzman asked with a certain vengefulness.

I think he deserves a lot better than Deena-Gotmor-lips-and-boobs surgically.

Boy, me too, she and her common sense agreed. "I think he's a big boy and can make his own decisions without my opinion."

"When the real Jeremy said I'd be taken care of"—Betty changed the subject to the one at hand—"this is what he meant." She tapped the preliminary plans with her finger. "But I meant like family would look after an older person. Help out with appointments and shopping, check on you every day, take you places you'd be afraid to go alone. I got enough money."

Charlie and her best friend exchanged helpless stares.

"You can't hire people to do what family and friends do out of kindness. Hired folks beat you and steal your money. I really didn't know the house belonged to me. And Harry didn't used to seem so mean. He just kind of got worse all of a sudden. Jeremy warned me about him even after he was dead, poor man."

"But why did Harry frighten you so at the memorial service on the beach walk?"

"He'd told me on the phone he'd see to it I was blamed for Jeremy's murder if I told anybody about him. He just kept weaving in and out and behind people down at the beach, dressed different, wore a baseball hat, but I knew him right away. It was the way he looked warning at me that scared me so. I almost told you about him, Charlie, but then I remembered that look."

She'd confessed to Amuller that Jeremy didn't trust his brother, who had been in trouble more than once. So he kept secrets from him. "They didn't either one say anything about no woman. And when Jeremy died I still never thought Harry done it."

Jeremy, or maybe both Jeremys, had worked out in the home gym in the redwood house's walk-out basement. Gladys apparently acted as the lady of the house, and there was always a Jonathan Phillips at home as there was a Jeremy Fiedler in the compound.

The *P-T* revealed that an enormous inheritance had befallen the three, none of them named Jeremy. When they saw how much the government would take of it, they'd decided to ensure they'd give up no more when they realized the fruits of their investments on the rest of it. Most of this was probable conjecture, since the injured cousin whose name was neither Harry nor Jonathan had refused to talk.

The three had built their own illegal trust out of distrust, and come upon the scheme of disguising their profits by using false names and phony companies until the capital gains couldn't be traced. Ultimately they and the money disappeared in the electronic melange of a fast-growing, only-partially understood transfer of record keeping to an even-less-understood, more confusing, and ever-upgrading medium known as "software."

Record keepers at the lower levels have never been well paid and as a result have become increasingly less educated and, according to the morning's *P-T*, totally overwhelmed by the constant changes in technology. Computerized records of the government and particularly of law-enforcement and tax-collecting agencies are held hostage to hackers, and this induced the "Jeremy brothers"—their true names still not revealed—to mastermind this scheme, largely utilizing the computer skills of teenage hackers—in this case, the unusual use of *female* teenage hackers.

Under the guise of being a dirty old man, they could induce young girls to do highly illegal hacking for a chance to run away from home for long periods and scare the holy shit out of their parents so that when they did return they had really big negotiating rights. They could make good money in cash they didn't have to declare to parents or to government and could spend as they pleased.

A few had turned up dead, which is not unusual for young women anywhere—who's more vulnerable than a rebellious teen? Still, Charlie figured the Jeremy who was Harry did some work on his own there. One Jeremy knew how to work women, the other knew how to terrify them into submission or kill them. Harry must have hired the young girls to leave bouquet bombs in an attempt to scare occupants out of the compound so he could search for the stash, too.

One of the fathers had come forward already, and there would be more parents talking hard with more runaways as the story continued to break in the news. One of the fathers would have been the voice on Jeremy's answering machine heard by his neighbors when they forced their way into his house.

"Betty, when did you know there were two Jeremys?"

"Not till about a month ago. You know how nosy I am." She looked around the table with a nod and a lift of the chin. "Surprised I didn't notice sooner, but my eyes had been going for a long time and I was worrying more about myself and being alone in my old age."

"Didn't you want to know why there were two Jeremys?"

"Jeremy promised me if I kept still about it and didn't ask questions I'd know soon enough and he'd see I was taken care of. He was always so dependable, I believed him. But I still got good neighbors, don't I?"

Charlie hadn't thought Betty capable of keeping such a secret even for a month. But she'd never thought to question Jeremy, either.

Johann Sebastian Amuller had come to collect the loot in the Hefty bags. He gave Charlie a suspicious squint, but made no new threats as to her imminent arrest for Jeremy's murder. His brother offered a far better motive and obvious intent to kill as witnessed by neighbors, a noted lawyer, and a well-known ex-Lieutenant in the Beverly Hill's homicide department, all able and willing to testify on Charlie's behalf. J. S. knew he was right, but he couldn't prove it. He trusted his gut and his prejudices and *Good Cops, Bad Guys.* Charlie hoped she'd never have to deal with him again.

"I wonder what the good Jeremy told Tuxedo that day we all sat here and called him up from the dead?" Libby said out of the blue where she came from, bless her. " 'Cause what he told me sure came true. 'Watch out for Rory Torkelsen.' "

"Me too," Betty said, and so did Maggie. They all looked to the top of the refrigerator into the half-lidded eyes of the inscrutable feline. Tuxedo's yawn was the only answer.

"What do you mean, yours came true?" Charlie the mom overreacted. "Rory Torkelsen—"

"Yeah, tried to strong-arm me into one of the little boys' rooms last Friday at school. Had some friends in there already telling me how I'd pay if I ever told on them."

"Did they—?" Charlie started.

"You didn't break his spine, too?" Maggie the lawyer broke in. "Or those of his friends?"

"His friends are fine. He's still walking kind of funny, though. Mo-om, don't look at me that way. I saved everybody from the wrong Jeremy and you still think you have to protect me." Libby left the room, disgust hovering in her wake. Tuxedo jumped from the refrigerator to the counter to the floor and pranced after her with a look of disdain for Charlie.

Charlie gave him the bird, but he didn't notice.

Betty Beesom did but she said, "He warned me against Harry, too. 'Watch out for Harry,' he said in my head, and I didn't listen."

"You too, Maggie?" Charlie asked.

"Yeah, 'watch out for Mel.' Yesterday while Libby was protecting you and outsmarting our murderer, I took the liberty of listening to Mel's answering machine while he was in the shower after never mind and guess how many girlfriends he's servicing? I thought it would be full of his wife's savagery, as he described it. These were all women wanting to know why he hadn't returned their calls, or—" She shrugged. "You and Jeremy were right I guess, Charlie."

"Oh, Stutzman, I didn't want to be right. It's just you're way too good for him. Way, way—"

"Yeah, well, now that Hilsten's engaged we can go bar hopping and pick up guys together. Right?"

Charlie knew they had all imagined Jeremy's individualized warnings because of the stress caused by murder in the compound. She didn't give the matter, or her own warning from Jeremy, another thought. Until the next morning on her commute to work on the 405.

CHAPTER 41

———◆———

C HARLIE SAT IN a grid on the 405, drying her hair and drinking coffee. What did Mitch want with a bubblehead and fake boobs? Oh well, he must really be lonely. Before traffic resumed she'd talked to Keegan Monroe, so excited to be back in his own house—a very nice habitat in Coldwater Canyon—and enjoying having to fight off the press, something rarely required of a writer. He rhapsodized over the food he was cooking for himself. He couldn't sleep yet, but the nightmare of prison would take a while to lose its hold. And last night he'd even been out to Residuals on Ventura Boulevard, a restaurant bar that displayed the tiniest checks ever to get through the entertainment industry's cookbooking to the folks who did the work.

She'd finished her bagel and, in pain the whole time, wrestled her pantyhose on. She got one call off to New York, and stuck in her earrings before traffic started moving again. As always it roared past going the other way. But not bad for one grid.

Mostly Charlie was enjoying not having to face a trial and jail time, cherishing the traffic sounds—(please let them last), rejoicing in being in charge of the Toyota and her life and her work and the routine of it all. An exciting job full of stress beat the hell out of being handicapped. She was blessed. She and her kid were alive.

But Charlie would never again try to put her pantyhose on in the car until her rib had mended. Even getting in and out of the Toyota without twisting your torso was impossible if you were the one behind the wheel. In the ER they'd suggested she let her husband drive for a few months. *Grrrrr.*

But she was not about to complain because this morning looked wonderful after her catastrophic vacation. She vowed to work till she dropped. That was the only safe way for Charlie Greene.

That was also about the time a semi going the other way jumped the meridian between north and south on the 405 and headed straight for the Toyota after taking out a few SUVs in front of her. It was too late to change lanes. Or was it?

Jeremy and Hairy and Tuxedo were not staring at her from the big rig's windshield either, and she did not accompany the Toyota up its radiator like in her dream. She did hear herself screaming and cursing as she wormed the little, crushable, parkable, familiar Toyota over between two other SUVs.

The one in front of her climbed the semi's hood. She managed another worm into the next lane over where traffic was really slowing down, and then to the next. Where she and her ribcage and her beloved Toyota joined she-couldn't-tell-how-many cars and trucks and everything-in-between in a crunch that shoved it all into what looked like a grassy ditch before the dependable old gray Toyota bent its ribcage in the middle, and Charlie, too.

"That one alive?"

"She's breathing. Cut some more metal and I think I can pull her out."

I have my earrings on. I can hear you. "Don't leave my computer behind. I already have a broken rib."

"She say something?"

"Gibberish. Now, pull—"

Charlie was almost resigned to coming to in life or death with talking heads leaning over her. The three in focus at the moment were Edwina, Libby, and Mitch Hilsten. They were all grinning. Grinning expectantly, sliding quick glances at each other, waiting for her to say something first.

She'd let them wait.

Something had happened on the 405 but she couldn't remember what. Something bad. But she could hear, so that was good. She could hear hospital sounds, people being paged, squeaky wheels moving down the hallways, the purposeful steps of sensible rubber-soled shoes as staff moved about, the scritch of privacy curtains pulled back or forth between beds. The lighting above her and drip stands beside her clinched it.

Nothing hurt anywhere on her body, not even her rib—drugs. In fact, she felt unusually optimistic—good drugs. She wiggled her fingers and toes, wrinkled her nose, tried feet, hands. It couldn't be too bad or they wouldn't be grinning so hard.

Edwina's hair had morphed from a lank, dishwater, salt-and-pepper brown to a fluffy beige bob. Breast-cancer surgery and its everlasting aftermath had turned her mother into a total stranger. She even wore makeup and earrings.

Mitch was just Mitch—after Larry Mann, the second best-looking man in the world. But looks weren't everything.

The fact Libby Abigail Greene was standing next to Mitch

without snarling was really amazing. They were all focused on Charlie and they were all happy—what?

The 405—hospital—Charlie tried to sit up and the drips rattled on their stands and her rib tweaked through the drugs and she said, "The Toyota? My car? Is it—?"

Edwina and Libby stopped grinning. Mitch let loose his full extreme gleam, and female grunts and sighs emanated from the other side of the bed, staff. He put out both hands and her daughter and her mother slapped some bills on his palms. A bet. They'd bet on her first words. He'd won. What did the women in her life think she'd say first?

"I thought you'd want to know about my new friend." Charlie's mother typically answered the unasked question instead of the one Charlie had voiced.

"You were supposed to ask about Deena Gotmor," her daughter griped.

"The Toyota's gone, Charlie, but look at it this way—you have an excuse to buy a new car," Mitch said.

"Mom, it was the color of dead fish guts anyway. You should be glad to be rid of it."

"It was an old and loyal friend, wasn't it, Charlie?" When your mother actually understands you, you really feel old. Charlie felt something like mourning through the drugs. Mourning for her office on the road.

"Anyway," Libby said, "your warning from Jeremy came true, too. Now they're all in. So we don't have to worry about that, like waiting for the other shoe."

There was a mirror over a sink directly in line between Mitch and Libby, and for a breath-stopping minute Charlie could have sworn she saw Jeremy Fiedler in it, looking back at her.

"Except for Tuxedo," Libby continued. "We don't know

what Jeremy told him. But he's got nine lives. And Tux is still dragging chewed up hundred-dollar bills into the house."

The Jeremy Fiedler, who was dead and could not possibly have any reflection in any mirror, winked at Charlie and disappeared from over the sink.